RANDOLPH S.

V

THE ACHILLES

A Tale of Failed Leadership, Courage, Killers, and Women

This is a work of fiction. The events and characters described herein are imaginary and are not intended to refer to specific places or living persons. The opinions expressed in this manuscript are solely the opinions of the author and do not represent the opinions or thoughts of the publisher. The author has represented and warranted full ownership and/or legal right to publish all the materials in this book.

The Achilles
A Tale of Failed Leadership, Courage, Killers, and Women

v1.0

Cover Image by Randolph S. Wardle

Outskirts Press, Inc.
http://www.outskirtspress.com

ISBN: 978-1-4787-4168-8

Copyright Registration Number: TXU001888390

PRINTED IN THE UNITED STATES OF AMERICA

Chapter 1

It was a cold night, about ten degrees with limited visibility across the northeastern border of Pakistan. Why do Decembers always have to be cold? The valley below my vantage point was lit only by the moon, stars and some random campfires. The lack of ambient light allowed the galaxies, over a million miles away, to peek through the clouds. I was truly at momentary peace in the forested ridgeline overlooking the village of the Badabers.

My body and clothing were dingy and covered with all types of infectious matter from two weeks of traveling, killing and taking care of one widow and her child. I remember my drill sergeant always telling us to take care of our feet first. I had failed this requirement because, instead of covered combat boots, I wore open-toed sandals. From sores, blisters and cuts, my feet were fairly destroyed. Hopefully I would have the Achilles tonight and we could get out to Torkham Gate by tomorrow morning.

Because I was living amongst the animals and people, an unmanaged beard had shown up all over my face. It rose halfway up to my eyeballs and down to my t-shirt line. Lice, from what I could identify without a mirror, had been living in all the orifices of my body. My brown hair was long and close to curling on the edges. Smelling of dirt and human waste due to a lack of toilet paper, and with lips that were peeling beyond repair, I was clearly beyond taking care of my issues. Without a drug store to cover down on my personal hygiene needs, life was difficult. Life for me at this point was at the basic level of subsistence and survival. The human need to survive was the only thing keeping me alive.

My weapon of choice and for most others in Afghanistan was the Chinese-made AK-47, a knockoff of the Russian Kalashnikov AK-47. It could get dirty all day, take a beating, and still keep shooting. I had received this weapon graciously from a dead Taliban warrior a few weeks back. The best stolen property I had ever been associated with. Hell, he was never going to use it again anyway! Ammunition was easy to get as it lay everywhere after a fight or in any village throughout the tribal areas. I dumped my Army issued M4 weapon prior to crossing the border in Shkin, Afghanistan.

We had been traveling for hours by truck that day to reach this over-watch position into South Peshawar. It placed me in position to gain intelligence of the objective and safety for the child. Waba, the Pakistani assassin, was still hot on my trail. Hopefully, I had shaken him off earlier in the cemetery.

Dropping some gear in the truck to lighten my load, I only kept my AK and a knife. Taking position just inside a tree line overlooking the Pakistani Frontier Corps basecamp, I took a seat and remained there for hours. While I observed movements of tribal and military personnel moving in and out of the camp, timing was everything at this point. I also looked for positions to run to, if required, as I began to assault forward. Once clarity was achieved, I rested and watched the valley. It was very calming.

My mind began to wander to how I had gotten myself into this mess of locating a U.S. secure radio tracking system that would require me to kill so many people. Where was my ex-girlfriend Daisy tonight? Was she worried or with someone else? I had not written in over nine months or been home in over five years. The time spent away had made my mind wonder negatively about her. She had been the only female memory that I had up to just two weeks ago. But, that wasn't important now; I needed to concentrate on Laima now.

In a flash, I awoke from my thoughts to a rope around my neck and a man screaming into my ear, "This will be your last night to breathe the air in his country. River, you will die tonight by my rope and knife and Laima will be my house slave!"

I could smell the animal within his body and his stench breath that spewed from his mouth. It was Waba. His anger and saliva ran down my ear to my neck as he confessed my life was ending. I could feel his face against mine, beard to beard, the transferring of heat and sweat. Lucifer had arrived and he had picked me tonight; death was now upon me on a Pakistani hilltop.

Struggling to free myself, I placed my hands over my throat and worked my fingers in between my neck and the rope, trying to free my airway. I moved around, trying to free myself from his grasp. Spinning and spinning, we began to wrestle on the ground. He was strong, and I had been weakened by my journey. Within seconds, I was finally face to face with the greatest Pakistani assassin, Waba. He was within an inch. I finally could tell the color of his eyes: They were black and cloudy from his life on the battlefield.

The spinning had placed the rope on the back of my neck. Waba continued to apply pressure until I began to lose consciousness. My mouth was open; gasping for air, yet nothing was coming out as my forehead lifted up to the sky. Death seemed near as the last of my dreams appeared. There she was.

Dreams and realities appeared that showed Daisy and me at home in Hippie Hollow, Texas, in the 1970s. We were running and playing along the lake. We looked like we were only three years old. She was the only true friend I had ever had then. I had visions of my German-born parents when they were young, in love and extremely happy.

I had learned in college that, when under threat of death and disease, God allows you to think about love, friendships and who really counts in your life during your last few breaths. I could only think of five total true friends that I had in my entire life. You know, the ones that will come get you out of jail anywhere, drive you home when you're drunk, pull you out of a fight just before the police show up—you know, real friends. They are few and far between. Once you get older, people you know are mostly acquaintances at best. It's just real life.

The love of a parent and a soul mate are rare. With death upon me, I found that I would never feel their love or share life ever again. So, what was it like to lay in bed with a true love and just waste a day away? The birth of a child, it was something I would never experience, other than watching a Pakistani girl give birth ten days ago. That girl took the pain like no man could. Pushing out a small child through that little hole and then cooking dinner a few hours later. Dedication and resilience without the requirement of painkillers. The Rangers look for people like that!

As I began shaking my head mentally from the experience of watching childbirth, the rope was suddenly tightened again around my neck from behind; Waba began bending my neck to the breaking point. I tried to break free as the cold settled over my body. My legs began to freeze just as my stomach knotted. I could feel urine flowing from my body. *My God, I am going to piss on myself before I die.*

The only good side to that was that my family would never know or see me. When you die doing covert actions at this level, you are never recovered. And, because this was an unsanctioned mission, no rescue was coming. I starting drifting towards my last breath, and I began seeing the beginnings of life. You know, the whole-life-flashes-before-your-eyes thing. This was where I was to see my maker, good or bad. Opening my eyes one more time, I saw Laima standing in front of Waba and I, holding and axe, crying.

Chapter 2

My name is River Rochman, and I was born in Hippie Hollow on Lake Travis, Texas, on May 2, 1967, to Baron and Ada Rochman. Their real last name was Reichmann, but they changed it in the mid-nineteen-fifties due to negative American feelings towards Germany and their desire to move to America. They could see a better life in America with the coming of the hippie culture and their newfound spirituality. The hippie culture would provide a freedom of expression, freedom to grow and sell pot, and freedom to follow their true love, brewing beer.

They even worked on their accents to include my own, to not sound so German. In private, we spoke German, but in public, we spoke our best English.

Baron Rochman was a small man, weighed very little, and arrived in Hippie Hollow at twenty-seven years old. My mother was of the sweetest nature, even more when she was smoking pot and brewing beer. My father would sit around pruning his pot plants and talk of our future in Hippie Hollow. He rarely discussed the old country; the effect of war on him was great. My mother, Ada, was also a small woman but had some wide hips that could have born more children than just me. She was a great cook, kept a clean house, ran our family like a military outfit and was really smart. That was the German engineering in her; everything was precise.

They had only general labor skills, with great common sense. They did yard work and road work with the county, but mainly sold pot and home-brewed beer to locals. Hell, even I was peddling the stuff through the 1970s. I was smoking pot by the time I was ten. Customer satisfaction was my motto; I had to prove to my customers that the stuff was good and cheap. I mean, heck I was smoking my own product. I was only ten years old and had no money, so it must be cheap, right?

"River 'The Potster' Rochman," the pot heads in Hippie Hollow would say when I passed. My father was proud but my mother knew that this was the wrong thing for a ten-year-old to do. Needless to say, I was the breadwinner at times.

I would bring back the money, or even sometimes food that was traded for pot. My mother, the "banker," would collect that money into a pickle jar. This banking method allowed my timid and sometimes unemployed father to claim success as a German immigrant. When my father wasn't around, she complained about his inabilities. I hated to hear my mother talk ill of my father; I found it disrespectful at times. I am sure she loved him, but just needed to vent to her only child.

Respect for my father was deep; he had moved my mom and him from Germany to Hippie Hollow, a nudist colony with a population of over one thousand people. The colony was located along Lake Travis. Signs saying "Nudist Colony Ahead" lined the roads leading in. Those signs were magnets for mostly men with binoculars. My parents seemed happy, and it was a simple existence.

During my younger years, clothes were not a requirement. Well, not until puberty hit. That's when I couldn't hold my manhood together when Daisy came around. I think I got my first arousal at the age of 11 when Daisy showed up one night and could not sleep. This was not unusual as her parents were always wasted on something and left Daisy alone a lot. She trusted me and my family.

Our house was an old bus with a plywood hut that looked like a storage shed. Colorful sheets and rugs hung from the roofs to block wind and dirt. It didn't cover down to the ground, so your feet were always dirty because the wind would blow. My father moved the bus around several times to block the wind each year. Then he reattached the bus back to the plywood section of the house.

There was no running water or power in our area. Lanterns, buckets and gas generators were traded and purchased more than anything other than food. The restroom facilities were mobile public outhouses that moved around Hippie Hollow each month. There were very few outhouses, because it took energy to dig a hole each month. The labor forces around Hippie Hollow were not that motivated to burn or dig a hole for shit. Needless to say, it got full fast, and then it took forever to dig another.

An old man with no clothes would sometimes ride around telling everyone the new location of the outhouses. That didn't help a teenager. I just stopped looking for it and walked away from the house and left it for the animals to work it over. Sometimes my mother would smell something offensive and claim the raccoons did it and then give me the "eye." She knew what happened: Her only son was the culprit. Mom had to be proud!

The religion of the community was Hindu, a spiritual following that was not so much about religious beliefs but daily morality and karma. It always confused me when my mother discussed Hindu and the daily morality requirement. Daily morality discussions came early in one-line statements like, "The earth is our mother. She clothes and feeds us, and the milk of the cow runs in our blood." The statement "clothes and feeds us" gave the green light for pot and beer distribution because it provided everyday care for our family.

Oh, well, Hindu and incense burning was a positive morality check. We all smoked pot and brewed beer illegally all day. According to the great state of Texas, this was morally, ethically, and legally wrong to do. Fifteen minutes after each conversation on this matter from the local law enforcement, everyone was back to smoking pot and I was back on the beer kettle brewing the immoral brew.

My father's horticulture techniques on pot were second to none. Proudly, he was the best German pot developer and I was the best first-generation German-American pot seller in Hippie Hollow.

One summer when I was sixteen years old, my mother asked me what my plans for college were. I was shocked to hear her discuss this idea for the first time in my life. I had harsh memories of her dropping me off at kindergarten in 1972 and never dropping me off or picking me up ever again. Maybe it was because Daisy had mentioned to her recently that she was going to go to college at the University of Texas in Austin.

"You should go with Daisy to school," she said.

"Mom, my two-point-oh average will not get me into Harvard, OK?" I said. I guess she had become wiser over the years. Maybe she now felt that she may have been an absent mother and finally felt bad about it.

"Mom, no teacher or principals are calling, so I must be OK! Listen, at no time will I ever have a sign in the front yard saying I was student of the month or year." It was just not in the cards for me academically.

Daisy was always concerned about me, we were very close. We had been dating over the summer in 1983 and I felt something very strange with her. I liked her, maybe even forever.

Education with Daisy was important, and she wanted me to go to school with her so she would not feel out of place. She still dressed a "hippie way," with long brown hair in a ponytail. It looked hot and normal for me! I still was wearing bell bottoms with rhinestone designs and a tank top with peace signs and drug references attached. My clothes still had not changed much from the days of the Vietnam War. Clothes were passed around in Hippie Hollow, as we got the most out of what we had. This was the beginnings of the recycling revolution.

Daisy was a straight-A student, while I was focused on pot and beer development at my parents' bus-shed home on wheels. One day, Daisy brought me a college scholarship application to Texas State University and wanted me to fill it out. Daisy applied and received a full-ride scholarship her senior year to Austin. All I received was an acceptance to go with no money to assist. Daisy begged me to find the money and she would help work with me that year to raise the tuition money. Daisy was the best; I owed a lot to her as she helped me. I related this help to love. Later I realized that I was wrong.

One night, I showed the acceptance letter to University of Texas Austin to my mother and father, and my father was stunned and my mother was excited. Yet, they both realized they didn't have the money to give me. My mother said, "We are poor and have no money to help right now."

I knew that was coming, so I said, "Maybe I could grow my own pot and brew my own beer to sell for profit."

Baron and Ada Rochman were excited with this motivation, initiative, and idea. They both said they would help me grow and brew illegal substances to pay for my college education. We were all excited and my mother ran around Hippie Hollow half-clothed telling everyone.

"My son is going to college!" The pressure was now on to get the money. When the pressure is on, mistakes will happen.

My father began to make space for my future pot and brewery development venture. There were exciting times that would only last few years as the police raided Hippie Hollow and broke up the operation. My father and mother took the rap and went off to county jail on a six-month stint. Man, I loved my parents!

During their incarceration, I ran out of money for college tuition after the first semester. The pot and beer distribution cash flow system was a month-to-month scheme. I had only a few weeks at the end of December 1985 to come up with the money to continue. I wandered around campus to gain inspiration.

As I moved slowly through campus, destined to lose my girlfriend and my future, I saw a sign for Army ROTC that said, "Be All You Can Be." Below it read, "College money for four years as an officer."

Be All You Can Be! Hell, I wasn't being anything right now. I went to the army recruiter to see what I could do to save my college career. I signed the next day as my parents waited in jail.

It was the biggest decision I had ever made. When I told Daisy, she was furious because she was an Anti-War believer. That was the day I felt the beginnings of separation between us.

"River, I can't believe you did this to us!"

"Baby, I have signed a contract."

It was law now and I had to go the following summer after I graduated from college to the army basic training and officer school. Daisy stormed off and left me standing there looking out into the university's agricultural fields and all I saw was a cow. How Hindu, dammit!

By signing that document, I had just created a downhill life struggle that would later bring me to death's door multiple times. The army would lead me to a great life, death, pain, and sacrifice. If I could have only seen into the future, I would have turned around and ran. The cow should have been the karma!

It was now June 1993. I graduated, barely, from college. My parents came to the graduation—wasted, proud, and incarceration free. It created an extremely happy moment for my parents as I walked across the stage. They didn't know anyone in our family that had graduated from college. Under my graduation gown was my army dress uniform. I wanted to show my pride as a new second lieutenant in the army. A few months later, I left home for basic officer training. I should have looked back one more time! Just one more smile...

Chapter 3

Within two weeks of starting officer basic training, I knew I loved what I was doing. There was better food, housing, healthcare, and more money than I had ever had before. I was probably making more money than half of the people in Hippie Hollow combined. Growing up poor was not my choice, but was part of my parents' newfound, American-arrival Hindu religion and a Rochman laziness that had given us a life of simple wants, needs and desires. My mother had hinted to this reason for our poverty when she was high on pot. This truly made her verbal and mental credibility even more suspect as I look back on it now. They were my parents: Everything they said was golden, but it just started to seem a little jumbled and confused as I became more aware of the outside world and its politics.

Army healthcare was straightforward for the easy stuff like a cold, flu, dental, and stitches. When it came to glasses, they were black-rimmed ones that looked like they had been on Buddy Holly, black and rigid. The army sergeants called them my "birth control glasses." I would never go on a date with these things on. My looks were downgraded with them on and my I.Q. increased in the eyes of women. Looks were more important than I.Q. for women in bars at this stage in my life. Let's thank the Hindu gods for Lens Crafters and two pair for a hundred bucks. I started looking like a GQ-smart type of guy. One set for work and the other for "play"? Add some nice clothes, and I was converted from a hippie child to a middle-of-the–road, college-educated man. This was a changing moment in my social and mental standings. Life was a brighter color with an education, money, and a solid job.

My first physical the army gave me, I came up "hot" on a piss test for pot. Yet, they needed officers so bad that the doctors stated, "Remember, you took the pot only experimentally!" I walked out of that office freed from my chemically induced past. The sins of yesteryear, they had been given a clean slate. All I had to do now was survive the next four years of required military service to pay off my college loans, and I would go back home to Daisy and Hippie Hollow. Maybe even smoke a little!

I never planned on marrying Daisy right after college, even though we had dated throughout. We needed to find jobs and get our own affairs in order. Daisy was not personally, politically or at any level mature enough to handle the political, social, and sometimes isolated life of a military spouse. Crazy thing is, she easily understood when I told her that I would not be back for a while. I walked away with a lump in my throat; I guess I had expected her to be a little more broken up than that. Like, "Oh, baby, please don't go!" stuff.

"River, I love you to a point, but not enough right now to move from Hippie Hollow and live against my political morals," she said to me without a tear in her eyes. The undertones of that statement led me to believe that she was over me enough and we should move on. We would write rarely but no phone calls, it was a quiet relationship, you might say. That was the last I would see Daisy for many years.

I was commissioned as a signal officer and was placed in an infantry battalion in Europe. My love of the outdoors and living like a minimalist matched my old lifestyle, minus the pot and home brew.

Sleeping on the ground, foraging for food, surviving hardship and pressures on my personal soul somehow fit with my younger years in Hippie Hollow. Heck, having nothing and moving towards an objective to get something were easy and satisfying to grasp. This army life was great! They even placed shitters on wheels in the field that didn't move around and fill up. Some guy showed up in a tank truck with gloves on and pointed a hose into the shitter hole, and magic! It was all clean. Then he sprayed blue chemicals and it smelled great. I was so spoiled in the area of chemical toilets!

Those three years went fast as I had some German girlfriends and I did a lot of field exercises. It was a cool thing; I could pass the time away with having fun with my job and someone. Daisy wasn't waiting around for me anymore, as I had changed and grown apart from her. Changes in my life and career started to give me purpose and direction, and I needed that. A career in the military became my life, and I believed I was ready to commit. I decided to make this my career.

The realities of life outside of Hippie Hollow and the United States showed the happiness and sadness of our world. And me, I was in the middle of it all, working towards making the world better. United States' pride and direction are extremely powerful aphrodisiacs that can lead you away from the past towards something better. A patriot I had become, working for the cause of freedom and believing I was ready to give my life to that cause. Yet, I had never been tested in combat.

Soon enough, I was at ten years of military service and holding the rank of major. Money was coming out my ears and I was spending and selling it like a cheap whore ten minutes before the end of the world. It was magnificent; I had a sports car, an apartment for entertaining of all sorts and types. Still, I had Daisy on my mind all those years. She was the marker that all women I had ever seen would have to stack up to.

I wasn't unusual; a lot of majors were not married. They had dropped all their lives into this career; it was everything to them. Life was that way for me too. Loneliness would later haunt me and my choices would be questioned in a foreign country.

Being single would soon be the ticket to hell a year later. I had come down on orders to Fort Bragg, North Carolina, in May 2003. At the reception station, I was lined up with other captains and majors by highly decorated brigade commander; his name was Col. Edwin Stanton. He was a decorated hero from the Afghanistan invasion.

Col. Stanton had done an airborne operation into the northern part of the country in late 2001. Some Northern Alliance warriors and Afghan locals that were held hostage in the notorious Mazari Sharif prison by the Taliban called him "Alexander the Great" after he rescued them. The name stuck with the media, and he was an instant international hero.

As Stanton was walking through the ranks of officers, he seemed to be looking for something in particular. He talked to some and not others. He asked questions, such as how to operate certain radios that included satellite systems. Even secure devices to drown out voice transmission to the enemy. They were easy systems to operate, from what I had heard. From the multi-band radios to the Iridium satellite phone system, they were common operator-type questions. I just wanted to blurt the answer out, but I kept my cool. Not kissing ass, just assisting the conversation.

Col. Stanton came near me and could tell by my body language that I was either ready to answer the questions or just plain scared of him. Within a few seconds, Col. Stanton passed up three officers in the formation and came right to me.

Stopping and looking into my eyes closely, he said, "You been listening to every word I have been saying, so go ahead and answer the questions." I started with the multi-band radio through the

Iridium satellite phone, and I could tell you from front to back what these systems could do and how to operate them. The Iridium satellite phone was even easier to explain because I used to carry one in Kuwait during post-Gulf War duties.

"Very good, River. You are on my list of good officers." Col. Stanton seemed impressed and moved on to others.

At the end of the inspection and testing by Col. Stanton, he asked me to fall out and stand by for further instructions. Whatever it was, I was excited and ready. Stanton seemed like a steely-eyed killer that needed assistance in his unit to "get them squared away." *Hell, I am your man. Major River Rochman at your service!* I believed this was that moment in my career where I would get out ahead. Shifting gears from the middle of the officer pack to all-out forward.

An army specialist came to get me and lead me into Col. Stanton's office. I waited for over thirty minutes before he came back to his office. His office was lined with awards, flags, and pictures of warriors from Afghanistan, Iraq, and Panama. It was extremely impressive. As I was walking around his office looking at them all, Col. Stanton showed up and scared me a little.

"Major Rochman, please take a seat."The seat was cold and made of stiff black leather; I guessed not many people had ever sat in it to warm it up. He began by reading my personal file. It laid out where I was born, my parents' employment, and Hippie Hollow activities.

"So, you lived in a nudist hippie colony and your family provided to the community marijuana and illegal alcohol?" He pressed me for hours on my private life and why I hadn't visited or talked to my parents in years. I was broken down emotionally that he knew so much about me, from pot to beer sales in Hippie Hollow and coming up "hot" on a piss test entering the army. It seemed my life was in his hands if he decided to tell anyone in the military.

"What the hell is going on, sir? What is it you want from me? I left that life and I knew if I went back, I could be in trouble with the army," I said rapidly.

"So, your military career is more important than your parents at this point," he said, almost coldly.

"Sir, they have not contacted me either, so I believe it's mutual."

"The answer then must be yes, River."

He slowly handed me some water as my mouth was drying out from being scared. Col. Stanton leaned forward to me and said, "Have you ever heard of the Bards tribe in Northeastern Afghanistan?"

My mind was blank, as I could only think of Russians and communism. He said, "Not long ago, some Special Forces were lost carrying secure radio equipment with enough technology that the Taliban could soon locate all secret operatives on the border between Pakistan and Afghanistan."

I soon became unglued from that ninety-eight-point-seven-degree leather seat and began to squirm.

"Everyone from the Central Intelligence Agency and Delta Forces will be hunted down by some of the most hardened terrorists alive today," said Stanton. "River, your country needs a favor: your patriotism!"

We stood up and went next door to a secure room where he showed me files on a known terrorist group that was claiming to have these systems and was prepared to use them. "The clock is ticking, River. You need to help us go in and locate the radio systems and the terrorist organization that is planning to bring harm to your brothers," stated Stanton.

I started looking around the room with confusion. Maybe someone from Candid Camera was going to jump out and laugh at me. I waited a few more minutes, but no one jumped out. My intestinal area and my ears heated up over the gravity of what I was being asked to do. I thought, *Afghanistan and Pakistan, where the hell is that even on the map?*

Col. Stanton looked at me as if it were the last time he would ever see me. As we walked back into his office, I looked on his desk. There were pictures of Hippie Hollow and everyone I knew from the days of pot and beer. He even had the drug test from the army doctor. I was screwed beyond belief.

"Do this, River, or we will deal with you by the law. You lied and you knew the consequences." Coldly staring at me, he continued: "You will be in Leavenworth by next week! Or you can do this mission, with security assistance from U.S. Special Forces and the Afghan National Army. It's not that difficult, as you know how to operate these systems, confirm their location, and obtain them. We will take over from that point with your extraction."

Stanton waited for a reaction from me. None came within his time limit, and then he said, "There is no choice; you leave tomorrow for Kabul, Afghanistan. You will pick up all required gear and information needed to begin the mission there. Key personnel will meet you at the airport and transport you through security to a vehicle waiting to transport you out of the city. River, you can tell no one!"

Chapter 4

Paranoia is defined as an unfounded or exaggerated distrust of others, sometimes reaching delusional proportions. Paranoid individuals constantly suspect the motives of those around them and believe that certain individuals, or people in general, are "out to get them."

When I was boarding a C-17 aircraft at Fort Bragg, North Carolina, to Kabul, Afghanistan in the dark hours of the morning, paranoia was what I was feeling. What I was doing seemed legitimate when it was told to me verbally, but with no operations order, the mission requirements seemed unsanctioned.

When I showed up at the air terminal, I gave the desk officer my name. He came back and said, "Sir, you are not on any manifest for anywhere." I called back to the brigade staff duty officer, and he connected me with Col. Stanton's home residence. No one answered. I hung up and gave it a few more minutes to call back.

"Hey Sergeant, can you write the phone number for the staff duty?" I took the number on the slip of paper and put it in my wallet.

Not being on the roster to fly should have been a red flag to my hippie nature, but it wasn't, because I had been off-list before to include promotions. Just an administrative oversight, I guess. I continued to work the brigade staff duty officer to get him to connect me to Col. Stanton. After an hour with no luck, I took a break. The desk officer just kept nodding his head west and east, as if to say, *I have nothing and have heard nothing, sorry!*

Two hours after I arrived and thirty minutes before the only plane going to Kabul was to leave, the phone rang at the flight desk. I jumped up and walked over to the desk to see who it could be.

"It's Col. Stanton on the line for you, sir." I picked up the phone.

"This is Major Rochman, sir." No one answered me; I was waiting again with a phone in my ear.

I waited a few more minutes for Col. Stanton to answer the phone call.

"Sir, they do not have me on the list to fly! Am I at the right terminal?"

He yelled, "Stand by and let me talk to the flight officer at the desk!"

I handed the phone to the guy across the desk to let him answer the question.

"Sir, sir, I do not know of any Major Rochman taking a flight to Kabul," he said in a rushed manner. "Yes Sir, I will see what I can do, but I cannot promise anything." The flight officer looked at me with a tempered look. "I will get you on a flight, but it will be a cargo with no seats."

I grabbed my bags and headed for the flight line, following the officer. He pointed to a van that was headed to drop off pilots on the flight-line. I took off my helmet, put in my ear plugs, and threw my bags into the back of the van. The van smelled of men in a locker room with a hint of flatulence. What a way to begin a trip to the Middle East, with a little added paranoia.

The flight would take over thirty hours to get from Fort Bragg to Kabul. We would stop at Ramstein Air Base, Germany, and Kuwait International Airport to refuel and get new pilots. These were the only moments where you could clear the stale air inside the plane. It was the worst flight ever; it smelled of jet fuel and constant heat. The emanated mixture at times was sickening.

Nothing is comfortable about flying with cargo—it has space priority. During the trip, I must have moved around on top of the cargo, from the front to the back ramp, just to try to get comfortable multiple times. Some places I went back to two or three times.

With these flights, there are no such things as in-flight meals. You eat what you bring; I brought nothing, so I stole a Jimmy Dean Box Lunch from the cargo stash. It was still frozen but time was of the essence, so I ate it quickly. Water was minimal, but one of the air-load masters gave me some bottled water to survive the frozen and stolen Jimmy Dean. He was a life saver.

As the hunger began to pass, I started thinking how jacked up this mission had started out. It seemed nothing was coordinated at any level. I had to fight and call people to get from Fort Bragg to Kabul. Who the hell has to fight to get to a war zone? *Look at me; I am just a nerdy guy from the radio world going out to get some radios and equipment from some bad guys under Special Forces and Afghan National Army security.* It sounded just OK, but there still was confusion as to the end state of this mission without any formal operations order. Col. Stanton said it was my mission until extraction. *How does extraction work? Why should I worry? That's the Special Forces' job, to get me out. They pull security, right? I will be fine.*

As the aircraft neared Kabul airfield, the plane began to circle around, starting at about three thousand feet. The reason was to avoid surface-to-air missile attacks on the aircraft. The Taliban were known to use stinger missiles given to them by the U.S. against the Russians in the 1980s. They could easily use them on us as we flew in.

The plane began to shoot flares out the wings to provide a heat signature in case any other weapon system they had was heat seeking. I was becoming sick to my stomach due to the plane's constant rolling, the heat, and the smell of jet fuel. Plus, I had been on this airplane for more than a day with very little "get off and stretch my legs" time. River Rochman was not your average soldier; I was a former liberal hippie kid who had never really had a life of danger. I was truly not ready for the hardships of this life. Patriotism had to be earned from suffering while trying to gain freedom for others. All I had known was peace, love, happiness, and extra money-making opportunities in the army until this moment. When we finally landed, I somehow felt in my chest I would never leave from this airfield ever again.

The back door dropped on the plane, and all I could see was black sky. A few minutes later I saw the lights of a forklift coming from a distance. The load master told me to sit and wait until he unloaded the aircraft. The engines remained running so they could turn the aircraft around in case of attack and fly to Kuwait for a rest. Kuwait was still a six-hour flight from Kabul. These pilots earned their money every day.

The load master said, "Stand up and move to the rear of the aircraft, and walk straight out until you see a soldier holding a ChemLight. That soldier will take control of you and move you to the in-processing center. The in-processing center will confirm your arrival and unit of assignment. You will wait in the barracks until your unit comes and signs for you."

I began to move out the door of the aircraft, and I had forgotten my ear plugs, and it was loud and windy. The farther I walked away from the plane, the more heat I felt. The fuel and exhaust smell was really strong at this point. My face and neck were extremely hot from the airplane exhaust, to the point of feeling like they were on fire. I tightened up from the heat and I tried to block my skin from direct contact. The high-pitched engine sound was minor compared to the heat. Thank God it was only temporary.

We moved towards a dark spot ahead of us, following the green

ChemLight. Within minutes we were all marched into the in-processing center. A young army private yelled out to us all to get out a copy of our orders and hand them over.

Shit, they gave me none; someone was supposed to meet me. I looked around as paper copies of orders flowed by me to the clerk, but I saw no one for me.

Here was that moment where the officer is looked at like an idiot in front of the soldiers. *Jacked Up from the Floor Up!* That's what I could tell myself at this moment. I had no pickup name or phone number—just that I was linking up with the Special Forces.

"Sir, what unit are you supposed to go to?" asked the clerk.

"Special Forces," I said hesitantly. The clerk gave me the look again, and it was embarrassing.

"Sir, sit over there until I get everyone else done."

I moved slowly—feeling as if I just got smoked and cussed out by a 7-11 clerk after I tried to convince them I was 21 when I was really only 17.

Three hours later, the clerk came with a phone number and said to call this guy. The "guy" was Col. Stanton with the next part of the messed-up schedule of events. I called the number collect, and Col. Stanton answered and stated, "River, a vehicle will come by and pick you up in twenty minutes. You will get in and they will drive you to the Afghan National Army Training Center east of Kabul. From there, you will get your transportation to the Afghanistan–Pakistan border. First, you will travel to Shkin to meet up with the Special Forces units. They will be your force protection during your search. From there, I will provide you the intelligence needed and way forward to your objective. I cannot give you any further information at this time in case of capture along the way. Good luck, River."

Stanton hung up and didn't even say goodbye, just an abrupt end. I never said a word as he talked and I listened. He did that all in under thirty seconds on an unsecure line.

Twenty minutes passed and, sure enough, I was picked up by a civilian that looked like he had just come from a killing. He acted pissed off, because I probably woke him up from sleeping. Forty years old, I guessed by looking at him. He probably was a retired spook or black operations guy that now made a thousand dollars a day to go outside the wire and hurt people.

I felt comfortable with him until we left the airport and drove straight into the city that was just liberated by the United States. "Just act like you belong here and do not look too long at any one person," said the Scary Man. I didn't believe him until I got the stare-down by a ten-year-old boy at six in the morning. He was pushing a small wheelbarrow filled with bricks. He looked tougher than me and could probably survive the Ebola virus if asked.

The sun was beginning to rise and the clouds began to show themselves in the distance. "A storm is coming," said the Scary Man. He wasn't kidding, because right as he said that, the Muslim call to prayer music started to play. Some people stopped to pray, while most didn't. I guess they were not strong and devout Muslims.

"In the name of Allah, Most Gracious, and Most Merciful," he said in a low tone. He just stared at me, with an extremely stern look of respect yet hate and said, "You are my replacement, River!"

"Oh shit," I said.

I would soon learn to distrust anyone over ten years old, find that everyone was suspect, no one meant what they said, lying was part of survival, and there are a third and fourth wind when you're running for your life and you still have to kill folks as you run away. Hippie Hollow personal survival was a verbal discussion about peace and this place would be the physical presence of the machine gun. I would soon have to be good with both!

Chapter 5

I turned and stared out the window of the truck in disbelief. Was it fate or the lack of a religious upbringing being paid back by God himself? All the drug sales, illegal liquor stills, or out-of-marriage sexual fantasies of Daisy—could God be that cruel? Or, was I just the good soldier doing something that sounded relatively easy with a little danger involved? What could go wrong? I had protection by the Special Forces and Afghan National Army soldiers. And solid personal protection to ensure my safety had been promised by Col. Stanton.

As we arrived at the Afghan Army Training Center west of Kabul, the capital of Afghanistan, I could see old stone brown-colored headquarters buildings with a few A/C units dangling from the windows. Rugs and clothes hung out of the windows where soldiers and officers were living on the second and third floors. It was a dusty yet acceptable area to train soldiers. To most soldiers, this was a palace filled with food to them. Most all of the men came from poor families that couldn't afford to feed them, where marriages were inept, or they were propositioned by terrorists from Al Qaida. The poor conditions in Afghanistan meant poor health and dismal work conditions beyond imagination. Rampant crime and corruption by government officials led to most social failures throughout the country. All these men knew were grief, loneliness, destruction, and death. These four things always survive, after all else fails.

Some U.S. troops were there assisting in training and mentorship roles. Other contract U.S. civilians were clearly there for the money. The mission looked to be difficult—the Afghan soldiers were mostly illiterate and unmotivated to be soldiers and defend the broken government against the Taliban. They were to train these Afghan soldiers and then send them out to protect their own nation. Once completed with their service, they were released to go home; just as poor as when they came. AWOLs were also high among these ranks. At least a third left, taking their equipment with them. U.S.-provided weapons would soon be used by the terrorists, as the AWOL soldiers sold their weapons and uniforms for money or became terrorists themselves.

The U.S. military trainers knew they were coming back a year after they left. It was the rotation—in one year, out the next—to be followed up by another tour in Afghanistan or Iraq a year later. For some, it was the money, and others, the excitement of war itself. The only romance there was to war was when you were alone in the mountains; the air is a crisp cold, with people moving around the village below making the noises of morning. It somehow reminded me of home in Hippie Hollow. We too had very little, and it made things simple during the mornings.

As we drove into our sleeping area, Scary Man said, "River, this is your tent. Get some sleep. I will be back at 0200 hours to leave for Shkin."

Grabbing my bags, I headed for the tent and laid down on a metal bunk with only the bottom springs exposed and sagging. "Perfect," I said. I rolled my sleeping bag out, laid down and did not wake for another nine hours. When I awoke, my face was extremely oily and sweaty. It was only four o'clock in the afternoon.

I headed for the shower area, passing those coming out in

flip-flops with a towel thrown over their shoulders. I loved every minute of it—this was real soldier stuff. I was now just one of the boys, and life was good. Just as my euphoria peaked, I ran into the guy I was replacing, and he looked like shit. I mean, way worse than I ever have. The war had turned him skinny and frail. Earlier, when he picked me up, he had a lot of gear on him so he looked intimidating. Now he looked like a smoker on the verge of a vitamin deficiency. Health was not a priority for this man!

"Hey, what's up?" I said. Scary Man could tell I was concerned with his looks and condition.

"Yes brother, this will be you in one year!"

"One year! I was sent here for only three months to find some radios!"

"Yes, me too," he said with a laugh.

I gingerly sat down outside the shower area, confused, nervous, and outraged. Did Col. Stanton lie to me and this guy? Could this be the first of many lies?

Scary and Frail Man came to my tent later to just say hello and ensure I had not gone missing after the first day. "River, this is not what you signed up for. It's a little more involved than just looking for radios on the border in Pakistan. You will be dropped off at the border camp known as Shkin Fire Base. From there, you will move up to the border and cross with Special Forces and local work force support. You will then travel by vehicle and then move dismounted to the village of Shawal to get supplies. From there, you will walk about thirty kilometers east to the city of Miran Shah. There you will locate a communications site that overlooks the city. You can't miss this place. That's where I believe the system is located.

"Once you get the system in your hands, run like hell. Only two exit routes out of the area are feasible: One goes to the Afghan border and the other is north towards the city of Peshawar that links to a highway to Torkham Gate. Either way, you have to come out of Pakistan into Afghanistan and return the system to U.S. control. That way it's accounted for, and we know you are still alive."

"You only have yourself to rely on inside Pakistan and along the tribal areas of Afghanistan. Col. Stanton led you to believe this was not all that bad, River. It's dangerous and has limited success written all over it. If this was a bet in Vegas, you would be at one-thousand-to-one odds. Initiative and the desire to survive are all you have."

"How big is this system, really?" I said.

"The brain of this thing is the size of a cell phone. You need to leave the rest. It's too much to carry and run with. This is a snatch-and-run play, like high school football."

I looked at him and said, "I didn't play football in high school!"

"River, this is not a normal radio you are looking for. This system tracks U.S. forces movements along the border areas. Soldiers have already been killed and injured due to this system being in the wrong hands."

"How did these systems get into the wrong hands?" I said.

Scary Man said, "Col. Stanton had them stolen from him when he was a commander here. He has been claiming he still has them, but really he doesn't. That is why I am here; I have the information on where they are at, but have not physically seen them. We know there are four of them spread amongst four tribal areas inside Pakistan—Mian Shah all the way through to the northeastern border of Pakistan. This is about one thousand miles between these two locations. These areas are extremely dangerous to navigate as the mountains are steep and covered in snow."

"Will I have a vehicle at any time during this operation?" I said.

He smiled and said, "I walked from Shkin back to Kabul, any questions?"

I turned away as he stood up to leave. I couldn't believe this. Col. Stanton was trying to save himself, while we roamed the countryside looking for his radios that were being used to kill our own troops.

"River, I too was just a simple man with a family. I don't know if they are still waiting for me." What you had in your life, if anything, is gone for good. You will never mentally or physically recover from this. Stanton owns you now!

"At 0200 hours tomorrow morning, you will move by ANA convoy to Khost Province, stay overnight, and then move the next day to Shkin Fire Base. From there, you will receive your marching orders to move across the border to begin your search by Col. Stanton. River, I have only my experience and stories to move you ahead from here. Oh, and another thing, when you are walking and gathering intelligence, it takes weeks to get information from the tribes. It's about building relationships, and once achieved, they will trust you if you're useful to them. Nothing is free, so be prepared to give everything.

"You are Stanton's greatest and final hope of finding these systems. He will leave command next year and he's got to have them on hand. If not, he will go to jail, as will you if you survive at all!"

"What about those that have died?" I said.

"He only cares about himself and his career," said Scary Man.

"I am in a world of hurt, correct?"

"Yes, and just know, you are now starting the downturn of your life. You will never be the same person. The future memories that you get from this mission will remain. Those you love and care for will see through these bad times every day. Stay calm and remember that violence can and will take you over when threatened. Never drink alcohol when you are thinking about these days. You will fight to the end with whoever gets in your path," said Scary Man.

"Scary Man, how did you get into this mess?"

"Same way you did, River: You have no clear ties to anyone, you have a past that could get you put out of the army, and you are a strong patriot! Be ready by 0200 hours tomorrow morning. We leave for the border. I will see you then."

Chapter 6

I couldn't sleep that night; I was too nervous and scared to do anything. Walking multiple times during the night to the chow hall to drink and eat Otis Spunkmeyer muffins, I clearly was suffering from fear. My face was heating up; stomach cramps couldn't be controlled by food.

Scary Man came to my tent at 0200 hours to police me up.

"Damn, you are here and on time," I said. He was dressed like an Arab tribesman loaded for bear, while I was dressed like I was going to the field at Fort Benning, Georgia, for the first time. I had all the military and spy gadgets hanging off of me as if I had just raided a military surplus store.

"You do not need all that stuff," he said as he began to throw off my spy gear. "You are going to get us all killed like that. Take all that gear off and only keep your pistol and rifle. When we get out of town and into a village, we will get you some clothes that you'll need to survive as a local. They will be the only clothes you will own this year. You have to blend in like you belong here. If not, you will die before you get to the border. "The secret to Afghanistan and Pakistan doing covert operations is to blend in, act like they do, learn some language, walk like they do across open ground, and at some point, get a donkey to pull behind you."

That would be some of the best advice I would ever receive from anyone. And, it would later come in handy.

We jumped into his pickup with a truck bed full of Afghani army soldiers dressed in green uniforms, weapons, and looking around with confusion. They had the same look on their face as I did: *Oh shit!* You could hear the soldiers talking to each other behind me as we drove down the road. I had no clue what they were saying until Scary Man started laughing. I asked him what they were saying, and he said, "You look like you don't know what the hell you are doing either."

Great, a bunch of newbies, including myself, a truck of fools! Col. Stanton even suckered these guys, or was Scary Man just as jacked up as Stanton? Had he lowered himself to self-survival at the expense of these soldiers?

"We will link up in West Kabul near the 'Glass House' with a patrol from the Afghan National Army for movement to Khost Fire Base. We will stay there for a few hours to get some sleep".

The "Glass House" was exactly that: a house that was made with green glass. Every building structure around it was destroyed and dilapidated, except the Glass House. They said that, during the war, the owner had paid off the enemy forces to not damage his home, and it worked.

The owner was in the brick-making business. His brink factories were dirty, nasty, and unsafe places to work. These factories created "black lung"-type health symptoms among the workers. Most were under the age of fifteen and looked as if malnutrition had set in. The skin of these children was stained with black carbon, their noses were filled with it, and their eyes looked red and irritated. They made less than one dollar a day and remained illiterate.

Our ride through the city to the linkup point took only about thirty minutes. The convoy force was sitting there waiting as we pulled up. Some had army vehicles but most were in trucks like ours, overloaded with soldiers hanging on for dear life. A few machine guns atop a few vehicles would act as our weapons for protection along the way.

Looking bewildered at this rag-tag organization, I said, "Are we safe with these guys? They look too young to even have an idea of what's about to happen."

"The scary part is, River, they look scared because they should be. They know what's about ready to happen. Most have experienced attacks and the death of family members. These guys are being forced to protect someone they do not even know. I am a devil and a possible casket ride home for them by just being around me!"

"They see the look on your face. You're scared and confused, and they know it. If we get into a fight, they will look to us to lead them. They have not one leader amongst them, so they will be looking for any help to save themselves. Not one hero exists among them, River!"

Convoy movement started after Scary Man gave a safety briefing. He talked actions on enemy contact, vehicle breakdown, medical, and medevac procedures. It took a few minutes to get through it because the translation between Afghan and English had to take place. The looks on these soldiers' faces made me extremely nervous. They had no clue what really was being said. Most of them could not read or write. The money they made as soldiers was sent home to their parents. These soldiers were only brave enough for a few hundred dollars each month. As I looked into these soldiers' eyes, my gut told me that some of them would never make it home alive in the next two days. We were looking at dead men standing around us.

Our convoy speed was about forty-five miles per hour as we headed out of the city through the valleys to the west. Roads were decent for the first half of the trip. The second half would be through mountain regions where you barely moved due to the rocky terrain. You didn't want to break down in these areas. If you did, the odds of being attacked went up dramatically. If attacked or ambushed, it would end up being a turkey shoot and a Mexican standoff!

A few hours into our movement, I was looking out the window; I could see ridgelines surrounding the city of Gardez. The city of

Gardez stretched north and south down the side of a valley. It had a water source and green agricultural fields stretching out from it. Farmers, both legal and illegal, developed an industry of subsistent living and illegal drug trade with foreign backers. They could farm for a hundred dollars a year, or they could make a thousand dollars a year from the drug trade. Easy choice: Foreigners wanted opium over wheat.

As the sun was coming up, I could see old Soviet tank positions on mountaintops overlooking key cities and villages. They all had graffiti on them and looked very weathered. Only children played in them these days.

Destroyed Soviet tanks were a sign of victory for the Afghans. They won and they knew it without question. The Afghanis had the Soviets eating rats and squirrels and running for their lives for about the last three years of that war.

"The more your enemy suffers mentally, the greater the victory," Scary Man said as we passed battlefields.

The Afghanis were patient, they had history on their side, and they could wait you out. Their children would run you out in ten or twenty years.

"Allah gives them hope, courage and patience," he said.

"What a great traits to have," I said.

"Americans have none, and that will be our downfall if and when the time comes."

We drove by villages along the Kabul-Gardez Highway that were built with sticks, mud, and rope. Nothing looked level or safe to live in. Streets were mud and dust with a little added human waste and empty water bottles in the pathway of children playing. When the children saw us coming, they would run to our vehicles and ask for anything. When we said no, some would flip us the bird! That's when I was sure Americans had been through here. The icon of America in this village was the middle finger. What a legacy we had left behind. I too would probably leave behind bad habits and memories for the Afghanis and the Pakistanis. War is hell, but it's the little memories that you leave behind that will affect the American ideas of democracy and hope.

Food looked scarce for these people, yet the roadside markets looked filled with items to buy. Some products looked Chinese and Indian made. Very little was locally made, and exports were few and far. Exporting, to them, was the next village over. International business capabilities were not a part of their mind-set. Bricks and other farming items were made for local consumption and trade.

We cleared the city in about one hour and headed west towards Khost. Meandering uphill and moving through switchback roads that were dropping down in elevation, roads would soon become unimproved. The roads began to get smaller as large trucks got closer to our side-mirrors. Based on the driving capabilities of the truck drivers coming towards us, they must have not been trained. There isn't a Department of Motor Vehicles or a highway patrol out here!

Yet, who would need a license? The trucks they drove were known as "jingle trucks." They got this name because they had small metal chains with silver metal charms hanging from the side of each truck. You could hear them coming from a great distance in the desert. Each truck was painted very colorfully with mostly female religious figures. They were old–time, Allah-style paintings that brought good luck to their travels. The doors were mainly made of wood that looked like they went on your oak entertainment center. They were stained brown and very ornamental with carvings of religious figures. All truck owners took great pride.

As we hit the next switchback on the road down into Khost, trucks, people, and donkey carts stopped coming up the hill. The soldiers and Scary Man became a little edgy, moving themselves into position to defend themselves.

"Hold on, River, it looks and feels like this is going to head south on us," said Scary Man.

I looked over and mentally stalled and asked, "Why?" He double-taked at me with a look of "Unbelievable!" As I looked back through the window of the truck at the ANA soldiers, they had the pucker factor maxed out. Even these newbie soldiers knew this was not right.

This was my moment of naiveté of the world around me. Hippie Hollow was a place of safety that gave me the idea that the world was good within it. Here, I was tensing up for something I could not see or understand. Life and death were now all rolled up into one moment. This is where your mind goes crazy with thoughts of only survival, mentally asking multiple questions at one time: *What the hell am I doing? Can someone help me get out of this as I do not have these skills required to even save myself? Am I responsible for the soldiers with me? Is my weapon off of safe? Is there a round in the chamber?* And *I better roll down my window.* I mean, the mental craziness happens all at once. If my mind could have worked this fast during college, I would have been a genius.

As we drove closer to the center of the switchback road, we started seeing cars and trucks stopped in a traffic jam. "Oh, thank God, it is just an accident on the road. Maybe we can help with first-aid or something," I said. All the guys were still quiet, as if they didn't trust anything at this point. Our convoy was now stopped with no more than five feet between us. Scary Man got out and yelled to the ANA platoon leader: "Dismount and set up security!"

The soldiers moved slow and timid; they walked on the road as if there was a bomb nearby. They were really scared just like I was. Nothing professional about these guys, at all!

"What do you need me to do?" I said.

"First, get the hell out of the truck and stop acting like a passenger!" I was embarrassed at my inability to be a soldier in these conditions. Amateur as I was, as I opened my door and tried to make that first step onto the earth, I looked scared as hell. I stepped lightly on to the ground with the precision of a ballerina ready to get my ass beat. We were not even under threat of the enemy. I was scared, my teeth hurt, and my shoulders were tense. Man, I needed some Baron and Ada Rochman Hippie Hollow weed about right now!

I hunched down along the road, pointing my weapon towards the east, overlooking the Khost Valley off in the distance. My weapon was still on safe. You know, that is a hell of a mental move, to slide that lever on your weapon to automatic in order to kill someone. It's an adult commitment when you do this. You have to make the decision to use it or not! That's the choice you make when you have to shoot at someone: commitment in the blink of an eye. It's all about live, die, wound, or just scare with that much power in your hand.

We sat there for about five minutes, and I felt like that was about enough bravery for me. The ANA were ready to run also. Scary Man walked down to the accident area to look at what the deal was. He looked extremely comfortable as he acted like a local, shooting the breeze with the Afghan locals. He blended in pretty good, but the locals knew what vehicle he had come in. There was no hiding who he was and what he stood for.

Suddenly, up from the road came a girl dressed extremely warm for the temperature. She was zigzagging along the road as if she was drunk. I thought maybe she was handicapped, mentally ill, or on drugs. Everyone around her was getting out of her way fast. She looked extremely heavy around the midsection of her body. Scary Man started running back up the road, yelling, "Get in the ready position! Eyes into the hills!"

What the hell is going to happen? Get ready for what? Some drunken girl with her winter coat on. So what, right? I thought. That girl kept walking towards us, and the locals just let her keep coming. No social or local help for this girl. They must have known something I wasn't getting.

Scary Man pointed his weapon and started speaking in Pashtun: "Stop or we will shoot!" She just kept walking, slobbering out of her mouth, hands in her pockets and wearing a heavy blue decorative dress. That would be her death dress—the last one she would ever wear.

Boom! She was gone in an instant. She had exploded a bomb strapped to her body. I felt thc concussion and heat, and then I saw the flash of fire and light. It all came in that order. The strength of the bomb was intense. It ripped through the vehicles and the people around her. We were within seventy-five feet of the blast, and it took us to the ground. My ears were ringing as my skin was flash-burned and cut from hitting the road.

"What the hell?" I said, with my breath taken way.

I looked over in front of me for Scary Man; he was on the ground, shaken but getting up to return fire into the hills above us. He looked focused and in control, yelling, "Enemy at our nine o'clock!" as we pushed the Afghani soldiers and me to secure the area and keep our eyes out for enemy contact. The timing to get into position again was not enough.

"RPG, RPG, RPG"!

Chapter 7

The heat of the road on my face was unforgettable. Every pebble, rock, and grain of sand was touching my right cheek and eye socket. I remained focused on my immediate thoughts, only focusing on the heat of the road, the sound of gunfire, and the sound of a truck burning. The smell of tar and antifreeze reminded me of vehicle accidents on I-35 in Texas. When you smelled that, death seemed to be near. The smoldering legs, arms, and intestines were scattered around the area. Allah had just visited us!

Scary Man was moving up the hill to our nine o'clock, right towards the gunfire. Only a few Afghan soldiers followed in support. Most were scared or dead from the RPG explosion and its terrorizing effects of an unseen enemy.

The dust from on top of the hill became disturbed as the shooting and movement of the enemy prevailed down on us. I was still down behind a vehicle, pointing my weapon in the wrong direction. I was absolutely no help against the enemy. My face was frozen, my teeth hurt—I was only hearing my thoughts, looking for something to help someone, and still not having the courage or the will to take my weapon off safe. My mind had yet to commit to war.

Looking over the damaged vehicles, I saw an Afghan soldier crawling towards me, begging to be pulled to safety. He had one hand stretched out to me while the other dragged behind him.

"Help me, please!"

He was looking into my soul with empty, frightened black eyes and tears, visually begging for his life from someone he did not know. I think he was so scared and near death, anyone would have done. A Christian, Hindu or Muslim, he wanted to be saved by any brave soldier. I couldn't move to grab him. Bravery was not working as I thought of my own safety and no other's. I was not a good soldier for combat!

That man died on that hot road, burning from the heat and bleeding out from his kidney area on that day. There were three other ANA soldiers dead near him that could have been saved. That moment, your god or mine only gave bravery to one-third of us. There are those that fight to win, those that fight for their own personal survival, and those that died fighting for varying patriotic causes.

Screaming orders to the ANA soldiers in Pashtun, Scary Man kept them in a straight line to avoid them shooting each other during the assault. I could see ammo clips being thrown after us behind them. They were going through ammo quickly.

"Stay in line, stay in line! River, get your ass up here! We need ammo!"

I couldn't move. I was shocked from the event.

"River, get the ammo out of the truck."

I stood up to get the ammo out of the passenger side of the truck. There were two bags: I checked the first one, and there were only a few hundred rounds. The other had about fifty rounds. Grabbing them both, I began to run around the truck under cover. Just as I showed myself to enemy fire, tracer rounds skipped off the road and hit the taillight of the truck. As I hit the ground and backed into cover again, the ammunition was now left on the ground in front of me. As I stared at it, scared of it, even just to grab it, Scary Man continued to yell.

"Get me more ammo, anyone!" River, help us or we are going to die up here!"

All of a sudden, the sound of gunfire stopped. You could have heard a bird flying by, it was so quiet. That was it, the battle was over, and the ambush was a success for the enemy. Local civilians and soldiers were dead, and we were all angry and scared. The enemy's terror tactics had worked on us all.

Scary Man and two others made it to the top to find the enemy had run off into the distance. All that was left were empty water bottles, human waste, and manure from the donkey that hauled the supplies. In the distance, I could see dust and vehicle movement headed down into Khost. The enemy had slipped away. Scary Man looked through the scope on his weapon to look into the distance of enemy movement going into Khost.

"The enemy must be moving forward into another position to attack later. River, get up here now!"

I moved with a purpose up the hill, passing two dead soldiers, running as fast as I could.

"River, where the hell were you? We lost two soldiers because we did not have ammunition." He grabbed me by the throat, yelling, and forced me to the ground to look at the dead soldier. I could barely breathe as I looked into the face of the dead man.

"He had a family, people that loved him. Now he is dead for fifty bucks a month. You left us all to die right here on this road. You left us all here to die, River. If you are going to be a coward, walk back to Kabul. You cannot be trusted as a warfighter!"

As now a known coward in battle, who had been the cause of at least three deaths, I silently volunteered to pick up the dead soldiers and their gear. I helped swing them into the back of the truck. The Afghan lieutenant handed me some white sheet material and physically suggested I wrap the body.

"River, these dead men need to be wrapped in these sheets and buried soon, according to the Koran. We will not be able to do it until we arrive at Khost. Let's get off this road ASAP, and get through Khost in the next hour. So, hustle it up!"

These types of attacks are common along the roads. Road block, RPG, ambush, then run away. This was the cycle of violence for counter-insurgency throughout the Middle East. We would later see another attack with similar effects. Two enemy combatants would just whittle our numbers down so when we made it to our objective, we would lack combat power to be effective. It doesn't take a U.S. Army War College graduate to figure out effective counter-insurgency tactics. Most enemy fighters were just locals paid about eighty dollars for each rocket fired or per U.S. or Afghan soldier killed. That's a lot of money for an Afghan being sourced by unfriendly foreign nations like Saudi Arabia, Kuwait, Pakistan, and some even from the United States. It takes very few resources to stop a super power!

Once we had loaded the bodies into the back of our vehicles, the traffic and locals began to move around carefully. They stared, zigzagged, and then speeded up through the battle damage and the body parts, not even stopping to pick up bodies of those people they knew. These people seemed no different than Americans checking out the carnage on the highway back home. For thousands of years, it's the blood on the ground of the battlefield that makes people become less caring about the dead body and about considering their own mortality. They're just glad that it wasn't them laying there!

Scary Man yelled down to me to stop anyone over sixteen years old. He believed some of these people were involved in the incident.

"These people stopped the traffic to set us up to be attacked. Take the first two vehicles that come by. They are the most likely terrorists."

"Yes, Scary Man, I got it. Lieutenant, get your men on both sides of the road and halt those two vehicles coming up the road."

Lieutenant nodded, but only placed two men on both sides to avoid losing all his men if those trucks blew up. That looked a lot smarter than what I was going to do. The rest of the soldiers stood around the back of the truck to pray for their fallen comrades.

We stopped the first two vehicles and conducted a search. They had weapons and cash on them. They also had opium on them. It was in a paste form wrapped in green leaves shaped like a bulb. Drugs for traffic jam, I bet. The two vehicle drivers were both alone, but they resembled each other.

"They are brothers," said one of the soldiers.

I looked again and he was right. They both kept staring at each other with this look of guilt, as if to say, "Help me, please." The ANA officer took them into custody and said that he would hand them off to the local authorities in Khost. Scary Man knew this was a bad idea because the local sheriff in Khost was a Taliban supporter.

"We should keep them and use them if required against their Taliban brothers. They will be back to fight tomorrow if we give them to the Khost law enforcement," said Scary Man.

"I will handle this pig as Allah would like," said the lieutenant.

He took both brothers behind their vehicles and executed them as they struggled for their lives. You could hear them jerking and fighting up against the truck to get away. They died right there in the road. Nowhere near home, no I.D., no nothing in their pockets. Just a bloody entry and exit wound by an American-purchased 9mm pistol. With blood running down his hand, the lieutenant said, Allah was vengeful today!

I could see the blood and brain matter flow down the terrain with gravity. Both men had similar head wounds and lay within a few feet of each other.

I didn't know what to feel—glad, sad, or vengeful. They had tried to kill me. Why should I care if they were dead? The American justice in me felt that there was no trial by peers or a judge to validate guilt. Were we sure they were part of the crime? Should we have not investigated a little more than five minutes? It seemed that the road to Khost had changed the rules of law and civility.

"This is justice out here, River said Scary Man. There is no time to have to fight them tomorrow. Get rid of them now."

"Scary Man, how are we sure we did the right thing here? Should we have questioned them more than five minutes?"

"River, you do not have five minutes. You have less than five seconds to hand out justice. That's what they were doing to us. They were not going to bring legal justice, just death through ambush. Your day will come when you have the justice of River Rochman, and it won't be American justice. It will be hippie justice, right? Now get in the truck and let's move out."

As we got into the truck, some soldiers had tears and others looked as if they couldn't make the rest of the trip. They wanted to run for their lives as they sat on dead bodies of people they knew.

My mind wandered as I perspired profusely. I must have lost five pounds in about ten minutes. Cotton mouth and dehydration were evident on my lips. Trying to drink water, my gag reflex wouldn't allow it to go down. I just kept throwing it back up from just being scared and a coward. I shot no enemy; I only got three of my own killed.

"River, get out of that truck and come over here. Where the hell were you?"

I tensed up like a school boy ready to take the paddle. I had no excuse to give other than I was scared.

"When all hell breaks loose, you have to fight; you have more training in fighting than these men do. You must lead these men or more will die like today. I need you to help me and not coward down behind a damn truck."

I looked way off into the distance; I was a complete failure and contributed to the deaths of these soldiers. Never had I felt lost like this. These dead soldiers would never have anything ever again. My failure ensured their death! Tears began to fill my eyes and I began to choke up to cry. I was shaking and weak in the legs, and I just wanted to die right there. I wanted to take the place of those soldiers that I could have helped or even saved.

"Get the hell back in the truck, River!" he yelled from the depths of his throat.

He grabbed me by my man-dress and shoved me back to the truck. The shame was so great—I was a true coward and I still had to cross into Pakistan. I questioned myself: Was I that violent of a leader that couldn't be killed by man alone, like him? Shit, I was this guy's replacement! Was deciding the death of others better than choosing a possible moral right-to-life and legal due process of two enemy Taliban soldiers? What do I do next time? All I could see was that soldier looking to me for help, and I did nothing! So, what justice did he get? Death and only death!

Chapter 8

Extremely disappointed in myself, I got back in the truck once all the soldiers were loaded. Looking back at the soldiers, we were missing two people. The reality was that I was partly responsible, and that was evident to these soldiers. They too questioned my ability. Their lives were in my hands. They blindly trusted me. I am an American soldier, enough said. I waited another half-minute, but my driver didn't show up. I suddenly realized: That was the soldier looking to me for help. The one I failed to save, even when he begged.

"Get in the truck, lieutenant. I need someone in the passenger seat."

I slid over to the driver's seat as the lieutenant crawled through the back window. He seemed to be afraid of stepping out of the truck; he must have felt safe by not touching the earth. I couldn't blame him after what had just happened. He looked at me, terrified, but later seemed at ease with the metal door protection of the truck. Those in the back were exposed to the enemy and the elements. I became increasingly aggressive all of a sudden. This event had changed my life forever; I would never see the world through Hippie Hollow eyes again. Looking at the lieutenant, I gave him a look of "Strap it on, and get brave."

"Point your weapon out the window and look for bad guys."

"OK," he said with the small knowledge of English he had learned through the ANA officer's course at Kabul.

Troubled and confused about what to do next, I started the vehicle—and it took more than a few tries to start. This just increased the tension.

"Dammit, please start!"

It finally started on the third try, just before I flooded the thing. Getting that truck started and letting out the clutch was two of the hardest things I had ever done. The last time I drove a stick shift truck was with my dad back in Texas. It was a 1962 Chevy truck we used to haul around beer and weed. It's also where I kissed Daisy for the first time.

Letting out that clutch meant commitment to move closer to the enemies of hell themselves. A troubled destiny was out there; a destiny that could only be provided by the enemy—they get the first vote. This was my "destiny by enemy fire!"

We began our movement down the switchback road into the city of Khost. Immediately we began to see the life of the city. Rural meets destitution through most of the city. Visions of *National Geographic* pictures of the slums of Calcutta came rushing back from childhood. Trash laid everywhere, with goats, dogs and poor people searching through it for food. Motorcycles drove by with tough guys carrying AK-47s or all their wives and kids. They stared at me like they wanted to kill us rightnow. A lot of black turbans were being worn by the young men in the area, and they looked like they meant business. We seemed to have just entered the outer corridor of the Taliban nation, and it was evident.

Pointing to my head, I said, "Lieutenant, why do they wear the black turbans?"

"Black turbans mean Taliban supporter or bad person."

"Why do you not arrest them?"

"The town is filled with them. We would all die."

"OK, keep your weapon pointed out the window at them and keep looking out for motorcycles or cars coming near us."

Buildings and businesses never made it beyond two stories due to lack of safety inspections and standards. There was no OSHA out here. Everybody seemed to be a contractor or salesmen of some sort, but with no training. If an earthquake hit, the city would be collapsed on the people of Khost.

"When I was a child, I use to visit here with my parents. My brother died on this street when he was ten years old by Russian soldiers who came looking for food."

The lieutenant became very quiet and looked out the window. He clutched his weapon tightly, exposing his white knuckles. The loss of his brother was still fresh in his mind, and revenge was an option. These people had been invaded so many times that sadness and revenge can take as long as it likes.

The side streets were uneven dirt and some gravel. Alleys were filled with boys smoking old cigarette butts, standing by doorways with very little opportunity to make anything of themselves. Girls would be separated and playing together amongst the trash and dilapidated buildings and houses. You could smell wood burning along with the stench of old blood from animals having been killed for food in the streets. We saw a man slicing the throat of a goat, as the animal struggled to live, its legs kicking and jerking until they stopped, and the blood slowed as its heart gave out. As blood drained into the streets, little girls picked through it with sticks. Mangy dogs also smelled and licked the salty life of the goat; blood stained their lips like my mom drinking cheap Hippie Hollow red wine at a bong party. Survival had become their only human instinct; we were observing the lowest level of humanity. Khost was now my ground zero, the worst I had ever seen.

The ANA soldiers were keeping a sharp eye on everyone along the road. These boys were hardened from just twenty minutes ago.

Even I felt a little different, like more aware of what was going on. We were all tense with a purpose to kill if required. We had seen and felt death; the loss of our friends who were wrapped in the back of the truck reminded us. Having learned what it was to be a coward earlier, I put my weapon on full-auto before we hit the town. Yet my inexperience remained: I never had a magazine in the weapon.

Scary Man was ahead of us by two vehicles. I kept an eye on his vehicle so as not to get lost in the city. Taxis moved in and out of our convoy. The soldiers hung out the sides of the truck, weapons pointed out. They would point, stare, and yell at people to get out of the way. Facial stare-downs were quite meaningful and important out here. I tried it a few times and the local taxis blew me off as if it meant nothing. Scary Man was yelling out the window and pointing his finger at locals to get the hell out of the way. Boy, did they listen. There was something in his "flowery" use of the Afghani language and body gestures that obviously was universal. He was a master warfighter; I had to learn his ways in short order. My survival counted on it.

We cleared the city just before dark. There were no light street lights; the city and highways provided any nighttime safety. Khost Fire Base was about twenty miles outside the city. The roads were open but uneven and rough at best.

Just as we dreamed about arriving at the Khost Fire Base safely, a vehicle broke down just in front of me. It was overheating and stopped in an open valley, easy to ambush but hard to mortar our position. Most normal people would pull over on the shoulder. Not here in Afghanistan; mines and improvised explosive devices (IEDs) were the terror of all soldiers. I think they feared it more than shots being fired at them. *Always stay on the road. The shoulder is littered with death.*

Scary Man's front convoy vehicle finally stopped after they

noticed no one was behind them. We all got out and pulled security. I would soon be yelled at to go and see what the deal was.

"Open your hood," I said.

The soldier looked at me with confusion, so I opened his door and pulled the latch for the hood.

"Get out and help, dammit!"

Looking back at the lieutenant, I said, "Get these guys out and pulling security and get some water together. We need to fill this tank with water. Yep, it's overheated. Got any water, lieutenant?"

"No water left. Soldiers drank it all."

Scary Man yelled as if annoyed: "If you have no water, have them line up and have them piss into the radiator! Hell, they drank all the water, so I am sure they didn't piss on themselves!"

I grabbed my private parts and told them to piss, hop up and piss into the radiator. No reaction from my body part gesture, so I jumped up and pissed into the radiator as steam blew up and became uncomfortable to my Texas skin. The soldiers laughed, and I embarrassed myself. Once I finished, I grabbed the next soldier and told him to do the same. They got the picture. With six of them, we filled up the radiator to the top. That was a lot of water bottles.

The truck finally started, but you could hear the engine valves knocking. She was on her last legs, and we just hoped it would make it the last five miles. It didn't. We later towed it in, with soldiers riding in the back for the last three miles.

When we arrived at the Khost Fire Base, foreign and U.S. soldiers made a fuss that we showed up. The increase in chow hall numbers meant less for them. We used water, toilets, sodas, and medical supplies that Khost soldiers could have used. This was a military fire base with a budget, and we were not approved to be there.

Local residents looked at us as if we were not even worth knowing. The first sergeant of that infantry battalion walked out to investigate. Scary Man confronted him.

"First up, who are you? And tell me what your convoy number is."

"I do not have one. I do not operate that way."

"No one moves around my area without a clearance to do so!"

"I just did, First Sergeant, so what do we do next?"

"You are going to give me all your names and Social Security or ANA numbers so I can verify who you say you are."

"We are not going to give you a damn thing, but you are going to feed us, fuel us, get us water for the next three days, a place to sleep, and help us bury three bodies that died on the way here."

The first sergeant was in shock, and he trembled with anger. Scary Man and the first sergeant were ready to fight. All of a sudden, Scary Man said, "This can go two ways: I kill you or you kill me. If you do not kill me, I will continue to fight until you are dead. Right here in front of your troops, you will take your last breath, guaranteed."

The first sergeant could barely speak.

"What did you say to me?"

"You heard me, First Sergeant, so execute an ass-beating or get my stuff before this ends badly for you."

The first sergeant was in a state of shock, and he walked away as his soldiers stood around completely scared and nervous from the entire event. Scary Man showed no emotion as he started to unload his gear for the night.

A young sergeant reluctantly came up to Scary Man and said, "Park over by the wall on the back side of the camp. There is a Muslim burial site where you can take care of your soldiers. Chow hall closes in thirty minutes. "

"Thanks, Stud. Where is home?"

"Sir, you scare me too much. I do not want you to hunt me down and kill my entire family."

"That's too funny, troop. I only kill those that deserve it. Do you deserve it?"

"No, sir."

"OK, now leave and do not bother me again."

The sergeant moved out quickly in the direction of the first sergeant's office. Standing and trembling at the knees, the first sergeant just stood and showed no emotion. Scary Man had taken his dignity in front of his soldiers that day.

The dead soldiers were moved to a makeshift morgue on the back side of the base camp. It was also downwind so as not to arouse the wildlife to dig up the bodies. The ANA soldiers performed a Muslim burial as best they could in the dark. This was unusual for a Muslim burial they are supposed to be buried prior to sundown, but war sometimes changes traditions.

The dead were bathed and then wrapped in a simple cloth known as a *kafan*. This was the cultural custom. Usually, this would happen quickly after death but since this was a battle, it did not happen. Once the corpse was wrapped with the *kafan*, they began the funeral amongst the soldiers and a Muslim army chaplain. The *Janazah* prayer was recited by those Muslim soldiers who knew it by heart. Some just moved their mouths as if they knew it. I was spooked by the sound of the chant, but I knew I owed them at least to bow my head in respect. These were my soldiers laying there dead; they were my responsibility. One had looked at me as he died, begging for help.

Those soldiers were placed in an unmarked grave. No foot traffic was allowed in the area. It was holy ground. That night, dogs came from miles away and gathered around the new graves. They could smell death. They started digging, and I just turned my head and walked away. Shots were fired later that night—Bang! Bang!—from the guard tower. I heard a dog scream like a small child as it was wounded by gunfire. It limped away, dragging its hindquarters, being attacked by other dogs. That dog was only a bloodstain and bones the next morning in the sand.

My first day was my worst day in combat. Moving back to my truck under the light of the moon, I knew what great responsibility, human loss, and cowardice meant: me!

I didn't sleep that night…

Chapter 9

Dogs outside the wire howled all night, while moving around those dead soldiers' graves. I had never been in a cemetery at night in America to know if American dogs did the same. Maybe not, but we put them six feet down. These soldiers were only a foot below the earth with rocks piled on them.

U.S. soldiers were starting to walk around and moving to the latrines to conduct personal hygiene. They dressed in only their fatigue pants, t-shirt and boots, with a towel over their shoulder. Some had flip-flops instead of boots because they were the ones that would take a shower. It seemed a quite simple moment in a soldier's life. Normality was upon me for those minutes.

Breath flowed like steam, as I began to feel safety behind the walls of this fire base. It was the first time in hours that I realized I could breathe and feel safe. Thank God that my body pumps blood and gets oxygen on its own. The calmness of post-battle is comforting, maybe because I was still alive. In the last twenty-four hours, I became an adult, a coward, and a patty. Control of my destiny? None. The enemy and C. Stanton had a vote at this point.

The latrine needed to be my next stop. We would soon leave, so a shower sounded good in order to relax. As I began to walk by our vehicles to get my rucksack, Scary Man was sitting there in a sleep-like trance. He jumped up to his feet, half dressed.

"Let's get going. Wake everyone up. We are gone in thirty minutes."

"All right."

Scary Man had jumped out of his skin! It must have been just a reaction to the last year he had been screwed over by Col. Stanton. I must be looking at myself a year from now. Could I ever go back into society? Would I go home and be pissed off at everyone, start fights, and not talk to my family? No one will ever understand my story. It's only been a day. What happens next?

"Get up, fellas; it's time to move out."

The ANAs looked at me like with confusion. So, I gestured and pointed at my watch. They started to move around; they sounded and smelled terrible. With the lack of motivation to get up, taking a shower was now off; I just continued to blend in with the ANA. Maybe tomorrow I could clean myself.

The sun was starting to come up as the cold of the morning intensified. I put on my coat and gloves while staring at the sun, the eternal heat tab. There is something extremely beautiful about the first time the sun peeks over the high desert mountains. The glow of red and brown together made the area look safe. You could hear Afghani families in the distance waking up and moving around. The smell of fires burning in the air reminded me of home, except these people around here had better weapons and training than they do in Hippie Hollow.

As a kid, I never saw a gun in my neighborhood. Crazy thought. We sold drugs and brewed beer for distribution with no weaponry. We were simple and peaceful people that believed everyone was a good person in a hippie colony. Trust here in Afghanistan meant so many different things.

The vehicles were packed and ready to go when we realized that again we were down one truck. So, we doubled up in the back and front of all the vehicles. Scary Man seemed nervous and ready to go; he wanted me in charge right now!

"I hope to hell we do not have to fight out of these trucks again."

"What are the chances moving through this area?"

"Real good!"

The truck convoy pulled out of the fire base. Being down a truck, we had to double up soldiers in a few trucks. We picked up speed to about thirty miles an hour and moved about five miles to the south. The roads were maintained and well-traveled; moving through valley areas went well with little to no slow-downs. Soon, we pulled over and Scary Man yelled for all drivers and the Afghan platoon leader to come to the front for a safety and route-of-travel briefing to Shkin Fire Base. Shkin was about 180 kilometers from our current location.

Shkin Fire Base was located right off the Pakistan and Afghanistan border. This place was known as "Hell on Earth" because of the fighting that goes on this area. No mistake, we needed our "A" game for this movement.

"We are moving south-southeast to Shkin Fire Base along Route Warrior. It will take us about six hours to get there if nothing happens along the way. Our route of travel will be through the villages of Almara, Ayitay, Faqir Kalay, Dabawri Kalay, Sarobi, Gol Kowt, and then into Shkin Fire Base."

"Make sure all your medic bags are ready to go, weapons pointed out at the terrain, and ensure you have one crew serve weapon in the front and one in the rear of the convoy for protection. Weapons go on semi, and the crew serve weapons need to be on full-up auto. Be ready to go men, so mount up!"

Those Afghanis sure understood him when he talked. Something in his voice meant, I lead and you follow and do what I tell you to!

"We get in a shootout again; you better engage and help me, because in a few days, this is your donkey to ride."

"I got it. I will make it happen!"

"You better!"

"OK, so go back and talk to those soldiers in your truck. Explain you are in charge and they better do what the hell you say. We move in five minutes."

Here was my moment. I had to lead and understand that engaging the enemy meant to save the lives of soldiers and civilians. When I got back to the truck, I spoke in a stern voice and gave guidance.

"If someone starts shooting, you guys dismount and return fire, and I will do the same. When I move, you two soldiers will follow me Understand?"

Shit, they actually nodded their heads as if they got it. Maybe these guys could speak English and were educated at Harvard. No way, no Harvard grad would put himself through suffering like this. Only a night school guy would do that!

I was still the driver and had yet to size up who could drive. These guys seemed to feel more comfortable carrying the weapon and pointing it at something. Driving a truck to them was multitasking when they carried an AK-47. Too much to handle, I guess.

This had now turned into babysitting in combat. I became more worried about saving them than killing the enemy. It took only a few minutes to figure that I was screwed during the next firefight.

Every so often, I would yell back to them to keep an eye out. "Keep looking out, fellas! Enemy everywhere!"

They became lazy after about an hour. Most soldiers start to become comfortable in combat as they get the feeling of safety and that everything will be OK. All that is a lie. The enemy picks the moment of time to attack; you must remain on the defensive and be prepared to go offensive in the same moment.

After about three hours of driving, we pulled over near the area known as Dabawri Kalay. This rural village was spread out over a few miles of riverbeds and waddies. In the center of the village along the road was a walled fort the shape of a pentagon—you know, five sides! The walls were still up, but inside was all destroyed with trash and animals moving around in it. Right in the middle there were a few tents.

Suddenly, a man waving his arms began to run at our convoy. Some children were running with him and kicking a ball. He seemed to be in a panic and wanting help, I assumed.

Soldiers immediately put their weapons on this guy. Being scared, I fumbled around for my weapon and got it hung on the gear shift of this five-speed truck. The vehicles in front of me went into a herringbone defensive formation and stopped. Soldiers began to dismount rapidly to pull security. My own exit from the truck was less than Fort Benning Basic Training standards, but we were not under any fire, so all was safe.

Scary Man started yelling at the man to stop and fired a few rounds into the air.

"Darawem! Darawem!"

That didn't stop him. Scary Man ran towards him with his weapon up and ready, grabbed the man, threw him to the ground, and said to stop. He put his hands behind his head and pointed his 9mm pistol to his head and told him to calm down.

The man was yelling and needing some help but we couldn't understand him until the ANA lieutenant came over to translate. They spoke Pashtun for a few seconds and the lieutenant said that his wife was having a baby and needed medical help. He kept pointing into the pentagon fortress towards a small tent in the center.

Scary Man yelled for the medic that was assigned to the platoon. He wasn't much of a medic as he was barely trained to hand out bandages and aspirin. The education level for most of these soldiers was very low. They were slaves to the Afghan government as they needed money and had nowhere to go. So, they went to the army to get paid "sometimes" by the government and they would, in turn, send it home to help their parents.

We moved two squads up to the fortress wall and surveyed the area and then moved in the compound slowly, working to avoid an ambush or any explosive devices. We left one squad back to guard the trucks. Once we cleared the area, Scary Man, myself, and three soldiers moved towards the white tent in the center of the fortress walls. The tent was made of white tarp that had the UNICEF logo on most sides and a wood frame to hold it up. UNICEF is a non-governmental organization that helps poor children throughout the world. They have also assisted refugee camps with tarp systems for living spaces.

Within a few seconds, I heard a bloodcurdling scream from the tent. Was it a child or a goat? I couldn't tell, but it scared the hell out of most of us. As we moved closer to the tent, I could see multicolored carpets running out the door of the tent with sandals on both sides. The wind was blowing slowly but no dust was moving around.

As we moved towards the door, we could see two dark figures; one looked older and the other looked like a little girl. Moving in, dogs began to bark and come around us to protect the girls. I moved my hand towards the dogs to warn them to get away. Looking into the tent, a nasty smell came straight at our faces with tremendous heat attached to it. The smell of old blood and female fluids from childbirth filled the air. The smell was so horrific, we almost collapsed from it. I first looked at the smaller woman who was having the child. Her head was covered with a light blue head covering that only showed her eyes.

"Hell, she couldn't be more than thirteen years old at best."

"This is a regular day, River. Make sure you clear the entire tent. Someone could be hiding."

Once we cleared the tent, I moved back over to the two women. The small girl had a colored blanket that covered most of her upper body, except below her knees. The blood and fluids were all over the blanket, staining all that came into its path. I went to touch her to let her know all was OK and we were here to help. She backed away towards the old woman watching her.

"It's OK! It's OK! We are here to help!"

She soon calmed down as if she understood my tone of voice. I asked the medic to get me some warm water and clean clothes to clean and wrap the baby. With the medic bag, we could sterilize what was needed. This would be my first delivery ever. Once in Hippie Hollow, I watched my mom deliver a baby. She asked me to get these same things for the birth. This was the only experience I had with delivering babies.

Pulling up the blanket from over her knees to look at the birthing canal, it was all bloody and hard to see what was happening. I used the warm water and cloths to clean it up. The fluids were mostly dry, leading me to believe that she had been waiting in pain for some time now. As I cleaned the area, I noticed the crowning head of a small infant. The baby had been stuck; the birthing canal was too small. The young mother was too young and physically not prepared to have a child. The baby was stuck and unable to breathe life.

"Oh, shit! We have to get the baby out now."

"Stand back."

Scary Man grabbed a knife, pushed me aside, and he immediately slit the bottom part of the birthing canal and the baby just slid out rapidly. The girl screamed with agony and leaned back as if to pass out. The old woman tried to hold her up as best she could. Scary Man just cut this woman like a pro, but could he stop her from bleeding to death? The baby had injured her further as the baby exited her body. She had already lost a lot of blood, and she was just a little girl herself.

I grabbed the baby off the carpet. It was a girl. She was bloody and slippery to handle. No breath came from her mouth, her chest did not raise, not a cry, or any movement. I turned her head to the side to clear her mouth of blood and fluid. No reaction. Pressing on her chest, I blew into her mouth three times and checked for movement. No reaction.

"Please, baby. Breathe."

I spoke to her and kept massaging her chest and looking in her glazed eyes. She never blinked—that's all I wanted, just a blink.

The medic grabbed my hand and said, "No... River, she is dead. She suffocated in her mother trying to get out. She was too young to have a child."

Scary Man was right. She was dead. Crying at that moment was enough. Confusion, anger, and asking why this happened spread through my entire body. I wanted to kill the husband, who was four times her age.

"What's wrong with these people?"

I ran outside the tent with my hand over my head, and tears ran down my face. I cried in silence—nothing exited my mouth but slobber; I just wanted to save the baby. When I thought I was bringing life into the world, I only brought death in the form of a small baby girl. Her husband looked at me with very little emotion.

"Your child is dead. She's dead!"

The old man ran into the tent, wrapped the child up in a bloody sheet, and ran back out towards the opening in the fortress wall. As he ran, a bloody arm of the child fell out of the cloth and flailed widely. Frantic and distressed, the child's father moved towards a mosque across the street. The ANA soldiers guarding the vehicles tried to stop him but were horrified at the sight of the bloody baby going into the mosque.

"Guard that mosque and wait for that old man to come out with the child."

I wanted revenge in some way. The soldiers moved towards the mosque but hesitated to show any offensive movements, so as to not offend the local mullah. We waited over thirty minutes and the old man never came out. Shaking and sweating, I wanted to put my hands on this man and not let go. He needed to feel this pain.

"River, we have to leave or we will not make Shkin!"

"I want revenge for him raping that girl and the death of that baby," I said violently, throwing my arms around expressing my anger.

"River, in this country, this is common to see girls like that marry young and have children. You cannot save them all. You cannot change these people. You have to accept it. If not, you are going to be killing a lot of people." Those words would affect me forever.

"River, let's go. The neighbors are not going to be happy that you are going to kill one of their own."

"We need to wait a little longer. The baby needs to be buried."

"They have their own customs and it isn't Christian. We need to leave now."

As we loaded the trucks, I kept looking back at the mosque. Our soldiers loaded their trucks very slowly; the effects of the dead child and the conditions of the child mother affected us emotionally. I took one last look over the fortress wall; the little girl was standing and cleaning her body. Blood discolored the water that ran down her legs as she scrubbed and cried. She never looked up; she only gazed down at the dirt. Dogs wandered around the child, sniffing and prodding the blood-stained water around her feet.

I hoped she would look up at me; I wanted to tell her that it would all be OK. Give her a hug and hold on until she felt safe again. Yet, I know she realized that this was the rest of her life as the second wife of an old man. A slave to the old woman, she would cook, clean, and have more children.

With the loss of the baby, she was now tainted as a failure in the eyes of the family. Blaming herself for the death of the child would be her lifelong fate. She was too young to realize it was the Third World conditions that killed the child. That village was a thousand years behind in civilization; medicine and medical capabilities were basic at best. Life or death was provided by the unknowing.

Would the young mother have died if we hadn't shown up? I'd say yes. The baby died before we arrived. Maybe the baby made it to a better place?

Inshallah, If God willing!

Chapter 10

As I drove away from the child and her dead baby, I couldn't help but know that this was the worst day of my life. Humanity had done a complete one-eight. Were right and wrong meant the opposite of each other. This was another world that was not on any chart anyone could find. Tears ran down my face. I tried to brush them away with my hands, which still were blood stained. I never remembered to wash my hands.

I rubbed my bloody hands on my pant leg. Rubbing so hard, I could feel my hand heat up uncomfortably. The heat caused the smell of the fluids to smell horribly. The blood had to go away, but my memory of the event would never wash off me.

"Clean hands. You will be sick."

"Lieutenant, I can't get the blood off. Screw this shit!"

The road was very rough headed to Shkin Fire Base. Signs of life were few except in the Orgun Town Square, not far from the fortress. It looked like a cheap swap meet with a criminal element attached. Buildings were colored dirt brown and stained with all types of matter. Most were one story and leaning. Some families seemed to be living in the stalls by night and selling by day. From toys, to weapons, to drugs, they were all available. The place was packed and they all looked at us as we rolled through the village. Not one smile or wave!

There were dry riverbeds running through the area that looked to cause problems with heavy rains. When it rains heavy in these areas, flooding occurs as the rain cannot be sucked into the ground, so it just runs down the path of gravity. Farming happens within a few hundred meters of these dry river beds. There is still water just below the surface that the roots grow to. There was some form or beauty to this area.

"What a beautiful field over there to our right. Flowers were blooming and it's still December."

"No flowers. Opium," said the lieutenant.

"Opium?"

"Terrorist make a lot of money, four times each year," the lieutenant conveyed to me.

I was starting to break through his broken English and understand him. He pointed to the north of us and said, "Americans." Off in the distance was an American fire base with a small contingent of joint military forces.

Scary Man seemed to not even get near these base camps. He would later tell me that the less contact with military commanders wanting to know his business, the better. Col. Stanton's mission was definitely a secret to everyone, including Scary Man and me. The intelligence I would receive would only be from what Scary Man and I picked up along the way. Limited contact with the good guys and the bad guys.

Lesson learned so far from this hidden gem of a mission was to stay to yourself, talk to no one unless asked, lie as much as you can, and make no friends. This mission was like selling weed back home to adults.

"Oh, yes sir, it's the best weed for the money!"

The next sixty miles to Shkin were uneventful, other than running low on gas. We carried some fuel but just enough to get to the next location. We ran the riverbed roads and waddies. Driving the truck tires through the same line as the trucks ahead of me, we avoided the potential of running over a pressure plate explosive mine. After a few hours of driving, we all began to become too comfortable with security. It was just human "lazy" nature for those with limited combat experience to feel comfortable faster than those with large amounts of "getting shot-at time." We were amateurs and they were pros.

I began to think heavily while I was driving. What would I be doing for the next year? Surely, not handing out flowers and feeding the homeless. This had now turned into "personal initiative" on me to make anything happen. What lengths was I willing to go for Col. Stanton and to gain control of the Achilles systems from terrorists? He told me that if I was caught or killed, they would deny any knowledge of my actions. I would be a failure in the media and to my prison parents in Hippie Hollow. Was this is a recipe for disaster or what?

Shkin Fire Base came into view in the late afternoon. It looked like Fort Apache meets an apprehended Panamanian drug lord's residence. Two flags flew over it, one U.S. and the other an Afghan national flag. The camp housed Afghani and U.S. soldiers that moved along the border to the east of us. The camp was bordered with Pakistan and guarded by the Pakistani army, and thank God, not the Pakistani Frontier Corps (PFCs). The PFCs were known to be in bed with the Taliban and allowed them freedom of movement across borders between countries. The PFCs were the whole reason there was no security in Afghanistan.

The Taliban are like a gang that controls the neighborhoods and do whatever they want. If you are not with them, you become an unknown victim to the world. In this area, your daughters are raped and taken to the Taliban base camps in Pakistan. Some girls survive; others work to kill themselves due to torture, seeing their family members killed, and continuing their empty lives with a lack of hope.

As we drove through the gates of Shkin Fire Base, dogs ran

around the vehicles, barking and looking for food to be thrown from the trucks. Only two vehicles, Scary Man's and mine, were allowed into the main compound while the others went to a separate ANA campsite within the wire. The lieutenant dismounted his troops while I began to grab what little possessions I had.

"Lieutenant, get your boys some food and sleep. I will find out what is next for you guys."

Looking back at the ANA camp, the men dismounted and headed towards an outside kitchen setup. The soldiers jogged over, acting like they had just come out of the desert completely lost, hungry, and thirsty. I headed towards the Tactical Operations Center (TOC) in the middle of the wall base camp.

The inside camp had four buildings that were just one story tall. Multicolored tarps covered some roofs to avoid leaking inside the living and eating areas. Stones and bricks held them down, as the winds even got down behind the walls.

The chow hall looked pretty cozy as it had some folding tables, plastic plants, Christmas lights, and pictures of Hawaii hanging on the walls. There was an area for snack foods like muffins, Pop Tarts, power bars, and sodas. You eat pretty well out here for a soldier. The cook came out; he was Afghani with a red dye beard. He looked about fifty years old and smelled like eighty years old and homeless. His eyes were sun damaged with cataracts protruding from his eye sockets. A pirate is what he reminded me of, based on his ragged clothes and head wrap. The only thing missing was a knife between his teeth. It seemed we had many characters that were not friendly in this area.

Scary Man walked in rapidly and stated, "We will part ways here at Shkin, and I head back to Bagram in the morning. Tonight at 1900 hours in the TOC, I will lay out all the intelligence: what I know, what I don't know, your known contacts inside Pakistan, and who you need to be concerned about. The Pakistanis know you are coming, so you need to be aware at all times. Avoid everyone over the age of thirteen. Once completed with the brief, we will telecom into Col. Stanton's office for final orders, so get some sleep."

Knowing I was taking command of the mission that night, I was in between excitement and terror. Was I still too naive to know what I was getting into? Hopefully, tonight I would have a better idea of what I needed to do. Maybe confidence of knowing the entire mission would help me settle.

That night at 1845 hours, Scary Man came and got me from my small, dirt-walled room.

"Let's go. This is the most exciting moment of my life. Today, I have made it through one year without being killed or losing any arms or legs."

It was a short walk to the TOC. As we moved through the doorway of the TOC, there were three members of the Special Operations group there to greet me. They soon took me to a back room, a semi-covered room that looked to be used for secret or above briefings. This is where they would give me the intelligence report on the Shkin area and my overall mission. This is where reality would hit me: I was alone! Within seconds, a picture of my enemy would be shown to me.

"The man is your enemy. His mission is to locate, injure, or kill you prior to gaining control of the equipment. He is the most highly qualified killer in the Pakistani army. With little to no support, this man can adjust and blend in to any location along these areas of the border through to Torkham Gate in the north. We have never seen this man beyond Torkham Gate area for some unknown reason at this time. He can shoot, fight, manipulate, and dismember you at any time he chooses. Eating and drinking is not a habit for this man. He has inhuman physical and mental range extension that allows him to go for days chasing you."

"What's his name?"

"The locals call him Waba, which means 'Black Death' in the Urdu language. His real name is one of the best kept secrets in the world. Even Col. Stanton doesn't know it."

"This picture was taken a few years ago in Peshwar, Pakistan, as he was purchasing weapons and bomb-making material to attack U.S. and NATO forces along the Jalalabad road from Peshawar to Jalalabad. Some local used a camera phone and was paid twenty dollars to get this picture. Once the picture was taken and sent to us, the individual was never seen or heard of again. No phone transmissions, no tracking from the towers, I mean completely off the face of the earth. Our assumption is that he was killed right after the picture was taken by Waba right there in the streets of Peshawar."

The picture showed a man about six feet, two inches tall, with black hair, and a scared face. He stood up straight and looked in shape. The picture looked a little grainy and was taken from a distance of about twenty feet. Yet, this was enough to get a sense of him.

"River, this man can change in an instant. He can add a beard, longer hair, clothing that blends in with locals, speak many of the local dialects, and operate almost any weapons systems in the world. He is truly one of the world's greatest and most capable assassins, and he knows you are coming!"

"The minute you arrived in this base camp, the locals here in Shkin probably contacted those across the border in Pakistan, and let them know someone new arrived. They know I have been here a year, so they assume I am to be replaced. You are the new guy, so it must be you. Get ready for enemy contact the minute you move past the border tomorrow morning. The Pakistani Frontier Corps to the north of Shkin will be your first contact."

"River, the Achilles system I believe to be spread out amongst the four brigades along the Pakistani border. The Taliban need logistical and freedom-of-movement support in these areas to cross and return successfully from inside Afghanistan. That's why we believe they are housed and used from these locations. Your first stop is Miran Shah, Pakistan."

"What is the distance from the border to Mian Shah?"

"About fifty kilometers east, but these systems are man transportable and can be used in any location with ten kilometers from the border based on the system's known effective range and accuracy. They triangulate between three systems for greater accuracy. When they get turned on, they have limited wattage output; this makes them difficult to locate rapidly unless you are very close. Between the local intelligence, spies, and Achilles, they are extremely accurate in locating and ambushing our troops.

"Once you get the first Achilles out of Miran Shah, head towards the Lawara Fire Base on the Afghanistan side. Located there are the U.S. Special Forces; they will take possession of the Achilles. Contact Col. Stanton from there and give him an update. He will provide follow-up intelligence. Intelligence will be given to you on a need-to-know basis based on possible capture and torture by the Pakistanis or the Taliban.

"Once you get the four systems out, you need to run for Bagram Air Field in Afghanistan. They will take the remaining system from you and inventory it to make sure you have gotten everything. We only need the brains of the system. It looks like an iPod with a touch screen. If you fail, we all fail and people you know like these men in this room will die from your failed attempt. I have searched for a year. Here is a folder for you to read tonight. You cannot take this with you. When you leave tomorrow, you go with what is on your body right now. You now become a local native, going across the border searching for work with no weapon. We will load you on a workers vehicle that will come through in the morning to the village. This truck takes workers back and forth each day to a mining operation about ten kilometers inside Pakistan. You will not be on that truck back here tomorrow night. After tonight, you will never come back here or see me again."

"Where will you go after this, home?"

He looked scared and empty and said, "I have no clue, but it will never be in the service of Col. Stanton or the U.S. Army. I plan to disappear somewhere in Europe. Absent Without Leave will be my status for one year, then missing after that. I will change my name, the whole nine yards. I am a wanted man with the Pakistanis and the Taliban. The family I have back in the States will be in danger if I return. The enemy knows my name, home of record, family locations, everything that can get them killed. My death would be of no difference to any government or legal organization in the United States. My life has changed and I'm on an unstoppable approach to hell.

"River, I will see you there in twelve months, *if God wills it.* Living in hell will be our only comfort and safety from the touch of Allah himself.

"Good luck, River!"

He walked out, leaving my mind to wonder. I never saw him again after that night…

Chapter 11

The morning came in a hurry as I was awakened by the S.F. TOC operations officer. "Sir, the truck going across the border will be in the village in one hour. You need to get into character to make this happen, so no shower, deodorant, brushing of teeth, or even washing your feet. You need to be dirty and smell like an old goat."

I was so nervous. Trying to eat was impossible. My stomach ached and twisted. Water seemed to run right through me; I must have gone to the bathroom four times in an hour. The S.F. guys were looking at me as if I would chicken out. Bets were being placed, ten-to-one odds that I would not leave the safety of the camp. Losing and staying between these walls might be an option at this point! I was scared!

Just before I left for the village, the TOC Commander called me: "Sir, Col. Stanton is on the phone for you."

I was thinking, why are you calling me now? I am committed at this point to walk across the gate into the village to start this thing. Any interruption at this point will affect my bravery to even do this.

"Yes, sir, this is Major Rochman."

"River, according to intelligence, Waba is somewhere near the village of Shawall, Pakistan. That's about six kilometers northeast of your current position. There is snow in the area, but the roads are passable. You could possibly cross paths with him in the next few days around Shawall. River, I do not have to tell you how dangerous that man is. He obviously knows you are coming. With him located within traveling distance leads me to believe, this is almost a guarantee."

"Daddy, Daddy, I am going to bed now."

"Baby, I am on the phone. Please go see your mother.

Sorry, River, I am calling you from home, but don't worry, no one is listening as no onc suspects." My heart sank at the sound of those children.

"Have you got the Iridium satellite phone with you? You should have gotten it from the guy you are replacing."

"No, sir, I was told I could only walk in with minimum assets. I am about to get on a truck into Pakistan as a day worker. I need to get going as the truck will be here in fifteen minutes."

"River, get a sat-phone from the S.F. guys and use that. Call me tomorrow morning at this time to confirm your status and if you are alive or not."

Just before we hung up, I could hear his kid asking questions and watching TV in the background. I heard someone's daily life as I was about to possibly end my own.

"Take care, sir."

"Godspeed, River."

"Goodbye."

"Do you have an Iridium phone I can use?"

"Yes, but these things are not all that reliable and you need to charge this thing once a day. These phones are not for long-term use. No charge, no use!"

"Sir, are you crazy by doing this? I mean, what training do you have to have to commit to this stupid mission of Col. Stanton's?"

The S.F. Commander looked at me and said, "Col. Stanton has

been looking for these systems now for over a year. Nothing has come out of Pakistan, so who is to say these things are not in the Iranians' or the Chinese hands getting reverse–engineered?"

"Your partner from last night that gave you the briefing, that's the first time we have ever seen that guy. He scares us just looking and listening to him."

The TOC radio operator said, "Society will not be ready for him. He will kill himself before the year's out. I take bets on it. Are you prepared to live that life, sir?"

My heart began to race and I questioned my judgment. It took all of three seconds to say to the TOC officer, "How do I get out of this?"

"Well, sir, you have five minutes to make your mind up. If not, you need to walk out to the village to catch that truck in ten minutes."

I grabbed my bag of food and headed out to the village. As I walked, with a lack of confidence, I pledged to myself that I would not die a coward, no matter how scared and misled I seemed to be right now. Hearing those children in the background had now solidified that this was not a sanctioned operation or even funded. Yet, I was committed at this point. The only way home was through Torkham Gate, I figured. That was my light at the end of the tunnel. If I died, then death would be before me.

The Afghani soldiers looked at me with confusion. What the heck was I doing walking towards the front gate to cross into the village? The ANA lieutenant started walking towards me, when one of the S.F. soldiers told him to go back inside and say nothing. I looked back at the lieutenant. I gave him the look of a dead man.

Crossing that front gate into the village of Shkin, I immediately walked by small huts with fires burning inside. Dogs were wandering around me, barking and sniffing. There was a group of men huddled together in the center of the village. That must be my group. I stopped about ten feet from them and waited for the truck. Old men were looking at me; I didn't see one young worker. These guys looked sixty years old all day. No Social Security in this place, I guess!

The truck arrived within a few minutes of my arrival; I didn't have time to question my bravery or brains at this point. Walking towards the truck, a visible lump formed in my throat. An old man, already on the truck, reached out to help me up. He said nothing as I had nothing to say. Only face shots and head nods at this point of thanks. Thank God that's universal!

We moved slowly towards the border. I looked throughout the back of the truck for the assassin. Paranoia began to strangle my mind. Fear increased as the border gates got closer.

All in one moment I thought, *Run River, as fast as you can! Now is your chance to get out of this mess.* My fearless leader, Col. Stanton, was conducting an operation from his house while he put his children to bed. Scary Man, I hadn't seen since yesterday. *Alone is what I am!* Intuition, hippie street smarts, and this old bag of bones were all I had.

The workers truck stopped at the border gate and ANA border guards talked to the driver and moved to the back of the truck with a flashlight. One guard pointed the flashlight around in circles, looking at faces. When he got to mine, he stopped for about two seconds then looked at his paperwork for the head count. It must have matched. He waved his hand to the driver to move forward. We moved only about a hundred feet to the Pakistani border guards' checkpoint and stopped.

The old men in the truck began to get nervous and start fidgeting. Something was wrong all of a sudden with the Pakistani border crossing. I heard the Pakistani soldiers speaking violently to the driver and throwing him out of the truck. The man fell to the ground and then got up and ran to the back of the truck to let the gate down. All the men got up and started getting out and lining up. All I could think was, this was shakedown or they were looking for someone. I was the last one to get out and I was closest to the tailgate. Guilty as hell is what I looked like!

Standing right in the middle of the gaggle of smelly old men, the sun was coming up. We all just stood there watching the Pakistani verbally beat down the driver right in front of the ANA border guards. The ANA said nothing. They feared the Pakistanis. The ANA soldiers were rarely ever paid by their government so bravery most times was in short supply.

Thirty minutes later, after yelling, waiting, and yelling some more, we were finally let back on the truck. The Pakistanis never looked at us; they just physically and verbally beat the driver.

It took all of one minute for us all to load in the truck and start to move. I got into that truck so fast; I ended up sitting in the middle of all these guys. Scared wasn't the right word at this moment. Staring out the back of the truck, I continued to pray to Hindu religious icons and ideas for the next twenty or so miles. We finally reached the work site near the Pakistani village of Shawall.

It was a mining area; they were looking for gold, it seemed. We all got out and began to get yelled at to get moving towards a tool shed that had mining tools, hard hats, and buckets to gather gold and any gems that we found. I had just become an enslaved miner. Off to the mines we went.

Chapter 12

The walk down into the mine was cramped and tight. I could feel the air thinning in the cave as my mouth filled with dust. As I moved down into the tunnel, hunched over for more than two hundred meters, the walls looked like they had been dug by hand more than a hundred years ago. This was an old mine that was constructed before heavy machinery was available to this area. Old-school mining, these guys had never seen a bulldozer or a tractor in their lives up here.

Swinging picks, we began digging for gold at about eight in the morning. It was extremely cold in the caverns; cold and damp seeped into the mountainside that December morning. The old men had no jackets or gloves; they were the toughest of the tough. American miners had nothing on these men. Safety procedures didn't exist. If you died, you died with no life insurance or medical help. Most of these miners' families would not miss them; they were one less mouth to feed. They just kept swinging their picks into the mountain, hoping to find something so they could make money for that day. If they found nothing, they earned nothing. This was commission mining at its worst.

Our first bit of gold wasn't found until after two o'clock that day. The amount of gold found looked small in the hands of the miner, but that was a week's pay to him. I found nothing and would have not known if I had. Gold mining was not a part of the hippie culture in Texas.

The work was hard and laborious. Water would be passed around to the workers by the same brass water cup every hour or so. It was just enough water to keep you going. My energy was weakening with little water and nothing to eat after six hours of work.

I had to escape today; going back to Shkin was not an option. The driver of the truck that brought me here would be one worker short going back. He was sure to be arrested and beaten by the Pakistani border guards for his numbers being short. The Pakistanis were meticulous when it came to head counts and immigration. The Pakistani Frontier Corps didn't care one bit. They just wanted a payoff to let you go.

At around three o'clock, they finally allowed us to come out of the mine and eat. It took me quite some time to back out of the mine, because turning around and walking upright was not an option. Once out, I walked in line with the others to a table filled with cooked rice, boiled chicken, and flat bread. It was served family style, everyone grabbing and crowding each other to get some food. I did the same, as I was tired and weak from mining.

As the miners would eat, they would every now and then look at me, confused. They knew I was up to no good. They would say nothing; no involvement seemed to be their motto. Within minutes, we heard a man yelling from the foreman's office. He was pointing at us and talking to an unknown man carrying a weapon.

The armed man was dressed like a local Pakistani; he had dark skin and had a weapon with a big hunting scope. By his posture and equipment choices, he looked like a professional soldier with great leadership capability and could scare any man to death.

You can tell a great warrior from his posture and the lack of posture from the person he is controlling. Then I heard one of the miners say, "Waba!" My head snapped back to look at the individual who said "Waba." Looking right at me, he said "Run!" in English.

"Where the hell do I run?"

"Toilet, toilet!" And he pointed over to a slit trench where you squatted down to go the bathroom.

"Do not run—walk!"

Who was this guy talking to me in English? Was he a Central Intelligence Agent or an MI6 paid informant? I began assuming and then didn't care. I walked towards the trench up in the woods and squatted down to act like I was going the bathroom. Both men at the foreman's building watched me carefully. I looked forward with concern in the trench. Contemplating a plan to escape, I looked into the trench. The trench was large enough for me to crouch into and escape without detection once they took their eyes off me. Looking back at Waba and the foreman, it was my time. I slid into the trench; it was full of human waste that allowed me to slide down the hill to a stream.

The English-speaking man at the food table told the miners to head back to the mine. This caused a distraction to the foreman, but I was sure Waba didn't fall for it. I followed the stream for about one-quarter of a mile to a heavily wooded area to hide in.

The Pakistani assassin was known to the local border population as Waba. Waba meant "Black Death" within the local language. He was cold and dark, known only to deep secret layers of intelligence. He had never been caught, and if caught, he would kill himself to avoid capture and torture.

He was the perfect soldier of death, trained by Lucifer himself, and would become a great martyr in the eyes of the Pakistani popular culture. *That's unless I get to him first!*

Running out with no water or food, I knew I had to head towards the village of Shawall. This was where I could gain food and water for movement towards the last known sighting of the system, a Pakistani brigade in Miran Shah. To get it in my hands, I would have to steal it while being surrounded by over four thousand soldiers, based on Col. Stanton's intelligence update.

The altitude was tremendous at over twelve thousand feet. I was at half speed, looking around as I moved to ensure Waba was not following me. I stopped after about a mile and hid in some bushes. Listening, I could hear movement but I couldn't tell from what. My mind wandered, my heart raced, and it could be heard a few feet away. The skin on my arms shimmered from the sweat. Ants could be seen near my legs as I had sat near an ant pile. They had become extremely violent towards my presence. Listening for a few minutes more to ensure the area was safe to move, I headed out in the opposite direction, due north along the Pak-Afghan border for about two miles, and then would move back to the east towards Shawall. I had about fifteen kilometers to get to the village to refit before dark.

Movement was all by terrain association and not by compass. If caught with a compass, they would know I was not a local. Locals know the areas, as they have lived there all their lives. I did carry a small map with general landmarks that was most helpful.

As I began to exceed my physical and mental capabilities, paranoia again set in every time I stopped to breathe. Getting to the village before my body gave out and nightfall became the enemy was my main goal at this point. With snow on the ground, it was difficult to travel at any great speed in some areas. Snow tracks trailed behind me; I hoped the limited snowfall for that year could possibly cover them up. Waba was a tracker. He would notice this right away if he was following me now.

The temperature began to drop to almost freezing by the time I had cleared the distance to Shawall. The moon was up and the sun was down, but there was enough moonlight to travel. Finally reaching the village at about two in the morning, I stopped about a half a kilometer out on a ridgeline to rest and do a visual recon of the area.

In the distance, I could only see one vehicle coming, with one blown headlight. Visually, I could only see one large truck in the whole village, which looked to have little to no transportation. They seemed to only use animals for transportation that pulled decorative trailer carts.

Shawall looked to be a small village that was used for trading and as a transportation pipeline to the west. The lifeline of the mountaintop village was the one road that came from Afghanistan and east from Islamabad. The snow was heavy in some areas but the roads were cleared for travel most of the winter. This was a major road infrastructure for both countries. It was also a known Taliban safe haven, based on U.S. intelligence. They used it as a route of attack between borders against U.S. forces starting in April of each year. This was known as the "Spring Thaw." That's when the mountain passes were clear of snow, and that eased movement in and out of Pakistan to attack foreign forces in Afghanistan. Taliban warriors were for sure in this village tonight, so I had to be careful.

Homes and businesses were spread out amongst the hilltop, and they slanted down towards a dry riverbed to the east. Farmers had their fields on the sides of the mountains. They had developed step systems because there was not a flat surface for farming to be found.

There were very few people around wandering the roads or in the fields. With the darkness and the time of morning, I would move down into the village to resupply by theft.

As I began to shiver as the temperature dropped below freezing, I listened to the wind, birds, dogs barking, and the sound of people moving in the distance. Calmness seemed to settle into my bones. Hunching down and wrapping my arms around a blanket, I just wanted to fall asleep. Yet, it was the best time to conduct a dismounted movement unseen into the village to get supplies.

Soon, the truck with the broken headlight arrived in the village. It stopped in front of a small hut in the center of town, and only one man got out. With the distance and moonlight, I couldn't tell if he was local or enemy. He walked into the house without even knocking. I immediately heard yelling in Urdu, and then he dragged a small man out, holding a weapon to his head.

Screaming and grabbing hair off the smaller man, he pointed a weapon into the mountains behind my current position while choking the man. Once released from the chokehold, the smaller man ran frantically into the house and came out with an AK-47 rifle, a coat, and a head cloth. He moved towards my position and then hooked a right through a cut in the ridgeline and out of sight. I had to move. There was no telling when the local would come through my area.

Now was the time to make a decision. Should I go into the village and get supplies, kill this guy coming along the ridgeline and possibly compromise my position, or should I skirt the village and look elsewhere to the east? Waba had arrived!

Hunger, dehydration, and possible hypothermia guided me to gambling and going to the edge of the village. There it was, along the tree line skirting the backside of the village. I would use it to gain supplies. If spotted, I could run into the woods for cover, if chased by locals. Off I went down into the village, slipping along the hillside to the right of the village to a lone house near the woods. There were clothes hung from a line that I could use. Hopefully food and water would be also available nearby.

As I neared the house, I could hear people talking and see a lighted candle moving around the back windows. No dogs seemed to be around. I was lucky. As I neared the clothesline, I could hear a vehicle starting up and road gravel being pressed to the earth from the weight of the moving vehicle. Stopping at the corner of a house behind a few fifty-five-gallon barrels, I looked around the corner towards the sound of the vehicle.

"What the hell?" I whispered.

The truck stopped, the driver pulled a cigarette out and lit it.

From the light of the match and the twenty feet between the truck and me, I could tell my worst fears had come true.

It was Waba, the same guy from the gold mine. He had arrived in the village looking for me. His warrior intuition knew I needed to get to my first objective through this village; it's the only place to get water, food, and clothing to continue east. Plus, I had limited navigation points to orientate from.

Waba shut the engine off and sat there quietly and listened. He sat for five minutes; he looked over in my area several times. He knew I was here! That was why he sent the man onto the ridgeline to smoke me out. It worked. I was just twenty feet from him now.

Chapter 14

In the world of assassins, there are those that are trained by their governments, those that were trained by a parent through tactics and beatings, and those that are abused and search for vengeance on strangers. Abbas "Waba" Mugal was no stranger to all three areas of the assassin trade. When Abbas was born, his biological father was Javed Iqbal Mughal, a Pakistani serial killer that admitted to killing or raping over one hundred people through the early 1970s near Lahore, Pakistan. One of the women he raped gave birth to Abbas in shame. In shame, she gave Abbas to an orphanage in Peshawar, Pakistan.

Abbas would live a horrible existence, begging and scraping for food in the violent streets of Peshawar. Many sexual deviates roamed these streets looking for young boys with no homes or families to go back to. Abbas continued until he was eight years old; that was when he committed his first murder. The victim was a sexual deviate that tried to overpower him in an alley in broad daylight, but Abbas had had enough. He grabbed a stick and began to beat the man in the head and shoulders. He continued to scramble to get to his feet while he screamed for help. As he ran away, he saw a piece of sharp metal, and, grabbing the metal, he turned around to face the rapist, and the metal pierced his stomach.

Abbas looked him in his dark eyes and said in Urdu, "Die, please die!"

The deviate fell on top of him and then rolled on his side. The blood from his stomach stained Abbas's clothes and hands. Yet, the rapist continued to breathe and bleed all over the alley. Abbas slid out from the rapist, crying, and he continued to stare at the deviate. Just as he was about to run away, he heard a voice.

"Do not cry, young boy. You did what you had to do!"

Abbas looked bewildered at all that had just happened, with a man in an army uniform telling him it was OK.

"I killed a man. He tried to rape me; no one would help me. I screamed for help and no one has ever come to help me."

"I will help you. Take my hand. What's your name?"

"Abbas, Abbas is my name," he said, wiping away his tears.

"Ah yes, Abbas, that means lion. That is a good name for a young boy that can kill a full-sized man."

"I am tired; I just want to be left alone!"

"Are you hungry, need a bed to sleep in?" The army officer reached out his hand and said, "Come on, Abbas, let's go eat."

"Please do not hurt me," he said, as his hands trembled from any touch of a man. He had also never felt the love and touch of a mother.

"It's OK. Let's go eat just around the corner on the main street. You look so hungry!"

Abbas and the army officer walked around the corner to a lamb kabob stand. There they ate and drank Coca-Colas. Abbas took some food and stuck it in his pocket for later. The officer pulled out the food and said, "You do not have to do that anymore. You will always eat. I will take care of you. Where do you live?"

"I live in the Peshawar Orphanage."

"Let's go over there and talk about your future here in Peshawar. Maybe I can help you."

Abbas walked slowly with the man. Not trusting of men, he stayed on the inside of the street in case he had to run through the alleys to get away. Soon, they reached the orphanage. The army officer walked to the front desk and asked for the headmaster. A small man with rimmed glasses walked up and gave the greeting of the day.

"Sir, this young boy here, do you know him?"

"Yes, he is Abbas. Has he given you trouble?"

"No, on the contrary, he has helped me greatly. I would like to adopt him, if possible."

"Really, Abbas has been much trouble and requires a lot of attention."

"Attention? I found him in the streets begging and being almost raped by sexual deviates. You will get the proper paperwork ready right now; I take him from here today. We will be back in two hours and I better have everything I need completed. If not, I will have you arrested and jailed for failure to care for these children. Do you understand?"

"Yes, sir, right away. We will get his things ready."

Abbas looked up at the officer and the headmaster and said, "I have nothing but these clothes and a blanket."

"That's OK; I will purchase you new clothes right now. Leave everything here; you will have a new life with me."

Abbas couldn't believe what he was hearing. Somebody was helping him. The army officer grabbed his hand and led him out of the orphanage for the last time.

"Abbas, my name is Captain Muhammad Akram Khan, and I am an officer in the Pakistani Special Forces, and I live in the Khyber Valley just west of here."

Abbas looked up at Captain Khan. "Are you going to be my father?"

"Yes, I will be your father and will take care of you. You are now my son. So, let's go get you some new clothes and sign some paperwork to make it official."

That was the day Abbas started his training as the great Pakistani assassin. Captain Khan took him into the Khyber Valley and began his training starting at ten years old. Abbas learned to shoot, knife fight, camouflage himself in any terrain or city, and kill without mercy.

Abbas found it easy by the time he was fifteen years old. By the time he was sixteen years old, his father took him into combat on the border and left him. That became his school, his mosque, and his family from that point on.

Abbas started off as the cook, and later moved to a foot soldier. After five years of cooking and infantry, he moved to the Special Forces School where Col. Khan was the commander. Khan made sure Abbas was abused when trained; he had a special reason for torture and training. Khan wanted to produce a super killer that had the stamina, skills, and the psychological capacity of a serial killer. That's why Khan wanted him: Abbas was predisposed by his father's DNA to be a serial killer. Khan could now unleash a world-class assassin and ruthless killer onto the battlefield to kill whoever he directed.

Years later, he would find out about his real biological father through now Col. Khan. His name was Javed Iqbal Mughal, and he was a convicted serial killer of more than one hundred people in the late sixties and early seventies. He had raped his mother in the early seventies. She would later be mercy-killed by her father, who was ashamed of her over the rape.

Chapter 13

As the smell of cooked goat meat spread through the air, my stomach began to tighten up. The sound of hunger gained audible tones as I leaned up against a hut. As I peeked around the corner to keep an eye on Waba, the warmth of the hut kept me comfortable for the time being. Waba continued to light cigarettes; the glow surrounded his face every time he lifted it to his face. His dark facial hair looked to be only a few days old. A beard had yet to form; he looked more professional and kept than anyone I had seen out here. Wherever he came from recently, he had been clean and orderly.

Who sent him and how much time does he have to continue to follow me? Am I a better soldier or just another individual that he has selected to kill? I wanted to believe I could hide long enough to get into Miran Shah and back to the border with the first Achilles. There I could come up with a better plan to move to Peshawar, Pakistan, for number two.

I could hear and see villagers going to sleep through windows of homes and huts. The moon reached high in the sky, lights began to dim, and distant voices stopped. Wild dogs could be heard clearly from great distances. And Waba, he continued to be patient as cigarette butts began to pile up outside the truck door. He gazed every now and then towards me. My leg muscles were burning from hunching down. I needed to move soon.

Suddenly, I could hear the sounds of crashing branches and footsteps moving from the rear of my position. It must be the villager that went to look for me. Over an hour had passed since he had left to search. Through peripheral vision, I could see the figure moving within fifty feet of me between two huts. He ended up at Waba's truck.

Waba's yelling and pushing consumed the tense moment. Exiting the truck, he threw the man to the ground, took his weapon, and pointed it at him. Shouting, Waba soon hit the man in the chest with the butt of the weapon, knocking him breathless. Taking his weapon and some cigarettes off the man, Waba started the truck and left slowly towards my position. The man's wife came outside to help him off the ground; she showed concern and started crying as she helped him up. His children stood at the door, seeing their father assaulted. As they spoke, I could not understand anything other than hate and fright.

Waba slowly passed my position. He stopped. Smoking the broken man's cigarettes, he looked towards my position. He took a long draw on a cigarette. It lit his whole face.

"River, I know who you are, I know your home, your mother's name, and that Colonel Stanton sent you. All those men at the mine, I killed them all, just for you. When they went back into the mine, I buried them alive."

My heart palpitated as he spoke in a graveled, low voice. This was an attempt to draw me out. I barely breathed or moved as he was very close. The only thing saving me was darkness and the sound of his engine running. He waited and listened. I gave him no satisfaction. Killing this man was now the only option.

"I will see you tomorrow, River. Have a nice sleep. While you are thirsty and starving, Colonel Stanton will have a nice night with his wife and children, warm and safe. You owe him nothing. He's trying to kill you for his mistakes, River. Come out and let's drink whiskey and smoke some good cigarettes. How about some nice food?" He waited for a response.

The assassin used psychology on me. He had some good points; I needed some food and water, and Stanton had been screwing me from the start. Yet, this man was a killer here to stop me from getting those systems. I remained quiet and still, it was my only option.

Within minutes, the assassin drove off, headed to the east, my same direction of travel. Waiting for the rear taillights to disappear, I began to finally stand up, stiff and numb from the crouching behind the hut. As I turned to look behind me, a small boy startled me; he was looking at me through the window. I looked with fright; he smiled and waved as I moved away.

Grabbing some clothes off a wash line and a handful of dried goat meat that was curing behind the house, I moved back into the wood line to the north. Stopping to see if anyone was following me, I could see lights from the little boy's house come on. The boy and another adult figure were staring at me from the window, waving for me to come back. Confusion about trust and safety for me was at the forefront at this point. I had no weapon or knife to defend myself.

I stopped and waited behind some trees to see what the family would do. Within a few minutes, they came running towards the woods and my position. They were both carrying something in their arms. They stopped within a few feet of me and laid down some food, water, ammunition, and a small, Soviet-made pistol in a small cloth bag.

The man gestured to take the items and leave quickly. They started running back to the house, just as lights from a vehicle moved towards us from the east. I grabbed the items up in the cloth bag and began to move north. Moving for only a few minutes, I heard shots fired from the village. Screams from a woman could be heard. A small child could be heard crying for his father.

"Abba, Abba, Abba!"

It only lasted a few short seconds.

Bang, Bang, Bang!

Nothing but silence returned after the echoes from the valley stopped.

I realized life was short for these people. Pakistani murders, Taliban, and Al Qaeda threatened their lives every day, took anything and everything they wanted. They were hostages in their own environment as their own government cowered down in Islamabad. Shall they ever have peace? I think not!

Moving slowly through the scarce wood line, I continued north three hundred yards to clear the village. I then pushed northeast along the Shawal Road that led to Miran Shah, the first location of the Achilles. The terrain was difficult as it was uneven and rocky with a lot of ridgelines skirting the Shawal Road. There were over one hundred kilometers to walk from Shawal; I needed a ride at this point. My hippie laziness began to exceed my safety standards. This would be my second stupid mistake of the night. I decided to walk the roads after only five miles, because the terrain was too much to handle, as my feet agreed. It slowed me down because it was also just too far to walk in the winter.

As soon as I could, I dropped down to a small vehicle road that was pointed in the right direction of Miran Shah.

I walked for hours, through the middle of the night; I saw no traffic or donkey carts. Most of my water was gone, but I still had some goat meat that still smelled OK. Needing to refill my water supply, I listened for streams and looked for houses along the way. Theft continued to be my only option. Yet, I would never put any more civilians in harm's way for me, so I would remain away from human populations that could help.

So far, some miners, a father, and a son had died for me. I didn't even know their names. Waba had a busy last few days. He had killed over fifteen people just to try and stop me. He used them as probable examples to anyone that might help me in the future: Death will become you!

As the sun started coming up, I began to hear vehicle movement through the valleys. People were beginning their work days. Feeling tired and worried over the distance I still had to travel, I saw a few trucks hauling hay and a few cows came up behind me. I moved onto the side of the road, covered my face, and waved as they passed. They too waved and stopped ahead of me and waved again. So, I ran up to the back of the truck and jumped on.

What a lucky break! I was asked nothing and I had to say nothing. The trucks continued towards the direction of my objective for hours. I was so exhausted that I decided to take my sandals off and rest for a few minutes. Just a few minutes would be no problem.... I would awake three hours later to the sound of Urdu farmers and cars.

"*Assalam-o-alaikum, Assalam-o-alaikum!*"

I was startled out of a deep sleep by the truck drivers. They were poking me with a wooden stick with a metal shank. I could only hear voices and cars moving all around me. The driver said, "Miran Shah."

"Miran Shah?"

"Ya, Miran Shah!"

"Oh shit, no," I said under my breath.

I had arrived in downtown Miran Shah at a Pakistani feedlot. The cows and hay had already been unloaded; the driver just needed me to get out.

"*Assalam-o-alaikum!*"

Jerking with agitation, I got up and slipped off the back of the truck bed, slinging my pack over my shoulder. I thanked him as I was walking away, "*Shukranlak.*" I remembered Scary Man used to say this to people when they helped him, even to Americans. Scary Man was a method actor; he was in character all day.

Assalam-o-alaikum and *Shukranlak*, hello and thank you, was all I knew at this point.

I had two problems at this point: I was in the enemies' city at ten o'clock in the morning and I couldn't speak the language.

Chapter 15

Terror pressed against my body until I lost my breath, and my direction of travel was unknown. It was time to blend in with the locals. The streets were packed with cars and people. My throat and shoulders tensed up as my legs seem to drag behind me. Scared was not the word for the moment, it was more like terrified.

Moving down the main street of the city, Ghulam Khan Road, I soon took a left into an alley that pointed to the south of the city. Suddenly, an older man pointed to me, waving his hand rapidly as if to tell me to hurry up and come to him. He wore light blue pants and shirt, a black beard, and a wrinkled face that looked like many desert trails of experience and hardship.

"*Idher ao, Ihher ao, jaldi*!"

"*Assalam-o-alaikum*," I said as I rapidly walked past him within a few feet. He tried to grab me to get my attention, but I continued on, lowering my shoulder to avoid being grabbed.

He kept calling me; I ignored him and continued on. As I looked behind me after about ten feet, he started running back towards the main avenue. He was yelling something like "American!" and I assumed it wasn't good. Picking up speed, I changed directions in the alley to throw off any chase that might ensue.

It took me over an hour to walk fast and jog out of the city through the back alleys and trading markets. Sweat was running down from my head, through my wool hat, and my clothes were soaked. The smell of cow manure had seeped into my clothes on my backside. Plenty of women would duck their heads and cover their noses as I passed. Cow manure and sweat had now become a disguise from the locals. I began to look like a poor peasant villager from out of town. I became a local at this point.

Thirst and hunger started seeping into my mind and became the next problem to solve. I looked at my old watch, a fake Rolex that I got at Shkin from a mobile vendor. It was a silver diver's watch-looking thing. You had to move your arm to keep the thing working. For how much I had walked and run today through Miran Shah, this watch should run for the rest of my life.

Suddenly the air filled with the screams of a woman coming from a small house on the outskirts of the city. I looked to my left, at about one hundred feet and saw a man beating a woman and a small child in front of this house. He pulled her hair and smacked her in the face with a closed hand several times. The small girl—I assumed it was her child—tried to push the old man away. The old man kicked her in the waistline area and she went to the ground.

Screaming and crying, the child tried to get up, but was too hurt and frightened. The mother endured the beating for more than half a minute.

"What the heck?" I said with a low voice. The American in me wanted to run over and stop the man and save the girls. The question was an ethical one at this point. I wanted to keep walking and not get involved, as that was the tribal way and I still had a mission to complete. Here in the tribal areas, girls were not to be saved or educated, just beaten and turned into house slaves.

So I moved quickly away into the woods, to avoid contact or arrest. More screams and cries continued. They haunted me. Visions of my own mother or Daisy being the victims of this crime ran through my mind. There was only one thing to do: Save them right now.

Give these woman five minutes of saving and then beat the hell out of the husband. Once completed, I would slip back into the woods and run for my life. Good plan, right?

Moving back into the outskirts of the city by the woods towards the screaming, I hid behind some trees and trash. Looking back into the man's yard, I saw both girls on the ground. I could see blood coming from the woman's mouth; dirt was in her hair and face. The dust made her hair look gray. The little girl had her arm wrapped around her mother as they both lay lifeless. The husband could not be seen in the yard, as he must have moved into the house. Within a few minutes, the husband stood in the doorway, drinking something then walking back into the house. He never came out to check them.

"That's it! That's it!"

Keeping my pistol tucked away, I moved and hunched over at a fast pace towards the side of the wife-and-child beater's house. I snuck up to the window to look in; the woman and child continued motionless on the ground. She must have been playing possum so her husband would not return for a second round. I listened and waited a few minutes. He suddenly stepped out in the yard. I looked around and listened for anyone nearby that could come to his assistance. There were none. Running at full speed with no weapon in hand, I attacked the man with my bare hands, throwing him back into the house. He fell on his back, hitting his head on the concrete-lined floor. Making no human sound other than bone on concrete after he hit, he was unconscious from the blow to the back of his head.

"You son of a bitch, you like beating woman and children?" I just kept speaking in English, hoping Allah would hear me and punish this man forever.

Snatching a handful of hair from his head, I kept slamming his head into the ground. The anger I felt wouldn't allow me to be merciful. I continued to slam his head into the ground, losing count.

Soon, no air seemed to be coming from his mouth. His chest didn't rise. Dead at this point was all I wanted for what he had done to his family. He was not coming back, ever!

I moved outside into the yard to check the woman and child. They stood there looking at me with horror. Not knowing what to do, I rubbed the blood from the woman's face and held my hand out to the daughter. They both backed away, as the mother clutched the child to her chest. They were both scared of me, as I was of them. They had every right to be scared: I had just killed the man of the house and their only source of livelihood.

Time was now ticking before she screamed for help, so I had to move. Looking back towards the woods for cover, I saw a water barrel with some cups hanging on the sides. Needing water for sure at this point, I ran towards it. This was my first opportunity to stock up before I moved to my first objective. I began drinking one, two, three cups of water. On the fourth, as I pulled my head back to drink, there stood the man I thought I had killed, looking at me, dazed.

Dropping the cup of water, I punched and kicked him as I hard as I could. My body was not in the fighting position to do this effectively, so it looked childlike at best. He fell back onto the doorstep. I grabbed his arm and pulled him back in, out of the view of any locals driving or walking by. I pulled out my pistol and pointed it to his head, and he just stared at me.

The wife suddenly ran into the house to the fireplace. She grabbed a piece of metal from her cooking fire. Running back towards me, she began to wind up her arm with that piece of hot metal, to swing and hit me. I jumped out of the way, and she hit the husband in the head. She continued to hit him multiple times. She wanted him dead for sure. His skull eventually caved in and brain matter began to seep out of his forehead and ears after about the fifth hit to the head.

She screamed in Urdu. I assumed it was *die, die and die*. I agreed with her desired outcome.

I grabbed the metal rod from her hands and restrained her. He was dead enough at this point and we didn't need any more noise coming from this house. I looked for the child, to ensure she hadn't run for help. She hadn't, as she was as quiet as a church mouse at the edge of the door, just peeking and looking at her dead father. No tears came from her eyes. She must have seen death before—or her father was just that bad to her also. I would go with the second thought.

Releasing the woman, I headed for the door to run. She grabbed me and implied that I shouldn't leave.

"Please, help me!"

She startled me by this, an English-speaking woman in Miran Shah?

"No, I must go before someone comes."

"Stay and help me. Nobody can stay here. We must bury him before find out, please."

"You want me to stay and bury this man?"

"Yes, I will help you, I will help you. Please help me!"

She cried in a low voice as if she only cried to herself and no other. She was a woman who seemed to have been beaten into submission for years. She only knew violence, slavery, and childbirth. Now she was alone, because I had just killed her husband. And when I left, people would wonder where the husband was. They would for sure come for her as the murder suspect.

Sitting down in an old wooden chair, the woman held my hand and continued to beg me to stay. The child moved closer, and her green eyes affected me so much, I said OK.

"Get a sheet to cover and carry his body into the woods. Do you have a shovel, axe, pick, something to dig with?"

She moved quickly out of the house with the little girl to get these items. I wrapped the body up in the cloth sheet from one of the beds. The blood from his head began to slow down from flowing, because the heart was stopped, yet it still stained the sheet for many hours to come.

The woman came back with a shovel and an axe. The little girl even carried the axe. I believe she really wanted her father dead and buried right now.

"OK, let's go. Help me pick him up."

"No, not dark yet. People will see us. Not until tonight."

"I must leave; it's too dangerous to stay."

"I will feed you, and give food and water for journey."

She handed me a large bottle with a strap attached to it to carry water. The bottle was wrapped in brown goat's leather, from what I could tell. With food and water, I had hit the mother lode of assistance. Yet, the price was the killing of her abusive husband and digging a hole so no one would ever find him.

I closed the doors and covered the front windows, all but one. I needed one that had a clear view of anyone coming to the front of the house. We were lucky; the house was off from anyone by about one hundred feet. The front of the house pointed towards the farm fields that were filled with poppies, so no one could get a clear shot into the house.

The woman and child began to bring some meat, rice, flat bread and water.

"*Shukran, shukran.*"

I scooped that food up with the flat bread like a potato chip scooping up sour cream and onion dip at a house party. There were no forks or spoons, just plenty of knives to be used. Yet, this was no house party I had ever been to. It was unbelievable and felt like this was a un trusted environment as I sat there and ate the food of her dead husband. Trust was now an expensive commodity.

As I ate slowly, I stared at the husband's body as he continued to bleed through the cloth. The body would remain in the middle of the house until I finished eating and it became dark outside. My stomach continued to nag away at me, nervous about someone coming to the house and the wife deciding to kill me. She just continued to smile and wait on me hand and foot. I believe she was happy that he was dead, and willing to help me if I buried the body.

"What are your names?"

"I am Seher and my daughter's name is Laima."

"What do those names mean?"

"Laima means lucky and Seher means early morning."

"Those are beautiful names."

"What is your name?"

"My name is River."

"River, like a big stream? Your mother gave you this name, why?"

"She wanted me to travel to other lands."

"Pakistan?"

"Crazy, isn't it? Pakistan is not a great travel destination."

"No!"

She just smiled. Laima just continued to eat, licking her fingers while she sat on her knees in front of me.

A few hours went by with very little conversation. She did relay to me that she was educated in English by her mother. Her mother had worked with the British when their army was in Miran Shah many years ago.

The daughter just sat in the corner of the house, playing and looking around. She looked very frail with her green eyes, just like her mother. Her body was covered in a blue long gown with a head covering that only showed her eyes. She would eat by shoving the food under her face scarf. It looked difficult and unclean.

"What do you plan to do after I leave?"

"I go with you; they will kill me when my husband cannot be found."

"You cannot go with me; I am staying in Pakistan for a while."

"I want you to take me and my daughter to America. I can help you get out of Pakistan and to Afghanistan. If you travel with a woman and a child, the soldiers will not suspect you. I can do all the talking. Please help us, it is not safe now."

She crawled over to me on her knees, begging me to take them out of here. Her hands reached out to me—they did not touch me, yet they trembled with fear. Rocking back and forth, she continued to beg me.

"It's dangerous where I am going."

"It's dangerous for me too. If I stay, I will be killed by the Taliban and my daughter will be beaten and turned into a slave."

Looking towards Laima and back to her, she had taken off her face scarf, revealing her tears and terror. Shock overcame me. I had just seen Seher's face, and it reminded me of Daisy's when she cried. Ethics of what to do invaded my every thought. What was the right thing to do?

I walked over to the window that looked out the front of the house. The sun had been down for over two hours now. A few lights from the distant houses could be seen and no cars were moving around. It was time to bury the body and hide the blood and brain matter. She had no bleach in this country, very little could be used to clean that mess up.

"How do we clean the blood of the floor?"

She jumped down on the floor and started wiping with a rag, but it just spread it around.

"No, stop, we need something to mask the blood. Do you have a goat or any animal we could kill?"

"Yes, a goat out back."

"OK, once we bury the body, we kill the goat right here in the house over your husband's blood and brain matter."

"I will get the goat right now?"

"No, wait until we have buried your husband."

"Blow out all the lights. I will check around the house to make sure no one is around."

Slipping out the front door, I slowly moved around all the corners of the house. I stopped and listened for movement. Nothing was heard after a minute or so. I slowly moved back to the front door. To my amazement, Seher had already dragged the body out the front door with the assistance of the daughter. Seher obviously wanted this man dead and gone. I was her only saviour and ticket out of here.

"Let me help you."

I grabbed his strapped legs and dragged him towards the farm fields to the south of the house. Laima followed at a quick pace with a shovel. Then Seher went to get the goat to kill it in the house. *I wish she would have waited*, I thought; *I need help digging the hole.*

Taking the body about two hundred feet into the fields, I located a good area to dig, bury, and cover up with vegetation. The body smelled after nine hours of being dead. He needed covering up. I grabbed the shovel from Laima.

"Stand over there."

She didn't move, so I grabbed her like a father and moved her away for safety. Her bones in her shoulder could be felt; she weighed very little and seemed to be affected by malnutrition.

"Stay right there, sweetie, and don't move."

I dug at a slow and soft rate, so as not to produce too much noise at night. After digging down about a foot, Seher showed up. Her hands were bloody as she had sliced the goat's throat in the same place her husband had died. This way we could hide the evidence to the local police. My guess was they had no CSI out in these areas. The goat was now the victim, and the husband was nowhere to be found. This would put time and distance between us and the local authorities.

After I had dug down about a foot in about an hour, Seher took over. Once we got to two feet, I stuffed the body down in the hole.

"Damn, his legs are too long."

"I fix it."

Seher grabbed the shovel and axe and began to cut and jab at his legs. She was cutting off his legs? There was some serious hate and moral issues going on here. I stopped her.

"Stop, stop, I will fix it! Taking his now heavily damaged knees, I smashed his legs tightly to the side of his body. He barely fit, but well enough for a murder. We covered him back up with dirt quickly. Then we placed dried hay, poppy shoots, and leaves to try and make it look normal. The terrain we buried him in was not used for travel. Somebody would have to be looking. The only concern was how long before the animals would dig him up. I figured we had a few days to get them out of Pakistan to Afghanistan. My only question was who would take them from me in Afghanistan? They needed asylum from the U.S. government. To do that, the government would know what I had been doing. Col. Stanton, I am sure, never told them about this, either.

"Which way is the Pakistan Frontier Corps Communications site west of Miran Shah?"

"I know. Follow me."

We picked up our water and food and began to walk through the cold night. Laima moved slowly. As we travelled, I began to carry her on my shoulders. When we stopped, we played. It started to feel normal as we travelled, like we were a family.

Five hours later, we reached the site of the first Achilles. The sun began to rise as I held Laima asleep in my arms.

"Sit down," she said.

"What is it?"

"See that building? That's what you search."

"OK, we sit and wait. I need to watch what they do. I will go in there tonight."

"Should we hide?"

"Yes, let's move."

We hid in between some rocks that had overhead cover. I immediately began my recon of the area. There was very little movement; it looked easy to get in and out. Tonight, when they ate dinner in the camp, I would move and begin to gain access to the Achilles.

Chapter 16

The reconnaissance of the area was fairly straightforward; the area we stopped in overlooked the compound from the south. It was a square, walled-in area with two openings in the front and the side. Bordering a cliff to its south, it only maintained three areas to exit if attacked. One guard monitored each exit with an AK-47 and one lookout tower with a larger machine gun in the center of the post. No lights seemed to be lighting the compound at night; at least, I hoped this was the situation.

Lying down behind a small tree and some rocks, I started to draw a map on some newspaper I had found on the mile walk to the overwatch position. This would be an extremely crude map that would work perfectly. This recovery of the Achilles would be conducted with less than what the true warrior Achilles himself carried into combat. I would sneak in with just a pistol and a map.

"Act like you belong there," Scary Man used to say. That meant, do not run or act suspicious in the first place, even if someone looks at you.

Suddenly, I felt something crawling on my leg. Jerking my leg, I looked back to see what it was. It was Laima sitting there looking at me, holding my leg.

"You shouldn't be here. Go back, please, go back!"

She grabbed my hand and tugged and said, in broken English, several times, "Come back, Seher."

"Trouble? Seher OK?"

"Come back."

Looking into her eyes, I saw something was wrong. She looked scared.

"Let's go, let's go!"

We moved quickly back to her location, and fifty minutes later, we arrived back at the hideout. Seher was sitting there waiting for me, looking into Miran Shah in the distance. She looked concerned and was pointing back to movement of personnel and equipment that concerned her.

"Soldiers are coming in trucks!"

"How many are coming?"

She pointed towards the edge of town to the west. Trucks were lining up and soldiers were loading to move out. Within a few minutes, movement of the convoy began. They were Pakistani Frontier Corps troops. That equaled border patrol that controlled the federally administered tribal areas that were located along the Pakistan and Afghanistan border. These troops were frontline fighters against or with the terrorist groups. They looked to be headed to swap out with another unit on the border. It was now 0910 hours.

This must have been the morning shift moving into place, but where were they going? Their direction of travel was north along the west side of the city on the Ghulam Khan Road.

"Where are they going?" I whispered to Seher.

"That road goes to the Tochi Scouts Memorial over there," she said, pointing to the northeast.

The trucks continued to move closer and closer to the entrance to the Achilles communications site along Ghulam Khan Road. Speed was about twenty miles an hour with a distance of about fifty feet between vehicles. These guys seemed disciplined with the way they conducted convoys.

As the convoy came to the gate of the Achilles compound, they stopped and horns began to blow. Soldiers began to move rapidly around the compound. They looked from a distance to be dressed up in clean green uniforms with few medals attached to their chest. Not one looked ready for a fight, more like a parade. Half the camp must have walked out and got into formation. I counted thirty men standing in line getting drilled by some officer or non-commissioned officer. They stood there for about ten minutes and then did a right face and headed down the hill. They couldn't march at all, but they were clean and washed.

Soldiers in the trucks below began to shift around; they looked to be making room for the communications soldiers. They began to load up in single file in each truck. Each squad of ten loaded up in individual trucks.

"Seher, do these soldiers guard the Tochi Scout Memorial?"

"Yes, there are guards, but I do not know how many."

"Let's hope that's where they are going. If they head northwest, they will be in our direction of travel back into Afghanistan."

"We cannot go that way; the snow in the mountains is too bad right now. We must go southwest to get around the high mountains."

"That will add a few days to our journey."

"Yes, but we will arrive earlier than crossing those mountains with Laima. You must take me to Afghanistan. I can help and I know the mountains."

She had a good point, but she also wanted political asylum from the United States. She must see this as doing me a favor. Seher was probably right; we would get there faster looking like a family. With her knowledge of the mountains and the seasons, she would get us to Shkin faster.

We continued to watch as the trucks started to move out of sight. Soon, the ridgelines would get in the way, and seeing where they ended up was impossible. All we could hope for was that they didn't come back before midnight.

"Seher, we will wait until dark. Be looking for the soldiers to come back. Hopefully they do not until late tonight."

"OK, let's eat something and get some rest, we will have to travel tonight."

"No fires, I want to remain quiet and unseen throughout the rest of the day."

Seher crawled down from our lookout position. Grabbing Laima, she said something to her. She laid down on the ground and covered her small body with her large scarf. Seher handed her a small broken doll. It was dirty and limp from its age, probably her mother's when she was little. Laima held it tightly against her chest and closed her eyes. It was a precious moment in the middle of a war. For a moment, it brought peace and civility, but just for a moment.

We sat there for hours, swapping out at the overwatch position. It was now 1600 hours, and there were no sign of the trucks returning. I only needed five more hours. Five more hours to move in and locate the Achilles. That's all I needed.

Food and water were running short. Travel to Afghanistan would take a few days, so we needed to resupply somewhere along the way.

"Seher, do you have any ideas on how to get more food?"

"Take it tonight when you get what you want from the army camp."

"What?"

"Take it, just like you did in Miran Shah."

"I might be a little busy to take food while I am trying to steal the Achilles!"

"What is the Achilles?"

"It's a system that kills Americans in Afghanistan."

"What do you plan to do with it in Afghanistan?"

"Give it back and go find the other three."

I started to look back out at Miran Shah and the camp to continue watching for the return of the soldiers and any other movements in the camp. Some vehicles were moving around on the road. Mostly farm traffic, from what I could tell.

"River, there is a truck coming up to the camp from the back side!"

I jerked around to see; it was a small white pickup. Driving around the back side of the wall of the camp, it stopped and one man got out.

"Please don't let this be Waba," I mumbled.

"Waba, who is the Waba? Waba means death."

"It's a man that has been chasing me from the beginning."

With the distance from our position to the camp, it was hard to see who it really was. The paranoia of Waba was obviously making me worried. I looked again, straining my eyes to focus. The man had gone inside the camp huts where he remained until the sun started to set at around 1800 hours. He came out and there seemed to be a loud discussion, with arms moving around expressing anger. I thought to myself that a few days ago, a man in a truck waved and yelled the same way.

After a several-minute altercation and loud yelling, the man got back in the truck. He started the truck and turned on his lights.

"Shit, he has one headlight out!"

"What does that mean, River?"

"That means this is probably the man they sent to kill me."

"They, who is they?"

"The Pakistani government!"

It was Waba, for sure. He just showed up three hours before I was to move in to get the Achilles. He knew what I needed and where it was being used. His intelligence obviously was better than mine at this point. Plus, he wasn't walking with two girls that could slow him down. I needed a new plan if Waba was in between the Achilles and me.

Sitting back in the hide position, I began to believe that this was now going to be extremely difficult at best. Seher then moved up into the lookout position. Looking back with concern, she said, "River, he moved to gate and stopped. There is no sound coming from the truck."

I jumped up and looked out over the valley to the compound. He was just sitting there, looking like he was guarding or waiting for someone other than me.

As darkness fell on the compound, Waba remained at the front gate. He was smoking, as usual, and the light lit up the inside of the truck. Smoke poured out of the driver's side window every few seconds. He was waiting for me, I could feel it. With most of the soldiers gone, this was the time I could sneak in, no matter whether Waba was there or not.

I leaned back towards Seher and Laima, looking to see what they were doing. Laima was just waking up. Seher was holding her to keep her warm. They both stared at me, and only their eyes were showing through their covered faces. They both had green eyes, pretty green eyes.

"Seher, how old are you?"

"I am eighteen years old."

"How old is Laima?"

"She is three years old."

My god, she was pregnant at fourteen and a mother by fifteen. Her husband, who we had just killed, looked to be forty years all day. My mind had a hard time wrapping around her situation as a woman and a mother.

"Do you miss your husband?"

"No, he beat us every day and was unclean. I wanted to kill myself just before you came to save us. Laima was afraid of him."

"Why did you not run away? Can't you go back to your parents?"

"Our culture does not believe in this way. My parents could legally kill or send me to prison for not going back to my husband. Even if he beats me and or even kills me."

Tears formed in her eyes. She grabbed Laima tight and hugged her. Maybe I had saved this woman for now. Yet, when I got her to Afghanistan, where would she go from there? I was sure Col. Stanton would not help her get asylum.

I didn't know what to say or do, so I just turned back around and looked at the camp and Waba in the truck. It seemed my life in Hippie Hollow was perfect compared to her life. I lived in a shack with an old bus attached. My home was a kingdom, I was safe, and my parents loved me. Tears formed in my own eyes at the injustice of Seher and Laima's situation. Was I God's tool that would save these people from death, or was this a chance moment to do the right moral thing? I felt no pity for her husband; he deserved it.

Deep into emotional instability, I began to hear yelling with authority flowing from the camp. A few soldiers ran out to the front gate holding weapons. Sounds of gunfire were coming from the direction of the Tochi Scout Memorial. Mortars and rockets began to fall in the distance. Soldiers from the camp jumped into the remaining trucks and left to assist. Waba just sat there as the Pakistanis rushed towards the memorial to assist.

Smoke continued to flow out the window from his cigarette. Waba just sat and waited. He was alone!

Chapter 17

Waba continued to sit and wait out the mortar attacks. The night began to freeze, and Laima and Seher held each other tight to stay warm. Without the fire, the night was extremely uncomfortable. I took off my head scarf and I wrapped it around Laima. She shivered and moved around a lot as I put the scarf around her. Never had a man touched or helped her in her short life. I guess it was not the custom in these parts.

"Stay warm, Laima."

"Seher, are you OK?"

"Yes, I am fine, but Laima is very cold. We must hurry and start walking to warm us."

I moved back to the overwatch position. It was now 2045 hours and my timeline was to start at 2100 hours.

Seher, holding on to Laima, moved over to me to take a look also.

"River, it's very dark and cold. The soldiers will stay in and not come out. Pakistanis eat at about this time every night."

"Seher, that's good idea, but I need Waba distracted somehow."

"Can I help you? I can go down there with Laima and beg for food and shelter at the gate. Waba is the only one at the gate right now."

Looking back at her with Laima in her arms, I was scared to put them in a situation where they could be hurt. I had become close to them. They were my responsibility after I killed the husband and father of these two. They could not go back to Miran Shah; they would be arrested and killed for murder. And that I would not stand for or live with. Afghanistan and asylum was the only way forward from here. I took a breath of air, looked at Seher and Laima, and knew she was right.

"Seher, are you OK with going down there and distracting him?"

"I want freedom and democracy. I want my child to grow free and go to school and maybe to the university. We will do it."

"In thirty minutes, I want you to walk down to the gate and ask for food and shelter. I will sneak up to the southside wall of the compound and get in from there. Try and get Waba out of the truck to help. Do not have him lead you into the camp. Do you understand?"

"Yes. How long will you be?"

"I do not know, maybe two hours."

"Do you know where this thing you search for?"

"No, but all those antennas on the roof of that center building must be the place."

"What does it look like? Is it heavy?"

"It's the size of an iPod."

"IPod, what's that?"

"Wait until you get to freedom. Laima will have two of those things with over a thousand songs inside it."

Seher looked at me with confusion. I had to remember, this was the same person that had never had running water, a toilet in the house, or a husband that didn't beat her. I was excited for her to experience freedom; I just had to get Laima and her to safety first.

"Seher, I am leaving know. Meet me back here in two hours. You will lead us to the Afghanistan border and then on in to Lawara."

"OK, what do I do if you do not come back?"

"Go to Lawara Fire Base Camp and tell them that River sent you. They will help you."

"OK, two hours."

I slipped over the watch position and walked the same route I had taken earlier. The terrain was extremely rocky and uneven. I tripped a few times; the lack of moonlight made travel difficult and increased my time to get to the wall. I hoped that Seher and Laima might find the same problem. The air was crisp and cold, my breath turned into white vapor as I became increasingly tired from the walk. After one hour I had arrived behind the wall of the southside compound.

Leaning against the wall to catch my breath and listen, I could hear Seher talking to someone at the front gate. She sounded like she was begging while Laima moaned, sounding like she was tired of walking. Discussions went back and forth; it started to sound stern from both sides. Laima continued to sound like she was complaining and Seher was telling her to be quiet. I had no clue how long they had been there asking for help.

"*Bahut bahut śhukriya*," I heard Seher say.

Sounding like they were walking up to the compound for food and water, Seher and Laima continued to talk in a low voice. From the tones of their voices, they were about fifty to seventy-five feet away from the wall. As their voices became silent, I looked over the wall to see who was near. No one could be seen or heard. I might have been lucky. Most of the soldiers might have gone to fight at Tochi.

Crawling over the wall, staying close to it to not be seen, I hit the ground and moved over to a truck. Hiding and listening, I could hear the radio room chatter from the firefight. A lot of orders being given, yet it was just one voice that I could hear.

I moved again, slowly, towards the radio room in the center of the camp, and again no one was around. Crouching behind the wall of the radio room, just below a window, I peeked in.

"Oh, my lord," I muttered to myself.

There was just one soldier; he looked like an officer. He was clean with well-groomed hair and mustache. He probably weighed a hundred and fifty pounds soaking wet at best. I could take him easy.

Sneaking around to the door of the radio room, I could still hear Seher talking to Laima. Laima didn't want to do something, by the tone of her voice. A soldier was with her and sounding upset that he was tasked to help this woman and small girl. Waba must have felt generous that night. Looking towards the front gate, Waba had moved back into the truck, listening to the firefight on the radio.

I decided to wait until Seher and Laima moved back to the front gate. Hopefully she would thank Waba and get a better look at him. I still needed a better description of him for the future. When she distracted Waba and the soldier, I could move in the communications room and grab the Achilles, if it was there!

Taking one more look into the door, I could see an iPod-looking system that was in a charger-type system. The officer was reading a manual that looked to be in English. I pulled out my pistol and pressed it against my chest. I didn't even know at that point if it was off safe.

Scary Man was right on this one: The first Achilles was at this location. The downside was that it could be the Pakistani officer's own Chinese-made iPod with dance party music. If so, this was a bust and I had risked Seher and Laima's life over it.

Seher, Laima and the soldier started walking back towards the front gate. I took one more look into the commo building; I jumped back against the wall. The officer had moved to the door to take a look out and see what was going on. He yelled something out the door to the soldier that was escorting Seher and Laima out the gate; they all stopped and looked back my way. My heart and breath stopped as they were all looking at me up against the wall. No one did anything; thank God, the darkness hid my position.

Within seconds, the officer walked out of the building towards

Seher and Laima, throwing down a cigarette butt. I could smell his aftershave; it was strong. The light remained on in the building, exposing the front door. Once the officer arrived to talk with Seher, I crawled in to grab the Achilles, not knowing if it was the radio or not. Never looking back, I grabbed it and placed it in my chest pocket. I heard no alarms going off from the removal of the radio. No green lights turning to red. Holding tight, I slipped back out, only looking back once at Seher and the officer. It all seemed safe. I slowly moved back to the truck and then up against the wall.

The officer began to grab the food and water that the soldier had given her. Talking ensued; Waba got out of his truck, walked over to the group, and pushed the officer away. Waba took back the food and water and gave it to Seher. Yelling and pointing in the face of the officer, Waba turned to Seher and pointed her to the gate. She took the items and moved quickly back out of the compound, with Laima running behind and starting to cry. Laima was scared; I felt sorry for her as she was so young to be in this situation.

Once Seher and Laima had cleared the front gate, I started to climb over the wall, but stopped. I heard footsteps and voices on the outside of the wall below me. Pulling my weapon out, I sat and barely breathed until the sound had passed. Soon, I made my move over the wall. Scraping my body against the stone wall, my weapon fell out of my belt, landing on the dirt below me. The sound was loud on a clear and quiet night. Looking first at my weapon on the ground and then toward the communications building, I saw the officer stop as if he heard something. He looked around and then told the one soldier to take a look. No options were available at this moment but to continue over the wall. So, I left the pistol to save Seher, Laima and myself and ran like hell.

I knew I had less than a minute before the alarm was sounded. Seher and Laima had to make it to the main road to hide in the farm fields. Praying, I hoped they would make it.

Within a few minutes and a hundred yards later, yelling and commands began to come from the camp. The officer arrived back in the commo building and found the Achilles missing. I ran for my life, focused on everything around me. With no weapon, there was no way to protect Seher or Laima. The remaining guards turned on some floodlights, but they were not powerful enough to see me in the distance.

After about a half a mile of running, I looked back towards the main road where Seher and Laima should have been. All I saw was Waba's truck moving towards Seher and Laima's possible location. He must have felt they had something to do with the theft. Continuing to move towards the overwatch position, I prayed that Seher and Laima would show up.

I made it to the overwatch in less than fifty minutes to find no one there. Looking back at the camp, it was lit up like a city, but no lights covered out more than two hundred feet from the camp at best. There were only about seven soldiers roaming the camp area, afraid to come out at night.

Waba was down below, driving up and down the road, flashing lights into the fields, looking for Seher and Laima. He was yelling something, and he sounded mad and impatient.

"Please do not move, Seher," I said in a low prayer.

Losing those two would be very hard to handle. Paranoia and sadness took over all emotions, as I walked back and forth, rubbing my face. Tears started filling my eyes. It had been too long; they were not back yet. Waba was hunting them down and was sure to kill them when he found them. I looked back over the rocks at Miran Shah, where Waba's truck continued to move up and down the road. Hopefully she ran to the east into the city to hide. I could only hope!

"River, River, grab Laima!"

My heart stopped when I heard those words. Seher was on her knees, holding Laima out for me to grab her.

"Seher, Laima, I thought Waba might have gotten you."

"We were hiding in the fields. Once he drove by, we ran to here."

"Oh, thank God," I said as I held Laima tight and I touched Seher on the hand.

"River, we must go now."

Seher was a lot calmer than I was. I guess she had been beaten for so long that this wasn't scary for her.

I looked back at the camp; they were still going crazy trying to secure the area. No change. Waba was now pulling people out of houses and beating them. The camp was still in lockdown but the fighting at the Tochi had stopped. No troops had been moved back to support the camp yet.

"Seher, we cannot leave until I am sure this is the Achilles."

I pulled out the box, I touched the screen, and it lit up. Seher quickly threw her scarf over the light, and we hit the ground. The screen said "Welcome to Achilles," clear as day. On the back it said, "Property of the U.S. Government." We had it!

Turning off the system, it was now time to move.

"OK, Seher, which way do we go?"

"This way, we go that way towards the south and then move west to Afghanistan. Will your friends be there to help us?"

"Yes, I have something they want badly. This little box is very powerful to my country."

"Will they help Laima and me?"

"Yes, since you have helped me, they will."

Since it was dark, Seher could not tell that I lied. Asylum, I had no power to promise this.

"Seher, let's move slowly. I will carry Laima and follow you."

2300 hours – Day 3
Thirty miles from Miran Shah to Lawara Base Camp.
I am on the run with a woman and child.

Chapter 18

As we moved out from our overwatch position, en route to Lawara Fire Base, I could hear Waba speaking loudly about an American. He was beating the locals, trying to get any answers he could from them. Since they knew nothing, they were beaten until unconscious. Once he realized that too much time had passed, I was gone. But, what he didn't know was where I was going with the first Achilles. Hopefully, he would assume Shkin, because that's where I had come from. He could possibly assume that I was with a woman and a child from Miran Shah, that we were moving slowly through mountain passes, and that we had to find food and water along the way. The only possible way out would be through Afghanistan. He understood that I couldn't take a chance with a woman and child in tow.

"River, River, I will find you!" Waba yelled from the compound through a megaphone.

The sound echoed throughout the mountain ranges several times. The sound was as chilling as the weather. Seher looked at me with concern.

"Don't worry, Seher, he will not follow us this way. He will believe we are headed back to Shkin Fire Base to drop off the Achilles."

"OK, we will walk directly west through the goat and camel trails used by the smugglers. They will lead us near Lawara. We will have to hide from the Pakistani border soldiers as they have an outpost in Lawara."

"What happens if the smugglers see us? Will they turn us in?"

"We must pay something if we get caught."

"Like what?"

"Money or me!"

I was stunned at how easily she handled that statement. She was willing to give herself to someone she did not know just for freedom and our safety? Seher was truly a woman warrior that understood sacrifice for the good of everyone.

We walked for three hours or so, walking goat trails that ran along the ridgelines. This was slow-going terrain at best. Snow, rocks, and cold streams created cuts on our feet and hands. Laima was still fast asleep in my arms, holding her small baby doll. The heat from my body kept her warm and secure. This was the closest I had ever been to acting like a father to any child. It felt so easy to assume the part of a husband and father. At this moment, I was their safety and they depended on me.

"River, we must find a place to have a fire and to get warm."

Seher was completely soaked in sweat and was shivering. Her hands were tucked under her clothes, as her voice trembled.

"Look for a cavern or abandoned hut."

We continued walking, searching for some form of cover for the night, for another hour. A fire was needed, and water and food to be eaten.

Finally, with the use of moonlight, we could see a small hut on a hillside at about sixty feet in front of us. It was dark with no lights coming from it. It was located in an austere location with very little foot or vehicle travel, which made it perfect for hiding and keeping warm.

"Seher, stop right here. I will go check to see if it's all clear."

She took Laima from me, and I moved slowly towards the hut.

I picked up a stick for protection and offensive requirements. I knocked on the door, for some reason. It was a war, right? Listening, I heard no movement. I knocked again—nothing. Pushing the door open, I could see nothing inside due to the darkness. Outside the hut, it had two windows covered by cloth that was nailed down to the wood window frames. The one-story hut was made of mud bricks and sticks and was maybe two hundred square feet. It had only three sides to the building, because it was built into the wall of a mountain. At this moment, it was a perfect place. I ran back to Seher and Laima.

"No one is there. Let's go."

Moving slowly back to the hut, I went in first and felt around to get my bearings. It was empty other than some rugs on the floor. Seher sat down, holding Laima in her arms. She let out a big gust of air. After ten miles of walking, she could move no more. Laying Laima down on the ground in front of her, she rubbed her hands and face to create heat.

"River, you need to rest also."

"We need a fire; we have stopped moving so we will get hypothermia. I'll go outside and find some dry wood."

"Pull it off the hut from the inside."

I looked up at the ceiling of the hut. Dry wood was being used as roof insulation; I pulled off a few branches, as dust fell to the ground and onto Laima sleeping on the floor.

"Sorry, Laima."

Continuing to pull wood from the hut, I made sure that the hut didn't fall down. Piling up the wood, I had enough for a few hours, I assumed. Building a triangle-shaped fire like a good soldier, I was ready to light, but there was one problem. I had nothing to light it with.

"Seher, do you have anything to light the fire?" She said nothing for a few seconds, and I could not tell by her face how surprised she was at my stupidity. Reaching down into her clothing, she pulled out a little bag that resembled a coin purse. Within it, she had two wooden matches that she used to light fires for cooking.

"I only have one more match."

"I will be careful, Seher."

Gathering up some tinder, carpet fibers, and old pieces of paper, I scratched the match on a small rock, and it lit fast. Putting it under the paper, it lit and I placed it in the pile of fibers and tinder. It started slowly and began to die.

"Oh, shit, it's going out."

"Get out of the way." Seher leaned over and began blowing on the fire to give it some air. The fire began to burn, and she kept feeding it with tinder and carpet pieces. The heat began to rush into my face and hands. Laima woke up as she felt the heat on her body. It was a great moment: Fire created a secure and safe place, all of a sudden.

Seher's fire-making skills and land-navigation skills were beyond anyone I knew. She could be the female version of an army ranger. Mentally and physically tough, trained in the arts of POW survival, and with one skill that no other ranger had: childbirth. Seher was tough!

The fire continued to burn for a few hours as we took turns sleeping, eating and drinking. We kept an eye out all night for signs of movement. The sun started to come up at about 0600 hours. There were clouds in the sky, and it looked like snow was on its way.

"Seher, wake up. It's time to go. Laima, sweetheart, it's time to wake up."

I touched both of them on the hand to get their attention. They were exhausted and weak; I knew the next twenty miles to Lawara were going to be tough for them. It would be even tougher if Col. Stanton didn't help with asylum. This might be a promise I could not keep. The look I would get from Seher if asylum was not given would be devastating. Laima will only know she was being left and her mother was crying. How would I live with this lie?

"Give me Laima. I will carry her."

"No, Laima will walk. This will look normal as we travel. Men usually do not carry a girl through the mountains."

"OK, let's get going. We have about thirty-five kilometers to walk just today. We need to be at Lawara tonight before dark. That gives us twelve hours to walk."

"River, the way we walk today will be by waddies used as smugglers' trails to the west. This will be dangerous so we must act like we are married and have a small child."

"You will have to do all the speaking. How will we explain this to others along the way that we come in contact with?"

She stood there thinking, and then ripped a length of material from her clothing. Wrapping it around my throat, she said, "Your throat was injured in a Pakistani army attack on our village, and you cannot speak because of the wound."

"Are they not going to be suspicious that a woman does all the talking and not the man?"

"No, there are many injured men from the terrorists and the Pakistani government. Most smugglers are Afghanis, so they hate the Pakistanis, and they will believe this story. You just move your head when I talk to others."

"Got it. It's 0620 hours. We need to get moving."

Chapter 19

The morning was extremely cold; my bones were tense from the shaking and shivering all through the night. My clothes were still damp from the sweat from just a few hours ago. Laima seemed to be walking and complaining at the same time. She would complain, stop, and then get scolded by Seher. That little girl was just like any other three-year-old in Texas. It was warming to my heart to be part of the moment; it seemed like a family. I was proud to help her, but sad that I might have to tell them asylum was not possible. They might end up in a refugee camp in Afghanistan filled with Afghanis that hate Pakistanis. She spoke Urdu and English, so maybe this could help her, but she could never say she was Pakistani. That could get her outcasted or killed in the camp. We could only hope that, if that happened, it would be a UNICEF camp where protection was just a little better than a government-run camp.

We traveled north along a dried stream bed about one mile through some high-altitude mountain ranges. It was straight uphill most of the way. Sometimes I would pick up Laima to speed up travel. Seher would look at me as if I should put her down, because she needed to be tough.

"River, let her walk. She needs to learn by herself."

"Seher, she is a little girl. This is not army training."

"Someday, Laima will have to walk these mountains to go home when it is safe; she will have to be strong for her children."

"Seher, she is three years old!"

"She could be a mother in ten years. She has to learn now."

"A mother in ten years. Why?"

"This is not America. We have no money or food, and children can be a burden on the rest of the family. Survival depends on finding a husband for a young girl. Some girls' families can get thirty-thousand rupees if they marry an older man."

I looked at Laima. She just smiled at me, not understanding what her life was about to become.

"You Americans think you can change our country and its ways, but you can't! I must leave with my daughter, and I need your help to save her from this life."

"I'm sorry Seher, I shouldn't have said anything."

"No, you must know. Carry this story back home; maybe that will help Laima when she is older."

We continued to walk up and down high ridgelines and mountains for hours, covering about ten miles by about 1300 hours. Yet, all I could think about was what Seher told me. I couldn't fathom Laima as a thirteen-year-old mother married to a forty-year-old man. Being scared for Laima giving birth to a child at that age was terrifying. I had already seen the death of a baby and the life-altering effects on a thirteen-year-old girl less than a week ago. Her washing the blood from her legs, crying into the bloody dirt still haunted me. Now with Laima, it was too close to reality and I just wanted to save her.

Figuring another twelve miles to go, I realized getting into Lawara Fire Base would have to take place after dark. This would require me to contact Col. Stanton to coordinate movement into Afghanistan. Hopefully the S.F. could meet me at the border and pull us both in. This would require me to use the satellite phone. It should have at least a little juice to make a quick call.

Throughout the day, we ran into other families and donkey convoys walking along the same trails and mountain ranges we were on. They too were up to no good or running from the Taliban. The men just looked at me and nodded their heads and waved. I did the same. Seher said and did nothing. She remained the disciplined temporary wife to me, never looking up, showing emotion, or speaking. Laima continued to walk behind her, and I stayed in front, leading her. Leading? I had no idea. Seher was pointing me in the right direction, and she could have passed the land navigation course at Fort Benning with no problems.

It was now about 1700 hours; we had cleared most of the mountain ranges and started into the lowland areas with dried river beds and waddies. This is where legal traffic flowed; we had no choice but to come out in the open around the Tochi River Tributary. You could stop and look down through the mountains to Afghanistan. A major road was to our south. I pointed it out to Seher.

"Look there, a major transportation route into Afghanistan. I can see trucks moving both ways."

"We need to stay in the mountains as much as we can. We need to cross that road and stay in the mountains. If we keep going, we will have to pass by the Pakistani border guards over there."

Seher pointed to the west of us, and by God, there was a building with a radio tower and mud walls with trucks around it. That was a Pakistani Frontier Corps outpost in the middle of Taliban country. This area was known as Waziristan, home of terrorism 101 and basic training for the world's terrorists. This is where the 9/11 attackers were trained and where Bin Laden was found and killed. No doubt, this area was dangerous. The people that were supposed to help you here, the Pakistani Frontier Corps, were in bed with the Taliban. If not, they would all have been found dead in their beds down in that outpost. Get along or die!

"OK, Seher, let's keep moving south along the ridgeline and cross down in the low ground and then move back up into the mountains. From there, we will be about three miles from the Lawara Base Camp crossing. I will call from there to get picked up. How is Laima?"

"She will be good. We are almost free."

My conscience was tearing me apart; I could barely look at her. What if she knew already that asylum was a lie? Leaving her home with a husband missing and two feet under was probably enough to take a chancc on a lie coming from me. If she would have stayed in Miran Shah, she would have been left with only prison, death, and a three-year-old daughter living in the streets alone. Yet, I was still doing the right-thing, just with my fingers crossed behind my back when I told the lie.

My stomach and throat seemed to hurt worse than ever in the cold night air; ulcers seemed to be forming faster than any doctor could imagine. The salt on my lips was heavy all of a sudden. This seemed to be a horse-to-water medical affliction. I could see the light at the end of the tunnel at Lawara, so my body was trying to slack off. But now was not the time. It's like how car accidents happen within a mile from your home. That was exactly how I felt about the distance between us and the border. A carless tactical move, any accident was the only obstacle in not reaching our objective.

"Seher, we need to move slow and cautious now. We are near a secured border that we have to cross. Guards will be looking for suspicious people at this point."

She agreed. We began our descent down into the low ground south towards the main road to cross. It took about an hour to get to the road. Darkness was showing its color. We decided to wait to cross until it was dark, so we hid behind some rocks to rest a few hundred feet from the road. Jingle trucks, military vehicles with heavy machine guns, and donkey carts moved up and down regularly until darkness fell. The cold started to creep up on us. Our sweat was turning cold. The wind was blowing slowly enough to make the situation worse. We had to keep moving and get out of the low ground because hypothermia could be a possibility.

"Let's get going. Follow me."

"River, Laima is asleep. Can you carry her? She is not talking anymore."

I grabbed her; her stomach was making sounds, and she seemed sick from the travel. Looking at Seher, I could see she was terrified and shaking from the non-reaction to her voice.

"Laima, Laima, wake up, honey!" I said this four times as I touched her face.

She finally opened her eyes and said, "*Ammi, Ammi, Ammi!*"

Seher grabbed her from me and hugged her tightly. She held her to her face and said sweet things that only a mother could say when she was scared for her child. Seher kneeled down to the ground and rocked her back to sleep.

With a few minutes, Seher was ready to go. We listened for vehicle movement and then crossed diagonally towards the next ridgeline that would take us to the Lawara Fire Base crossing. It took about three minutes to cross and get back into hiding. Soon after the crossing, a man and his donkeys pulling carts passed us below. He stopped and listened for a minute or so and then continued on towards Lawara area. This put this man just in front of us. This might be the time to follow this guy to the border and let him get harassed by the border guards. When that happened, we could pass on through while they were distracted. It was the entire plan I had at this time. Laima was not well, and Seher was too nervous and worn out from the experience. This also would shorten the distance to the fire base and the terrain was easier to walk. We could be across the border in a few hours; freedom was within distance.

I reached into my inside shirt pocket and pulled out the Achilles. This had gotten over fifteen people killed, a woman and child freed from a wife beater, and I had attacked and buried a man. How many people had I saved by getting this back? We would never know.

We continued to walk along a goat trail that followed the path of the road towards the Lawara. Laima was still asleep and weak. She weighed next to nothing, so carrying her was like carrying a weapon in my hands. The guy with the donkeys continued on at a slow pace. It was a comfortable pace for us as we walked a trail that rolled around boulders and waddies. I kept him in sight, because he was the distraction we needed to cross safely.

"River, how much longer?"

"We only have a few for kilometers until we get to the Pakistan guard post. We will stop just short of there and head due west across the border in the open. This is the only area that could be of concern."

"I want freedom. Please give us freedom."

I said reluctantly, "I will do everything I can to give you freedom, but we need to get across the border now. This will be dangerous; we need to be quiet."

"OK, River, thank you so much for what you have done for us." She was starting to cry. I grabbed her hand and she held it tightly.

Just that touch was all that was needed. She was going to get freedom, no matter what. My mission was now to save them. If they went back to Pakistan, she would be killed and Laima would be married by thirteen. I couldn't live with that for the rest of my life. Guilt and sadness would devastate the rest of my life. My conscience was attacking me!

"Seher, let's move and we can talk later. It's important that we move with the man ahead of us, please."

Seher began moving forward as I picked up Laima from the ground and followed behind her. It was now about 2030 hours; it was dark as hell and cold. We were shaking from the cold wind as it drove into our faces as we started to cross the open valley behind the man. Every so often, the donkey cart man would stop and look back as if he had heard something. We stopped every time he did. I just hoped Laima wouldn't wake up and make a noise, but she never did.

With just about a kilometer or half-mile to go, lights from a vehicle approached the man in front of us. He stopped and waited until the truck arrived. It was the Pakistanis checking on his cargo and identification. The man looked back in our direction but never said anything to the Pakistani guard. My feeling was that he knew we were there. He was helping us, from what I could tell. I grabbed Seher and pointed her directly towards the west. The border was just in front of us. Off in the distance, I could see the Lawara border crossing where the S.F. was stationed with Afghanis. Lights were on, flooding the crossing as trucks and people moved through. It was not busy at the time, and very few people were around.

"Let's move towards those lights over there. That's the place we need to cross. Just before we arrive, I need to make a telephone call to get us across the border without getting killed."

Seher moved at a fast clip, and even I had a hard time keeping up with her. She was using all her remaining energy for the last half-mile.

"Seher, slow down. We need to take our time. The S.F. and Afghanis will notice us through their night vision devices and might shoot. Slow down!" She finally slowed just about three hundred meters out.

I found some rocks and bushes to hide behind in an open area. This is where I would make the phone call to Col. Stanton and coordinate passage at the border.

"Seher, hold Laima and be quiet."

"What are we going to do?"

"I have to get us to freedom from the border."

Pulling out the satellite phone, I turned it on; hoping it still had enough power to operate. If not, we would have to walk in cold turkey, and that just wasn't preferable. Extending the antenna and pressing the power button, I saw lights and the word "search." The battery light said I had four minutes of talk time. What the hell? Somebody didn't update the phone card minutes. Col. Stanton's number was programmed into the phone by the S.F. before I left Shkin. Thank God, I would have had a hell of a time remembering the number. Looking at the time on the phone, I saw it was 2302 hours.

The phone started to connect and ring: one, two, three times. The battery timer was now down to three minutes. Finally it was picked up. It was Col. Stanton, but he answered as General Stanton.

"This is General Stanton."

"Sir, this is River!"

"Where the hell have you been? I counted you AWOL and dead three days ago. What do you have for me? You better have been busy."

"Sir, I have the first Achilles from Miran Shah in my possession." Silence was heard through the phone.

"Sir, I only have two more minutes on the phone. I'm hiding about three hundred meters from the Lawara crossing and need the S.F to let me through. I have a woman and child with me!"

"You have the first Achilles?"

"Yes, sir, now call the border and tell them to let me in. I do not want to get caught by the Pakistanis and killed by the Afghanis. I need help."

"River, this is great news. I am shocked; you are the only one to do it."

"Sir, let me in. Call the border!"

The phone died. I heard no confirmation from the now-promoted General Stanton on whether he was going to call or not. My body went cold, my mind wandered on what to do next, and we needed a new plan.

"River, are they coming to get us?"

"I do not know right now. Let me think, Seher."

Looking around, I thought south seemed to be the best route to go. If I went back, the Pakistanis would see us. Suddenly in the distance, I saw four U.S. soldiers standing at the border with night vision devices and full-up battle ready. They began blinking a red light out across the border, looking for a return blink. I had no flashlight, just the last match we had for a fire. Hopefully they had infrared devices that could see the heat from the match against the bush that we were hiding behind.

"Seher, give me the match."

I grabbed it from her and looked for a rock to strike it on. The wind was blowing slowly so I had to be careful to not blow it out. Seher grabbed some cloth off of her clothing and took the match from me. She formed a small break around the match using the cloth and lit it off of her shoe. It worked. The light burned and she held it steady. I looked back at the Lawara gate to see if they were seeing the light.

Finally, I got three blinks of a red light towards our direction. They blinked three times, four times in a row. That was good enough for me. I picked up Laima and told Seher to move quickly towards the border. We ran for our lives. Seher kept falling, and I kept picking her up with one hand. Laima woke up, and her arms were swinging around as I helped her.

"Be quiet, Laima! Shhhhh! Seher, keep running!"

I looked back up. The S.F. guys could see us coming. They went into a defensive mode as if to show the Pakistanis they meant business. The energy I had at this point was endless; we must have cleared two hundred meters in less than sixty seconds. Laima started to laugh; she seemed to think this was a good time.

As we got within one hundred meters, I could see off to my right Pakistani guards running towards us with a purpose. Seher started getting scared.

"River, they are coming!"

"Keep running! Keep running!"

The S.F. were yelling, "Come on, keep running!" Their weapons were pointed down at the ground to not tempt the Pakistanis to start shooting. They were yelling at the Pakistanis to back off; threats were going back and forth.

We kept our heads down and running towards the border gate. We had fifty feet left, with the Pakistanis running at full speed. They were within twenty feet of us. This was a collision course that would equal either freedom or a Pakistani prison for me and death for Seher.

Leaning forward: ten, seven, five, three feet was all that was left. Just as I hit that last three feet, a Pakistani guard grabbed my shoulder. I spun around, throwing his arms away from me, and fell to the ground just inside the border. Laima was still in my arms, laughing. Seher had beaten me through the border by about a foot. She was already in the arms of the S.F. I had to jerk my legs back across as the Pakistanis tried to pull me back over.

"Back off! Get away!"

The S.F. kept flexing their muscle at the border. The Afghani border guards did nothing except stand behind the Americans, confused and scared, wondering what the hell just happened.

"Are you Major Rochman? River Rochman?"

"Yes, yes, yes!"

"Do you have the Achilles?"

I reached into my pocket and pulled out the Achilles and handed it to them. An officer came running up and took a look at it and turned it on.

"Welcome to Achilles," it said in the screen. He turned it over and read the serial number. It was correct.

"Major Rochman, great job. Let's call General Stanton and give him the good news."

I looked around for Seher. She was holding on to Laima next to an Afghani guard. She was crying and talking to Laima.

"Seher, are you OK?"

"River, come here, please. Something is wrong with Laima."

I asked for a medic from the S.F., and they came running to check the child. After a few minutes of medical checks, they wanted to take her back to the medic station at the Lawara Fire Base.

The medic looked over at me and said, "She is suffering from malnutrition and needs medicines. We can help her."

"Seher, she will be OK. They will help her."

"Thank you, River, so much. You saved us."

The S.F. guys, hearing Seher speak English, became confused about who she even was. I later told them what had happened to her in Miran Shah; the S.F. officer wanted to kill the husband too.

"Seher and Laima need asylum here in Afghanistan and then need to be taken to the United States. It will be unsafe for them here. She is alone and needs help. You know what they do to females in these countries. Please help her!"

"Let's see what General Stanton can do. I cannot do anything but take her to Charahi Qanbar refugee camp in Kabul. Those can be a terrible place for single mothers, especially her age and the crime that she had committed in Pakistan."

"Just please, do what you can. She is good people. The reason I am alive with the Achilles is because she guided me through the mountains from Miran Shah to here. No way could I have done this by myself."

"Let's go call General Stanton and confirm that we have the Achilles, OK?"

Seher and Laima had already been moved to the medical clinic at the Lawara Fire Base. This would be the first time that Seher and Laima would ever receive true medical care in their entire lives thus far.

I had to now go back and discuss asylum or refugee status in the slums outside of Kabul with General Stanton. He had better fix this, or I would visit him tenfold if anything happened to those two girls! They had changed my life; I finally knew what love was just by watching Seher look and care for Laima.

Carrying Laima in my arms back to the fire base, I knew her safety was now my responsibility. General Stanton had better come through! Asylum!

Chapter 20

Getting them asylum was hard; sending them to a refugee camp in Kabul was easy. I knew this but it was worth pursuing for Seher and Laima.

"Asylum is that what you really want to do?" said the S.F. officer.

"Yes, they helped me get the Achilles."

"What else did she do for asylum?"

"She led me to here. I was given very little to complete this mission. I had no weapon and compass to get from Shkin to Marin Shah and back to Lawara. She risked her daughter's life and her own to throw off the Pakistani Frontier Brigade guards so I could run in and grab the Achilles. I couldn't have done any of this without them."

"OK, sir, let's go into my operations center and call General Stanton."

As we moved into the center, I couldn't help but feel hopeless about asylum. My gut told me they were going to the refugee camp in Kabul. Or, they would tell me what I wanted to hear, send me out for the second Achilles, and then send them to Kabul.

I needed a plan to ensure they were safe and not in danger tonight. General Stanton now had the rank to get what I needed, and that was to help this woman and child who had helped the United States bravely.

The phone began to ring, and suddenly General Stanton was on the other end, saying, "This is General Stanton, and how can I help you?"

"Sir, its River, and I am standing here in Lawara with the first Achilles."

"Oh my God, River, this is fantastic! How do you feel?"

"I am tired and broken right now; I need food, water and asylum for a young Pakistani woman and her child. That's all I need, and I will be back out for the next Achilles."

Silence was all I heard. I looked over at the S.F. commander. "Did the line drop?"

"Asylum for a woman and a child," blasted from the phone.

"Yes, sir, they assisted me in getting the Achilles and then led me to Lawara. They are very brave and deserve assistance from the United States."

"River, is her name Seher and the child's name is Laima?"

"Yes, sir! How did you know?"

"The Pakistani government is already aware of her assisting and that she killed her husband in Miran Shah a few days ago. They want her and the child back now."

"Sir, they will kill her. You know that. By the way, I killed her husband in self-defense in their home. He was beating her and the child, and I ran in to stop the probable death of the woman. She didn't kill him. I did."

"River, where did you place the body?"

"In a poppy field a few hundred yards from the house."

The S.F. guys looked at me after I said that. All of a sudden, I had street cred with them. I was a killer in their midst, and I looked like a half-local and foreigner that hadn't taken a shower in over a week.

"Shit, River, are you sure you want to take the blame? The Pakistanis are going to come after you when you reenter Pakistan in the next few days. You will be put up on murder charges and flaunted in front of the world. Then they will cut your head off on the Internet. If this is considered murder by trial, the U.S. cannot get you out of a murder conviction or a Pakistani prison. Damn, the U.S. government is not even tracking this mission; they will deny you, as I have told you."

"Sir, I need asylum for these two. I cannot have them go back to Pakistan and die. No refugee camp in Kabul, either. I need your help, please."

"I will see what I can do."

A recruiter once told me that I would never have to go to war because the Democrats would be in power. Peace, love, and happiness filled the air as I signed up for the military. He lied too! General Stanton would do that too: lie to me and leave them in Lawara to rot or be given back to the Pakistanis.

"Sir, I need more than that. These two are like family to me now."

"*Family*? River, your family is back in Hippie Hollow, Texas, smoking grass and being alcoholics. That's your family; go fix that! Now get your head on straight or I will have the police and the DEA raid Hippie Hollow and arrest your parents for selling dope! How do you want this to go, River?"

"Sir, I will get back out there and get your stuff back to save your ass, but when I am done, me and you will have words. Then I will go to the media and let them know what type of person you are. And, if I find that Seher and Laima are harmed in any way, I will come looking for you. I am good at getting away and hiding now. I can continue that life! You pick the outcome, SIR!"

"Now, River, calm down! I will do what I can to help your new *family*, but I cannot promise anything."

"You better promise, or this thing is over right now. Take your pick!"

"River, I will get them to safety and clean up the mess in Miran

Shah, but you have to leave tomorrow morning for Torkham Gate. You will cross in that area and get to Peshawar to get the primary brain for the Achilles. If you get that, you are done, River. You can then go back to your little girlfriend and kid. Last mission, River, for now."

"General Stanton, I will do this as long as they are safe and I am done after this. I want a full retirement from the army and to be left alone for the rest of my life. That's it, done!"

"Medical is the only way out. Hurt or go crazy is the only way. You better pick one!"

"I need a chopper and a few ground troops to help me get up to the border in Torkham. The Khyber Rifles Brigade and some Special Forces are in that area. They are the best they have, so I will need a weapon this time. Going for bear at this point, because Waba will be there, I am sure."

"River, I have intelligence on Waba. His real name is Abbas 'Waba' Mugal. His biological father was a serial killer of well over one hundred people, mostly children. He was also a rapist of children. Waba was put in an orphanage and later adopted by the current Khyber Rifles Commander, Colonel Muhammad Akram Khan. Khan trained him from the time he was about ten years old in Special Forces tactics and survival. He is the best they have ever had, a killer from the inside out. This guy will rape you and then kill you."

"I know how he kills; I have already run into him several times. Every person I came into contact with in Pakistan, he killed. Well over fifteen people at this point are dead because of him."

"You will probably have to kill him then. He knows you are looking for the brain of the Achilles and that it's in Peshawar. It's the key to the whole system. He just needs to sit and wait. Traps will be out, River. You better bring your best game."

"Sir, I have no game. I will probably die this time. You have left me with no resources for protection or extraction. Death is what you have brought me and fifteen other Pakistanis. And now I have a psycho killer and rapist after me. I have to go. Seher and Laima are being treated at the medic's hut, and I need to make sure they are not scared, and *get me that chopper and troops*! Goodbye!"

After I hung up, looking up I could see the S.F. guys staring at me. Their faces spoke volumes. I was a known killer, cared for a Pakistani woman that took a metal rod to the brain of her husband, watched over a three-year-old girl, and had a killer-rapist chasing me to Peshawar. Now, a small-time army officer had just become an image of death and glory for a few Special Forces troops.

"Take care, fellas!" I walked out.

Chapter 21

Time was of the essence. I needed food, weapons, ammo, and water, to start with. Walking towards the mess tent, I felt all eyes on me. The ANA squad and the S.F. soldiers were mumbling to themselves, "That's the guy that just ran across the border with the woman and child. They say he killed over fifteen men!"

I just let the rumors go at that point. They were worth the respect and the supplies I would need to continue on to Peshawar. Turning my head ever so slightly and looking in their direction, I saw some of them quickly look away. I had now become the scariest man alive!

Walking into the mess tent, no one was around so I started to load up with power bars, muffins, chips, and water. Anything I could carry. It needed to be small and stay good for a while. Junk foods and power bars stay good forever these days. I grabbed a whole bunch of salt, pepper, and hot sauce for the dead animals I would have to eat. This at least gave it some taste when I truly hated it.

"Hey, sir, here is a weapon you can use," said a young sergeant walking in as I stalked up on pogey bait. I filled the bag with muffins, breakfast bars, and bottles of water.

"This could be my last manufactured meal for the next week. What do you have for me?" "It's an AK-47, with grenade launcher, scope, and tripod. This baby has got it all. I tested it yesterday."

"Where did you get it from?"

"We got it from a Pakistani that was dressed up as a Pakistani Frontier Corps guard that tried to kill us with an IED last week."

"Where is he now?"

"Allah only knows," he said with a grin.

"OK". I grabbed it from him and ran through the handle action, cocking it back and forth to ensure it was free. This baby worked well; it even looked brand new. The sergeant did a great job with cleaning it up for me; it was perfect and ready for action.

"Where are the ammo and grenades?" I said, looking at the sergeant.

"It's all in the truck for you, with extra. You might need some for the movement to Torkham. There are plenty of bad people out looking for Americans and especially someone like you. You probably already have a five-thousand dollar reward for your head by now."

"Five thousand dollars? That's it?" Was my life worth so little?

"Yes, sir, but you have to remember the standard of living here. That means you have a million dollars on your head."

"That's pretty good. Yes?"

"I guess so."

I walked over to the truck to inspect my chariot that would carry me into battle. It looked used and weak at best. Tires were worn down, the shocks were bent, and it leaned a little on the right side. If this was a truck I got in high school, this would have been perfect and free. But, since it had to take me two hundred miles to the north through rough country, it needed some help.

Walking over to the motor sergeant, I spotted some blown-up trucks in a junk pile.

"Hey, Sergeant, can I get some parts off of those trucks to fix my own?"

"No problem, sir!"

Starting up the truck, the tail pipe rattled, and it sputtered as I let the clutch out. My chariot was clearly the only one available for a reason! With the truck sputtering and rattling, I moved over to the motor pool to make some changes. The motor sergeant took one look and shook his head and said, "I hope you make it."

"Me too. What can you do to fix the suspension?"

"Give me a few hours and I will have it ready."

"Thanks, Sergeant!"

Seher and Laima stayed on my mind most of the day. I had not seen them in the camp since I left the operations center. So, I went looking to make sure they were all OK. I found Laima playing with some of the soldiers with a soccer ball as Seher just watched. Her face was uncovered. She smiled with pride and the feeling of safety showed through. She was very happy watching Laima play.

Looking up at me, she said, "Hello, River, you look tired." She was sitting up against a mud hut on a spare truck tire looking at Laima playing.

"Seher, that's an understatement, after you walked me over one hundred kilometers carrying Laima." Seher just smiled and laughed.

There was pride in what she had accomplished, even if it meant killing a husband to do it. She and her daughter were safe from violence; protection from within the walls of the Special Forces comforted her.

"Will we get asylum, River?"

"I do not know, but I will do everything I can to make it happen."

"Where will we go if no asylum?"

"Kabul, to the refugee camps. That's where you will have to go."

"That's better than back to Miran Shah. I will for sure die there. Laima will be taken away and will become a slave to some old man, have children, and never get an education. She is destined for unhappiness." She looked away as tears began to fill her eyes. Laima leaned over to her and held her arm tightly and said something kind to her mother. It was a sad moment for a family. They knew they would be separated and never see each other again. Hell was upon them now!

"I will continue to talk with BG Stanton to help with your asylum request, OK? I will not forget you. You saved me many times from Miran Shah to Lawara."

I got up to leave, but Seher grabbed me and said, "Please do not leave. You will not come back for us, I feel."

"Seher, I have to go to Peshwar and finish the job or I will never go home."

Angrily, Seher said, "River, we will never go home. Help us!"

"I am doing everything I can." Tears began to flow from my eyes as tensions grew. People around us could hear the tone changing. This became complete terror for all of us as Laima quickly turned to look into her mother's face. Laima wiped away the tears from her mother's face. She then leaned over to me, wiping the tears from my face, and she said only, "River."

Oh my God, the touch of the child's hand and the tears of Seher were far more emotional than I could handle at the time. I got up and looked around the area and tried to breathe. Others looked at me with pity. The hardest of men couldn't have handled it.

Walking away, I told myself to not look back; it would be too much for me to handle. If I did, they would be in the truck headed out with me right then. Emotional trouble was upon me. I cared so much now for that family that I was prepared to put them in danger in Peshawar just so they could avoid the refugee camps, separation or the loss of Laima.

I looked at the ground as I walked towards the motor pool to check the condition of my truck. An SF captain said, "Do not think it, sir!"

"Think what?"

"You know the deal: That woman and child mean more to you than anything right now. You can save them only if BG Stanton helps you, and he has never helped anyone but himself. He is legendary out here in the hinterlands for not giving a crap for any of you guys. He blew it, and you guys are paying the price. Now you have this woman and child. Do you want to help them, sir?"

"Yes!"

"Then you have to take them with you. If not, they will end up in a Kabul refugee camp forever."

Putting my hands on the top of my head, I looked into the sky and wondered what the hell was now going on. There were only two choices to make: take them or leave them.

"Can they stay with you until I get back?"

"No. What the hell would we do with them? We would get attacked from the bad guys, or she would be sexually harassed by the ANA soldiers. There are no good options for them here. You need to take them with you. What about dropping them off along the way?"

I must have looked confused at the horrible thought of doing that to a human. I couldn't do that, I think! Leaving them here was now not an option; taking them with me was the only option. At least, away from here would be the first order of events. The second would be to hand them off to a good family between here and Peshawar. These plans only prolonged me telling them the truth, which was a hard proposition, but the easiest at this time.

Walking back to Seher and Laima, I said, "How would you like to come with me? Getting asylum right now was not an easy option; we needed more time to work this through the U.S. government." This was a lie, and I think she knew it.

"We leave in two hours; I will get food and water."

Seher stood up; there was joy on her face. Laima started hopping around, holding her mother's hand. Laima could feel the joy from her mother. Something only a child understands with her mother.

Seher walked over to the truck and started to prepare the front seat for travel, cleaning and getting bottles of water filled up. She placed food from my bag in the front seat. This woman was on a mission. Laima just stood there and watched the mechanic fix the truck. Even I smiled at the tender moment; it was a moment of calmness and had a family vibe.

Soon the vehicle was completed and fueled up. I picked up a few gas cans to ensure I had enough to get to wherever I was going. There's nothing more helpless than prepping supplies for a trip when you have no idea where it will end!

Best to pack for bear than squirrels, my mother would say.

It only took about two minutes to pack for this trip with the "family." We were ready to go. The SF camp all came out to wave goodbye to us. This was somewhere between embarrassment and a sheer "what the hell are you doing?" type of moment. The mathematical calculation of laughable plus dangerous equaled scary.

As we drove out the gate, the only person that looked back to wave was Laima. Laima knew of no danger. She was just a little girl who was loved by her mother for only a few more days.

Chapter 22

From Lawara to Peshawar, Pakistan was about a six-hour drive according to the map. Yet, the map didn't show road blocks and known enemy contact points. Seven hours really meant a few days in this terrain, which would go from rough to easy, back to rough in just a few miles. Night movements would need to be limited so as not to create attacks on a lone vehicle with a woman and child. This meant lodging would have to be acquired somehow. With the woman and child, this meant that camping in the truck was not an option. The mountainous terrain was covered in snow in some areas and the Taliban were known residents in this area. I was now to close to reality as a protector of a woman and child. The game changed from all-out war and devastation to a little war and devastation when they were around. I needed to become an insurgent myself!

Peshawar was gun central. That's ground zero for weapons manufacturing. Peshawar was no sleepy town; it had a history of violence and death throughout the centuries. The city was on the rigid edge of the frontier, the Pakistan-Afghanistan border. It was situated at the crossroads of central and south Asia and known as the political and business center of Khyber Pakhtunkhwa. Some of the greatest warriors to breathe air marched through this area into and out of Asia—Peter the Great and Genghis Khan, to just name the important ones. Hell, even the British in the mid-1850s had a foothold in this city.

The city was about one-and-a-half million strong today. Going into the city to the center where the Pakistan Brigade with the Achilles was located would not be easy. Maybe that's where Seher would come in handy. She could play the wife, and me, the muted and pale husband.

Peshawar was also the hometown of Waba, the Black Death assassin to those who knew, it seems. If Waba showed up in Peshawar, which I believed he would, trouble and death would follow. His human intelligence was outstanding, based on past experience. This city and its people were his and his father's. They would be waiting for us, no doubt about it.

"Seher, I am going to need your help again. I need you to play my wife and Laima my child again. I will not be able to speak so you have to do it for me."

"Maybe you should learn some Urdu!"

Surprised, I looked over to Seher. She had her face cover lowered, and I could see her smile. It was a smirk more than anything. She had a sense of humor; that was good. We needed that for this trip.

After only a few miles down the road, the truck began to make loud noises from the tailpipe. We must have punched a hole in the tailpipe, or it had separated from the engine block in some of the rougher terrain. Or it was old and rusted—we couldn't tell—but it was loud enough to give us attention as we drove down the roads and trails.

Seher and I, after an hour, became quiet. No talking, just looking around at the mountains and villages as we passed through, heading north to the Pakistan border. It was turning into one of those trips with your parents. You just want to pull over to the 7-11 store and get something to drink and eat—you know, one-for-the-road stuff. Laima was getting hot and thirsty. She began to complain to her mother about it, but she told her to be quiet and patient.

"Is she OK?"

"Yes, she is just thirsty and hungry."

"OK, let's pull over at one of the villages and you go get us something, OK?"

"Are you sure, River?"

"No, but we have to drink and eat. There is no other way. Let's just buy a bunch of food and water so we can last for two days or so."

"OK, but let's do it when we get to Khost. That's a big town and they see a lot of travelers. A village would be harder."

Seher was smart, maybe too smart for Pakistan or Afghanistan. She could lead a serious movement for women's rights. Her experience with her poor, deceased husband "wife beater" and her being a mother at such a young age gave her all kinds of credibility.

It took us only a few hours to get to Khost. That was because I wasn't hiding. I was out in the open like a local with his wife and child. I was driving at forty miles an hour and not taking goat trails all day. Heck, I could make it to Peshawar tonight if the roads were decent. Blend in, act like you belong, Scary Man said. He was dead on; I looked and felt the part. Seher and Laima made me feel safe, for some reason, as I drove with my arm out the window like I was in Texas.

I drove straight through Khost to the north side of the city. I stopped just short of the airport. It's not like an airport in America. It's like a dirt airport that flies drugs in and out of the area. Khost was opium central for farmers and Taliban drug dealers. I was now parked across the street from it.

Seher got out and walked over to an outdoor store that sold everything, including opium pods. Laima moved over into my arms and fell asleep again, I began to think she often gets car sick. Seher began shopping quickly: water, fruit, cooked meat, and flat bread. I love flat bread; I could eat it all day just plain. Seher paid them and began walking back to the truck just as a group of vehicles came. The truck was full of bad-looking guys carrying weapons and ready for the business of death. They looked like a Taliban gang that roamed the area, causing problems for the locals and protecting drug fields. The whole area around Khost was one big opium conglomerate. It was no surprise; they used the drug money to pay for their own war on everybody that was non-Muslim. We were looking at the Western problem right in front of us: The war on drugs meets terrorism. Drugs made the business of terrorism easy to execute; money bought weapons and loyalty.

Seher stopped, looking at the men, and they stared back at her. The truck stopped and began to drive over to Seher. My heart stopped. What was going to happen right here? Pulling up alongside of her, they began harassing her and grabbed the plastic bags full of food and threw them to the ground. One Taliban warrior grabbed some bread off the ground and began to eat it in front of her. They didn't unmask her but asked her name. She lied and used another common name. I couldn't hear the whole episode.

I put my hand on the keys in the ignition and my foot on the clutch to be ready to leave when they stopped talking to her. If they hurt her, I had no way to defend against it. What was I going to do?

"Laima, wake up, wake up! Go help your mother with the food."

She looked up at me as I was waving my hand towards her mother. I believe she got the idea to go help her mother. She moved out of the passenger side of the truck and walked towards the crowd of men harassing her mother. Grabbing her mother's hand, she began to tug and tug.

Seher looked down at her to stop, but Laima kept tugging. One of the men grabbed Laima's arm and moved her away. My grip on the steering wheel loosened as I thought Laima was in trouble. I opened the door to the truck, stepping out, and one of the Taliban warriors stared in my direction. Laima began to run towards me as I moved to the front of the truck. Seher began to chase her, and the men just watched as this all happened. The woman was chasing her scared daughter, while the husband came to get the child. I was hoping that was what the Taliban where thinking, but I was wrong.

They began to move towards our truck as Seher reached Laima. Grabbing her by her shoulders, she guided her to the passenger side and got into the truck. Staring at the warriors, I gave a weak smile and a hand gesture to indicate, "Please leave us alone." They started talking to me, but I didn't understand. Seher yelled something out the window, and they suddenly stopped. Seher waved to me to get back in the truck. I moved quickly back into the driver's seat, and Seher whispered to me to start driving away.

I cranked the engine, but the truck just cranked and failed to turn over. It just acted like it was getting fuel or something. I continued to stare every now and then at the warriors, and they seemed very interested in my lack of respect and speaking capabilities. Cranking, cranking and cranking, the vehicle finally started on the third try. Black smoke billowed from the rattling tailpipe. The smell of oil burning on the engine manifold filled the truck cab. Laima coughed more than a few times. The Taliban just kept watching and watching. Once the truck started, I never looked at them again. All my focus was on getting out of there and acting like everything was normal. I was just a mute husband and father with a broken old truck, a normal-looking occurrence other than the mute part.

"Seher, are we OK? Are they going to come after us?"

Seher was looking through her head cover, through the lace mesh that covered her eyes.

"No, but they are still looking at us. Just keep driving away."

I wanted to gun this truck and drive as fast as I could. Yet, that was not possible. I needed to act like this was normal and that I was showing respect by not burning rubber and creating a dust storm that would surely get us all killed right in the street. Immediate YouTube star!

Turning onto the road, we headed north to Peshawar. I never even looked to see if any cars were coming. I was just driving to save our lives at about twenty miles an hour. With the mountains of Tora Bora in the distance, I used that point on the horizon to keep focused on running away from the Taliban of Khost.

"It's OK, River, we are far away now!" Seher said.

Laima was sitting in her lap, looking out the window. Calmness was what she displayed. That kid's nerves were stronger than mine, and she was extremely brave for a little girl. I had nothing on these two, Pakistani mother and child. They could make it on their own in America, just not here!

Chapter 23

The Tora Bora Mountains on the central-eastern border of Afghanistan had such an unbelievable history to many countries such as the United States, Russia, Afghanistan, and Pakistan. Most memories were of war and loss of life since 1979 when the Soviets attacked. The region had not seen peace since the Russians, and the current intelligence showed terrorists hiding in these mountains in cave systems. These cave protection sites were said to be small cities that had all your needs met, including full hospital operating rooms. Terrorists and some family members became very comfortable in these mountain ranges until the U.S. and Coalition's forces attacked them in 2001 with dismounted, mounted, and air attacks the likes of which no one on earth had seen or even read about. It was a massive campaign that provided a deterrence mechanism. After these B-52 attacks, the landscape and the personal living here changed dramatically. In the end, not many terrorists were killed or located. Tora Bora was an outstanding information operations campaign against the Coalition forces.

As we got closer to the border crossing into Pakistan from the East, I could see the mountains filled with snow at about the 5,000-foot level. Tora Bora in English means "white mountains." You could believe it too: The mountains were beautiful as they held a three-dimensional posture that made them look closer than they were.

The mountains were steep and jagged with very few roads leading through back into Afghanistan. It was hard to believe there had been a major battle in such beauty. I guess beauty has its dangers, as it allows you to lower your guard to admire it. That's when it bites you!

"Look out, River!" screamed Seher.

I slammed on the brakes before I looked to see if was I was about to get hit. As I looked up, the truck came to a full stop on the side of the road. Dust filled the truck cab. Seher waved the dust away from Laima's face. I sucked in enough dust to coat my lungs and cough for the next few minutes.

Right in front of us was a mobile Pakistani border checkpoint; there was only about five feet before I hit one of their border enforcement vehicles.

"This is not good, Seher!"

"River, say nothing. I will do all of the talking. Laima will stay with you; hold her in your arms as if she is your child. I will tell them you are a deaf-mute and were injured during the war. Try to keep your face hidden behind Laima in your lap."

We both kept staring at the Pakistani border frontiersmen walking towards us with guns drawn. There were a total of six men at the checkpoint. They began yelling orders at us; Seher jumped out of the truck and began speaking to them. I had no clue what she was saying, but the frontiersmen were not showing any type of respect to her. Fingers and arms were pointing wildly back towards Afghanistan. My assumption was they were not going to allow us to pass. Danger seemed to be ahead of us. Seher kept talking and seemed to be insisting that we move forward.

Another frontiersmen moved towards me as the conversation began to get louder. Seher looked back at me and then over to the frontiersmen moving towards me. She was talking loudly and pointing to her ears and making the crazy gesture with her fingers around the side of her head. This was an Academy Award performance;

even Laima was acting out by rubbing my head and playing with my hair. I had to tell her to stop, but she just laughed.

I kept hearing the word "*mujahedeen*" said over and over. Seher kept shaking her head saying, "No *mujahedeen*, no, no!"

After about five minutes of discussion, the frontiersman that had been moving towards me was now up against my front fender, smoking a cigarette, staring at me. I just looked at his eyes while Laima kept playing with my face and hair. Air filled my stomach from nervousness, I had to go to the bathroom, and my forehead began to sweat. The man knew I was scared, and he was about to capitalize on it.

Seher was finally released from the border guard to move back to the truck. The man watching me moved around to walk with her back to the truck. He was whispering something to her. Seher kept leaning her head away from him but never laid a hand on him. If she did, she would be arrested and killed by them or the Pakistani government in Islamabad. Helplessness and scared was all I felt for all of us. The frontiersman continued to harass her and seemed to smell her as I could see him drawing in large breaths as he got close to her face. He was spooky and mentally disturbed. He could beat or kill her at any moment. A minute later he looked back at Laima and gestured with his tongue. A pedophile was all I could envision about this man. He didn't even look to be twenty years old.

"We must leave right now!" Seher said, extremely flustered from her engagement with the frontiersman.

"Where do we go, forward or back?"

"Forward into Pakistan! Hurry!"

I started the truck on the second try and off I went. The truck was jerking through second gear. My nerves were scattered throughout my body. No body part was acting right, and I think I pissed my pants after I hit second gear. Seher looked better after we moved through the checkpoint. Three men were at the actual checkpoint eating and drinking chi. They stared and then continued to drink and eat.

"Seher, do not stare at them."

"I must. I will remember their faces for the rest of my life. Revenge for all women and children will always be my fight. Those men have been bad to women and children—it's in their eyes and the way they treated me. They will hurt and kill for no reason. They must not be given this chance."

Looking forward, I thanked my lucky stars she wasn't mad at me. Her visual anger was incredible and intense. I started to believe I was nothing but a tool in her pocket to kill those that she hated. She knew I hated wife- and kid-beaters enough that I could commit murder. We were a perfect match to even the playing field in this country. This was feminism gone to the extreme.

Although I liked her enthusiasm and motivation to make things right in this land, I knew it was not possible on a large scale. Killing and hiding a body out here was easy. It was in Peshawar, a large city, where it would be hard to kill and get away with it. Keeping her temper down would be the key if she was provoked by a man that wanted to rape her or harm Laima.

Chapter 24

Do you remember when you were in your mom and dad's car and you said nothing to avoid possible repercussions from your voiced point of view? That's where Seher and I were in our fake relationship, marriage, and parenthood. Mom was mad and everyone else paid the price of her anger. Yet, this wasn't about cleaning your room or taking out the trash; this was about violence and revenge. She had a taste for killing those that hurt her; she was looking for someone else now. I was going to be nice for a while; no advice would be given, like "Hey, babe, you feeling OK? Or, can I get you something to drink or eat?" Hell no, I was now a mouse in a church—mouse in a church I say!

Was this how people became killers? Was it from society, mental illness, or crimes of passion? Seher fit all three reasons to become a killer. Her society allowed her to marry an old man at an early age. She was beaten with no legal ramifications against the husband, to a point where she mentally changed to a violent person. And three, I was there in her home to assist with the courage to kill her first two problems. I knew when she mixed the goat's blood with his, the respect and concern for his death had been lost rapidly. That was yesterday's news.

"River, you have said nothing for that last twenty kilometers. Are you OK?"

"I am fine; it's all good. Thirsty a little bit." Shaking my head more than normal to convince her nothing was wrong. She stared back, seeing nothing but scared.

"You are not a real soldier, like Rambo, are you?"

"I am an OK Rambo, just never this type of Rambo."

"Your commander wants to have his possessions more than your life? If he cared for both, he might have sent someone a little braver!"

"He sent someone a little stupider, in my opinion. I was looking for adventure, just not this much adventure. But, here we are together as one big happy killing family, looking for an iPod and being chased by another killer named Waba. You couldn't have written this in a book for anyone to believe." I said all this with a disdained look on my face.

"River, how much worse can this get?"

I stared at her. "It's going to get much worse!"

"River, where is your home?"

"I am from Texas, in the United States. I grew up there with my parents. They were from Germany but moved to Texas to start a new life."

"Are they proud of you? Do they know you are here?"

"No, my parents have no clue what I am doing. They are not fans of war and what comes with it. They were upset that I had joined the army, but I needed money for college."

"College means what? I am not sure what that means."

"I went to the university to study."

"I was educated by my mother. That's how I learned English. She was a great teacher. I miss her every day."

"Do you have any other family in Pakistan?"

"Yes, some in Peshawar."

"Great, keep them on speed dial. We might need them."

"Speed dial, what's that mean?"

"Don't worry, if we need speed dial, you will not need an

explanation. What kind of uncles and aunts do you have in Peshawar? Are they teachers too?"

"I do not think so. My mother told me they were poor and had been in and out of jail."

"What did they go to jail for?"

"Making bad weapons and selling chemicals for making heroin."

I thought for a second. They could come in handy in Peshawar. "Seher, put them on speed dial! Do you know where they live? If we need a place to hide or get some weapons, they may help us with the police record they have."

"Maybe they might, but I have not seen them since I married that dead old man."

Looking over at Seher, her eyes began to sink back into her head. The fury of the ex-husband remained in her DNA. She could never marry another man; the man would not be safe. Once you had the taste and touch of revenge tied with killing your husband, it was easy to transition to serial killer after the first one. Hate, due to repeated beatings and mental torture by her forty-year-old husband, was genuine rage. She must have felt free when she threw the dead goat's blood on top of his blood in their own home.

"Seher, are you OK? You got quiet all of a sudden."

"Nothing, I just wish my life was better, like yours in Texas. All I want is freedom for me and my daughter. Kindness, food, and a home to call my own is all I would ever want. Hopefully Allah will give me that someday."

I looked out the driver's side window and could see the snow on the Tora Bora Mountains. Christmas in Colorado came to mind. When I was about ten years old, my mother and father took me there to see the snow. That was the first and only time I had ever seen snow until I had joined the army. Being poor means you live and vacation where you live. Vacation for me was going to the other side of Lake Travis. That was considered foreign travel.

Chapter 25

Getting to Peshawar was no easy seven-hour drive. Triple-A would have been embarrassed over the difference in terrain travel vs. enemy contact. My advice to travel companies is: Travel the road yourself and then estimate the time. Provide other travelers a hint, such as: "This is what you need to be successful on this road: weapons, water, extra fuel, and maybe even a fake wife and child if you are a man traveling alone." These were just thoughts.

It's amazing what your mind begins to run through when you are under stress. It swings through positive and negative events in your life, like getting lost on a family vacation at the Grand Canyon where my mother kept telling my father, "You're lost. Pull over and get some directions, and I hope we have enough gas to make it."

Seher was obviously not an American fake wife. She just sat there calmly, smiling with the look of "You're lost." She didn't just say it outright in front of our fake daughter. If she was an American, she would have recalled it during a Christmas party twenty years later. It's hard to justify what the hell was going on twenty years in the past. The exaggeration factor is replicated tenfold as you justify her statement. Lies are like the fog of war: It's hazy and you just start saying anything to justify what you did. "I wasn't lost!"

"Seher, are we on N55 to Peshawar, right?" OK, here came the look of "You're lost, aren't you?"

"What did the map say?" My God, women are the same everywhere!

"No, I am not lost!"

"We are lost?"

"No, I just need to stay along this ridgeline road into Kohat. We should pass to the north of Kohat and then to N55 north into Peshawar. That's what I think. Any thoughts?"

"Where is the map, River?" I handed it to her, and she looked hard at it. Laima was looking hard at it, too. I thought, *Great, soon Laima is also going to agree with her mother that we are lost. Soon, it will be two for three against my navigating skills.*

"River, you need to go through Kohat to get onto N55. We cannot keep traveling through the mountains filled with Taliban and the Pakistan army that is fighting. We will get caught for sure. We need to go south to the road below us into Kohat. That way we go through with hundreds of cars and are not riding around up here in the hills lost."

"I am not lost, Seher."

Liama looked at me and then grabbed my hand and said, "Lost!" First word out of her mouth to me was "Lost!" It was not "father" or "friend." It was "lost"! I immediately turned south to Kohat based on their recommendations. I was now a father and husband in training.

We arrived in north Kohat at about two o'clock in the afternoon. The traffic was horrific. Eyes from men and woman in cars stuck in traffic stared at us. We were a little nervous, but not as much as a few days ago. I had started to become accustomed to the life of an "on the run" Pakistani family man headed to Peshawar for a weekend of stealing, killing, and being chased by an assassin. Just normal stuff, I guess.

Kohat was a large city that had experienced huge change over the years. They looked to be a large refugee area due to Afghanis flowing into the area in the last few decades of war in Afghanistan.

They spoke the common Pashun and Urdu languages. The city was filled with universities, major transportation hubs such as trains and trucking, huge transportation tunnels through mountains, and even a hundred-and-fifty-year-old British fort. It was shaped like a pentagon with gun turrets, similar to the one on Khost where that little girl delivered the baby that died. I remember that day often, and even when I look at Laima, it's terrible.

"Seher, look at that tunnel through that mountain."

"Yes, the Japanese helped Pakistan build it. It's very long and expensive. Many people died to build that tunnel. They call it the Pak-Japan Friendship Bridge and it's over two kilometers long. They should have used the money to save the starving people and to fight out the Taliban. They have done nothing good here."

There were a few guards on the side of the road leading into the Pak-Japan Friendship. Terrorist bombings of this 1.2-mile tunnel would be a huge political win for the Taliban. Hundreds of people could die in two blasts, one on each end, simultaneously. Boom, and that's all she wrote! They must surge when terrorist threats and intelligence require it. This must not be that day!

As we drove up to the tunnel guards, we slowed.

"River, I will do all the talking if they ask. Keep your window up and do not act like you even want to open it. Keep driving slowly. If you act like you will stop, they will ask questions. Look forward and do not look into their eyes. *Keep driving, slowly, slowly, slowly.* OK, we are through! Thank Allah!"

I must have stopped breathing for over two minutes. Focusing only on Seher's voice and my foot on the clutch, I didn't even put my foot on the gas pedal until I remembered to get the hell out of there. My eyes focused on the black hole that was the tunnel ahead of me.

"River, turn on your headlights." It was too dark inside, as the tunnel was not lit. Cars were honking their horns and flicking their lights on and off. It was a Pakistani auto disco tech at twenty miles an hour.

We cleared the tunnel in about five minutes with the traffic and the limited visibility. It opened up looking into the city of Kohat. It was your standard Pakistani city with crappy buildings, hungry people, and children playing in the streets, hash bars, chi and coffee houses, Cricket fields, and police stations. In some ways with the hash bars and coffee shops, it reminded me of the Pakistani version of Hippie Hollow in the early 1970s. Except here in Kohat, people acted like it was legal and accepted this way of life as normal.

In Hippie Hollow, anytime there were headlights coming into our area, everyone locked up their doors and windows, turned off lights, and waited for the car to be identified. Friend or foe? If it was a friend, someone would walk out and shake hands and then wave their hats for all clear. If it was foe, no one walked out and we stayed silent.

We continued on through Kohat via the Hangu Bypass that ran west to east. It was a fast highway that was well taken care of. We drove well over fifty miles an hour in that old truck. Seher and Laima thought I was driving far too fast for their own safety. This was the fastest they had ever driven before. Usually they drove just the mountain passes full of potholes and rocks. Laima just smiled as Seher held her tightly.

"Laima, are you having fun?" Seher translated and Laima moved her head north and south with her fingers in her mouth, filled with saliva. It was cute, as she giggled over and again as we sped through the city, bumping up and down. This was the funniest part of the trip so far for her.

We drove through Kohat through the Hangu Bypass, the Kohar Bypass through to N55, which was called the Indus Highway. This path allowed us to only hit one checkpoint going out of the city, and less contact with anyone was the key to safe travels. The checkpoint was called the ANF Checkpoint. It was mainly for weighing commercial trucks headed north into Peshawar. They waved us through and then charged heavy fees to truckers that were overweight. This area was known for extortion of goods and services. By the time the trucks got to Peshawar, they barely broke even.

The last few hours had been the most peaceful moments of this disaster. The hours prior to that, I had put this woman and child in more harm than anyone would get into in a lifetime. *Asylum*, I wanted to never hear that word again. Seher and Laima had been lied to by every man in the last three days. *Asylum* was not going to be possible, I felt. I was feeling that, as long as I kept them with me, I could protect them and give the U.S. time to think about doing the right thing for this family. Maybe even I was owed this by America. Look at what I had been asked to do! BG Stanton had better pay me was he owed. If not, I would visit him and his family. And hopefully Seher would be with me with a shovel in hand and a goat in tow. Pakistani female justice, I had learned, is violent and final.

Chapter 26

Once we cleared the north Kohat checkpoint, Laima started talking a hundred miles an hour and grabbing her legs.

"Seher, is everything OK?"

"She says she has to go to the toilet right now."

"I will look for a rest stop or a gas station. We need fuel anyway."

"Laima can go anywhere."

"No, that's OK; we will find a nice place for her to go. Look, right there. It's a Stop Shop gas station. We can try there."

"River, we have very little money left, maybe enough to get to Peshawar."

"Well, that's enough for now. We can get enough gas to get to Peshawar with a little left for some food. When we get to Peshawar, we will have to beg and scavenge for the rest. At least enough supplies to get out of Peshawar and drive to Afghanistan through the Khyber Pass to Torkham Gate."

"I hope you have better friends at the Torkham Gate crossing than at the last one. We almost died last time!"

Sternly, I said, "Seher, it probably won't be any better!"

"Your friend, General Stanton, is he helping us get asylum?"

"I believe so!" She knew I was lying to her at this point.

"River, we cannot keep lying to each other about this. I need to know if Laima and I need to have another plan. We have helped you and your government. Our lives have been at risk to get this Achilles. Will they not help us?"

"Seher, I will do everything I can to get you and Laima asylum, even if I have to sneak you two into the United States." I never looked at her face when we were talking; I just continued to rub my beard. She knew I was continuing to lie or that I had no clue what I was going to do. This was the married couples' version of lying. We continued to grow closer as she knew more about my reactions and facial expressions that could not hide the truth.

"We will leave you in Peshawar once we have the final Achilles. I will contact family and they may help me, or not. Laima and I have helped the American government and you, River, and they have chosen to not help." Tears began to well up in her eyes. Laima held her hand and wiped away her tears.

"Seher, please do not cry. I will fix this, OK?"

"You lie, River. You have no idea what you are doing. You brought us into something you are not in control of. What happens in Peshawar River? What are you planning? Where is the Achilles in Peshawar? Is the bad man waiting for us there?"

"I do not know, Seher!" This time I looked her right in the face.

"Yes, finally you have told me the truth. I see it in your eyes."

"OK, Seher, what would your plan be? What should I do right now?"

"First, I would get a map of Peshawar and at least understand the streets and how to get in without going through army checkpoints."

"OK, where do I get one of those?"

"Stop at the next roadside store. They have maps. We will then move to a safe place and organize ourselves to go into Peshawar, find the Achilles, take it, and then get out of the city in one day."

Eighteen miles later and thirty miles outside of Peshawar, we stopped in a small village called Matani. It was more advanced than most villages along the way that had a large population of Pakistani

Frontier Corps troops. In the past they had a lot of Taliban warriors in here. It took several years to get them out. Many people had lost their lives in fighting. But, the best part about increasing a government militia into these small areas is that technology increases, such as electrical power, running water, cell phone towers, and restaurants. This place had a few pay phones and a pay-as-you-go cell phone store that Seher pointed out as we entered town.

"River, stop here and give me some money for a phone call."

"Seher, who are we calling? Holy shit."

"What is holy shit?"

"Never mind, Seher. Who are you calling? This is a secret mission and no one is supposed to know we are here!"

"River, more than a few people already know we are in the country and in this area. We are no surprise to anyone right now. But, if you must know, I am calling relatives in Peshawar that will help us.

Seher got out of the truck and went to the pay phone. Laima, just sat there and smiled at me and then looked over to her mother. Seher just waved at her and looked at me. She had had her face covered ever since we entered the town. I could tell what was being said by her facial expressions from the phone call. Nervous energy filled every inch of my body as I looked for angles to run or drive like a maniac away from this town. I was asking myself, do I head back south or push on through the mountain passes back into Afghanistan? The problem with heading west at this point was the Tora Bora mountain ranges that were steep and rugged. No place for vehicle movement carrying a woman and child. It was south back to Kohat or go north straight into hell itself, Peshawar. It was our only option at this point, and we would have to leave without the Achilles, which was the mission. My concerns were now if the Pakistanis were now using this system to track me through the movement of forces to the north by the United States to now support my protection back across the border into Afghanistan via Torkham Gate.

Seher spent about five minutes on the phone talking to someone in a low voice. Her hands were moving around and then shaking as if she was begging for help. My theory at this point was, it was not working out; there would be no help from Seher's family. I mean, she was a known murderer in this country with a reward on her head by now. It had been only five or six days since we killed the husband. The Pakistanis surely had me on their radar by now with the fiasco at the border when we retrieved the first Achilles. Pictures had to be circulating by now. The only saving grace was the fact that no one knew at this point that we had reentered Pakistan looking for the main Achilles system. No one could be that stupid! Or maybe yes, there was still me with an asylum-seeking female murderer and her daughter. This could be the perfect cover of all time!

She hung up the phone and walked back towards the truck and bumped into several men with weapons. They started yelling, and Seher kept her head down and kept saying she was sorry. Soon, they threw her to the ground and kicked her in the stomach. I got out of the truck and rushed to her aid. This is when all hell broke loose!

As I moved towards the three men, everything around me went into slow motion. Why, I do not know, but confidence in what I was doing seemed to be operating within my mind. Looking at all three men at the same time, I could sense which one seem to be the most effective at weapons and the others that were better hand to hand. I was wrong on both counts. The man closest to me immediately went to pull his weapon; he was the biggest of the three. Fortunately, he was the slowest at getting it out of his man dress.

Pulling back my fist like a catapult, I let it fling just like when I hit Jerry Raymond on the playground in Hippie Hollow in the third grade. The power I had behind that fist was all I had. Hopefully, when I hit this guy, he wouldn't look at me and say, "That's all you got?" in whatever the hell he spoke. I connected with this guy's temple and ear. He fell towards the other two, out like a light. The other two fell back into the small cell phone store. I continued on to them and threw small boxes and then took their weapons away from them. The one closest to me stayed on the ground with an astonished look, while the other guy, the smallest guy, got up and wanted some more. No problem, except I started yelling and cursing in English. This startled all of them except the shop owner. He picked up one of the men's weapons and began to point it at the men. He spoke harsh and fast. He looked at me and said, "Get out of here now. Waba came through here this morning looking for you two. You must leave now; you are not safe for us now. I will take care of these three men. They are Taliban sympathizers so they will die."

"River, let's get out of here right now!" Seher grabbed me and pulled me back towards the truck. "Drive, drive right now!"

We rushed to get back into the vehicle, struggling to get the truck started as we heard sirens coming in the distance. In my mind I was saying, *Focus, focus, focus, River, get this thing started!* Soon, automatic weapon fire went off next to the vehicle. It was Seher back out of the vehicle. She had taken a weapon away from the shop owner and shot all three men right there in the cell phone shop. The store owner already had them lined up to shoot them but had not gotten to before Seher did.

"Seher, get the hell back in the vehicle right now. The police are coming! We have to leave right now." Seher just threw the weapon down on the ground once the magazine was empty. Dust and the smell of gunfire spread throughout the air. Seher ran back to the vehicle and off we went. I just pointed the truck towards the west, hoping to hit N55 or the Tora Bora Mountains.

We sped out of town in a cloud of dust like Bonnie and Clyde. That was the quietest ride driving away from a murder, ever. N55 was ahead; maybe we could make it out to the border. This mission was now over. Every policeman, army guy, and assassin was out for us.

"River, I am bleeding..."

Chapter 27

Blood was coming from Seher's mouth; Laima was helping to wipe it away from her mouth through her facial cover. Laima had a look of confusion, as she pulled up her facial hood to look for the blood. Seher began to breathe heavy, and pain began to seep from her nasal cavity. I kept staring at her and driving madly through Matani, looking for any way west to get out of town quickly.

"Seher, can you hear me? Say something!"

Nothing came out other than the sound of gasping for air. Her head turned slightly to look at me. "Help me, help me!"

Laima began to cry as she kept holding her mother's head up to wipe the blood away. I was in a panic, as the woman seemed to be dying right in front of me. This felt like when my mother had a miscarriage when I was five years old. My father was driving fast and talking to my mother: "You will be OK. I will get you to the hospital, and you will be all right." Tears came from my father's eyes as he asked me to rub a wet washcloth on her face to keep her calm and cool. I was so frightened and confused. My mother survived but would never have another child.

"Seher, we have to get you to a hospital right now." I grabbed our only map, which was in Urdu, and pointed to it and asked Seher to point towards a hospital symbol. She did it!

The hospital was just outside of the town at the N55 crossroads.

I just needed to keep on the same road through town to get to it. Once I hit N55, it should be right in front of us.

"Hold on, Seher! We are almost there—just a few more miles!"

Laima continued to cry and hold up her mother's head to wipe the blood away. It was the saddest moment of my life. My feelings for this woman and her child had become extremely close, family-like. All of a sudden, I was sure I would give my life for this woman and her daughter. There were no more questions of what was important; now it was not the mission. It was getting them out of harm's way and into safety for the rest of their lives.

Hitting the horn on the truck repeatedly, I flew through the town at a high rate of speed. Dust flew up and all the people in the streets held cloths over their faces as I past. We were now outlaws, hiding in the open.

Looking back to Seher and Laima, I saw that Seher was lying in the seat with her head next to my leg. Laima was now on the floor board holding her mother. Crying and screaming for her.

"Laima, it will be OK. Momma will be OK." I remember telling my mother the same thing, except she never was after that day. Every time she looked at a mother with two children, she wiped her eyes and nose out of sadness. I know this now, but not until now did I realize that I took her for granted and never showed enough love. Laima was only three years old; she was lying on her mother, giving all the love she had. The love she was showing might only last another few hours, then that would be it!

I looked forward at the traffic and the edge of town just a hundred feet way and traffic began to get out of the way. I focused on getting through; the hospital we were looking for was known as the Gulzar Chowk. It was at the crossroads of N55 and the Matani Bypass Highway, just another mile up the road.

Within minutes, I could see a building with a medical sign with the Red Crescent symbol on top of the building. The building was sparse at best, with a green sliding garage door-type entrance. There was a motorcycle outside under a tree with while plastic chairs surrounding it. There was one old woman sitting under it, waving flies away from her face.

Pulling up to the hospital at a high rate of speed, I slammed on the brakes. Dust and debris flew up in the air, and the old woman gave me an ugly look. I got out of the truck so fast that I beat the dust to the front of the truck as I ran around to the passenger side of the truck. I opened the door and there was Laima, holding her mother with dried tears on her dirty face.

"Laima, go get help, go get help!" She understood what to do. This was a hospital and her mother was hurt. Laima got out and ran to the door and cried for help and then grabbed the first man she saw. Pulling him towards the truck, he could see Seher. He barked orders and two women came out with a wheelbarrow covered with just a board. This was a makeshift situation but it was still medical care beyond what I could give her.

Seher was dying in front of my eyes. She had put her life and the life of her daughter on the line for me and the hope of asylum in the United States.

The doctor stayed back while two women nurses pulled off her face cover to check her pulse and see where all the blood was coming from. Pakistani culture didn't allow men to do this if they were not related. Laima couldn't let go of her; she just kept calling her mother.

As I looked at Seher bleeding and possibly dying from a beating in town by those thugs, revenge was now the target. The mission was off. I had to do the right thing as a man and a friend of this woman who had saved my life and risked her own child's. Seher deserved redemption, if I could not promise freedom.

The nurses picked her up out of the truck and placed her in the wheelbarrow and pushed her into the hospital. Laima grabbed me by the leg and tried to pull me into the hospital, but the doctor held his hand up as if to say, "No enter." Laima kept walking and pulling me as tears flowed from her little eyes. I was choking on emotion and had problems breathing as I held Laima's hand. Seher could not be seen from the outside door. All we could do was wait. A lot of talking and movement behind a dirty curtain could be heard. It was tense and active.

Laima continued to cry and then sat down on the ground in front of the door; she was still holding my hand.

"Laima, come on over here." Picking her up off the dirt, we walked over to the plastic white chairs under the tree. I held Laima tight in my lap and told her it was going to be all right. I was lying again.

A few hours went by before the doctor came out. He walked over and said something with a smile. Laima got excited and wanted me to let her down. I did, and she ran into the hospital, pulling the doctor with her. We followed the doctor into the surgery room where Seher laid in bed with oxygen, wearying a clean light blue nightgown. She tried to smile and could not talk normally; it was more a whisper. Seher held Laima's hand and then held mine. Her lips moved slowly as she looked at me. I got the feeling she wanted me to hear her. Leaning down with my ear to her oxygen mask, I heard, "I told them you were a deaf-mute." I nodded, smiled and squinted with understanding and emotional pain. Losing her was unthinkable.

"Please take Laima with you. I cannot travel. You must get what you search for. Please take care of her; she will be in more danger here than with you. If she stays here, she could be kidnapped and treated badly."

She stopped and then coughed extremely hard. Blood sprayed lightly into the oxygen mask. Laima screamed to her mother and started crying again. I held her tight and walked out rapidly to protect her from such a sight. Blood must still have been in her lungs.

I began praying as we moved back under the tree. The sun was out and the wind was blowing. If Seher died today, at least it was a beautiful day. Not moving from the plastic chair, I sobbed with Laima as if Seher was my own wife. This was something I had never felt before. In my mind, I knew we had to leave Seher here. There was no place to hide from Waba or the Pakistani military or police. Soon the hospital would report Seher's condition, I believed. How could I protect her from the enemy? Disguise her or give her another identity?

Looking over to the old woman sitting under the tree when we came in, I thought maybe I could lift her passport or identification papers. The problem was, this lady looked forty-five all day and not a teenager with blood coming out of her lungs.

I went back into the hospital and, lo and behold, there sat a young girl that was beaten and passed out all by herself. There was a plastic bag with what looked like her personal belongings sitting next to her. She must have only been about twelve years old. She had a medical chart with her information on it. I decided to swap them with Seher's. This was close enough.

Laima waited outside for me to come back. She looked at me as I ran out of the hospital. I pointed to the truck, and she got up and walked and then ran to the driver side to get in. She was too small and weak to open the door, so I opened it from the inside. She jumped in and I closed the door behind her. I started the truck, and Laima began to cry for her mother. I just ignored it and I knew Seher would have wanted me to.

Peshawar and the Achilles were only fifteen miles down that road. Maybe Waba would be there to meet me. My beard and the dirt on my clothes were only a few days older than the last time I had seen Waba. The only good thing at this point was I was only two people and not traveling with three. Laima was crying, lying in the seat. My heart felt heavy and tears flowed from my eyes as I told her that her momma would be OK, and we would go back and get her when she was better. She didn't understand me and didn't even care to look up.

"Laima, love you sweetheart! Momma loves you too."

Laima looked up at me as if she knew. She reached for my hand on the stick shift of the truck. I knew at that point she was now my child and my sole responsibility. The only time she let go was when I stopped for gas and some fruit. That's when I acted like the deaf-mute who was mentally sedated. Hell, it worked.

As we came over the mountains into Peshawar, I truly believed there was a light at the end of the tunnel. I would find this Achilles and get back to Seher before the next day. The sun was going down; reconnaissance of Peshawar was off for the night. Laima and I pulled over into a poppy field. We ate and then fell asleep for a few hours, off and on. It was quiet and still a little cold, and we felt safe, for some reason. Laima laid against me, and she stayed warm. I just hoped Seher was warm, safe, and still alive tonight.

The sun came up at about five-thirty in the morning. It was time to get to the work of stealing, killing, and protecting Laima!

Chapter 28

The morning was cold and wet by the time the sun came up in the poppy field. Off in the distance, farmers and drug lords were tending their fields for heroin. Poppies that morning were pink and beginning to bloom. The bulbs directly underneath the flower were swollen with a heroin paste.

The process of producing heroin at this level was simple. The paste from the poppy was extracted from the bulb by field workers who cut the bulb and let the white paste ooze out. Workers then scraped off the paste with a flat piece of plastic and stored it on a green leaf. They then shipped that green leaf full of the paste to drug factories that turned the paste into heroin. Simple at this level, except the return on investment was so high that the Taliban and Al Qaeda use the profits from heroin to fund terrorism.

"Laima, wake up, sweetheart. You want to eat something?" Laima just looked at me with some understanding as I was holding a bottle of water and a few figs.

"When we get finished and we go back to get your mother, I am going to get you a hamburger from some greasy burger joint. I bet you would like that. Maybe, I will get you a big Texas burger from Austin!" Laima just kept looking at me as if she understood. She just giggled a little. I felt like a father who was taking care of my daughter whose mother was in the hospital. You do things that are motherly and angel-like, and my mother came to mind.

Laima climbed up into my lap and wanted to hold on to the steering wheel. She wanted to drive. So, I started up the truck and put it in gear. We moved slowly, with Laima holding the steering wheel driving in a straight line. Laughing constantly with a little show of pride in herself. This could be the best day of my life, maybe even hers!

"Here comes a turn, sweetie. Hold on, hold on! Great job, Laima! I am so proud of you!" We stopped and I hugged her. "Great job, Laima!"

Suddenly, I heard a voice coming from behind me. There was a man in a farm truck trying to get by us. Pulling the truck over, I waved him on. As the truck came alongside, the man with a black turban on his head looked at me and pointed his finger, yelling something. I just looked as if I understood. He moved only another fifty feet and then stopped. He seemed to be talking on a cell phone and looking in his rearview mirror.

"Laima, I think it's time to leave."

Putting the truck in reverse, we backed out, turning around and going in the opposite direction as the cell phone caller. This guy was probably calling the local police as I allowed a female to drive a car. In a Taliban-infested area, women are not allowed to drive. It's against Sharia law to do so. We could be imprisoned or stoned to death for this crime. I had no plan to experience either forms. So, off we went to the east of Peshawar. We needed to get to a safe place; I needed to call BG Stanton to get the next bit of intelligence.

We drove deeper into the poppy fields, looking for an oasis lined with trees that provided overhead cover from air reconnaissance and was a long way from civilization. With the cell phone activity from the drug lord, being careful and out of the way of people needed to be the first priority.

After only fifteen minutes of driving through the poppy fields, I found a great location to hide and get my bearings. It was a large palm grove with thick brush. It was perfect for getting my mind wrapped around getting the Achilles and then exfiltration out through Torkham Gate on the Afghan border. I still needed to remind BG Stanton that he needed to coordinate air pickup at Torkham once we arrived. Laima and I would soon be the most wanted people in Pakistan if we got the Achilles and made it to Torkham.

Driving deep into the brush, I turned off the truck and just listened for thirty minutes. Laima was tough to keep quiet and to also keep from wanting to play. I had my hands full between both tasks. Sweat just filled our clothes; it was running down my back. You could feel that one bead of sweat that took its time running down my back. My bushy eyebrows also were retaining all the sweat running down from the top of my head. I just continued to wipe my face and focus on listening and getting used to the sounds of the area. Later this would help in me identifying a new sound that could be the enemy coming upon us, like Waba.

Time passed quickly. I was now comfortable with my surroundings. I thought, *let's call BG Stanton.* I pulled out my satellite phone, a piece of paper, and a pen. *Let's do this thing.*

Turning on the phone, I got connection and hit redial. It rang only once and BG Stanton picked up in a hurry.

"River, my God, where the hell are you at?"

"Outside Peshawar, hiding in a palm grove."

"Who is with you, brother?"

"You know exactly who is with me!"

"Just Laima, and Seher is back in some hospital damn near dead."

"I should have known you were following me the entire time."

"Listen, Waba is tracking you right now. We have been getting chatter through the NSA about you and those girls. Waba is headed right now to that hospital. He isn't going there to just chat about collapsed lungs or murder charges in Pakistan."

"Where is Waba right now?"

"He is in Peshawar at the old Peshawar Air Base just north of you right now. He should be leaving in the next few hours for that hospital. River, you need to focus first on getting the Achilles. The CIA is also coming to assist you if needed. But, they will not arrive for another six hours by vehicle from Islamabad. That's not enough time to grab the Achilles and get back to the hospital to protect Seher."

"Send the CIA to Matani to grab her!"

"Can't. This whole thing is secret and not sanctioned by Pakistan. If you are caught, you will be hanged on You Tube and then to the world on CNN. You will be a rogue soldier with no ties to the United States. What makes it worse, you have that little girl that could get killed in this whole mess."

"Mess, you're goddamn right, this is a mess! It's your mess that killed a lot of people. What's the deal with the asylum?"

"Calm down, River, we are working it. As I said, I cannot guarantee anything."

"You better guarantee it. She has done more for the U.S. than most people will do in a lifetime. We owe Seher and Laima this opportunity."

"They are not your family, River. Get your head together. You killed her husband; you have already paid her back. And because of that, you three have jeopardized the mission. You have got the local and national police, Pakistani Intelligence, and Waba, who is a psycho that will eat you for lunch when he catches you."

"Again, *sir*, you created this problem and when I get back, the news people are going to love to hear this story. I understand I could go to prison, but that's worth it to see you hang over this. You put a lot of people in danger to save your ass and get promoted. You will rot in hell with Waba or wherever Allah drops you off at."

"River, prepare to copy."

"Go!"

"The Achilles is located at the Peshawar Air Base in the Badaber section of Peshawar. It used to be an U.S. Air Force listen station and then an Afghan mujahedeen training center to fight against the Soviets back in the 1980s. That's why Waba was there—he was waiting for you to show up for that last two days. You need to get in there while Waba is gone. He should be out of the loop for the next five or six hours dealing with Seher."

"Do you think he will kill her?"

"I do not know what he will do."

"Sir, I beg you, send the CIA there now to protect her. Move her somewhere safe. Please do something; she has a beautiful little girl that needs her." As tears filled my eyes begging for Seher's life, Laima used her sleeve to wipe them away. Laima was much stronger than me.

"I will do what I can."

"You better do more than that; I will not let this pass, ever. Go get her now, or I will leave and go get her!"

"OK, but if you fail, she fails! Understand, without the CIA guys, you have no cover in Peshawar. They will go grab her if she is still alive."

"Even if she is not alive, I want the body so we can bury her. This child will need closure. I will do my job. You need to do yours. Goodbye."

Speed was now of the essence. I needed to get to this place called Badaber and take a look. Looking down at my watch, I saw that it was 0733 hours, and I needed to have a plan before 1933 hours. Then, I would grab the Achilles by 0200 hours and head to the border by 0500 hours to cross before the sun came up. Dismounted or mounted in this vehicle, we would see how it went. If it went bad, I would run the border in the truck, and if it went good, then we would walk across like locals.

"Laima, ready, set, go!" She just laughed!

Chapter 29

Looking down at the map, I saw it was still stained with Seher's blood. That map gave me strength to continue through with this task, yet it remained second to taking care of this child. We both studied the map; I was looking for anything that said "Badaber." I found an area to the northwest of our position that said "Badaber." It showed a helicopter pad and the sign with the letters PAF. My assumption was that meant Pakistani Air Force.

Close enough for now. It was all I had to go by. If this wasn't the location, I figured I would follow convoys leaving the place and see where they went. Hopefully, BG Stanton would guide me into the location. Yet, why should I expect him to do that? He needed to focus on getting Seher out of that hospital and back into Torkham Gate.

The gas tank was almost empty, as was the battery for the satellite phone. We need to find fuel if Torkham was even an option to drive there. The phone could charge on two-hundred-and-twenty volts, so I needed to find a power outlet to fix that problem. I could visualize a mission with four phases. My mind was clearer, my focus was simple, and I accepted death as an option if I failed. Yet, I could not accept the death or slavery of the child.

"Think, River, what do we do?" I said.

Phase I: Locate fuel for the truck and power to charge the phone.

The cost of these items needed to be free, as money was low and we needed food and water more than anything right now.

Phase II: Locate the Babader area inside Peshawar and recon all movements and base camp layout. We needed to see a large antenna farm with a satellite antenna that was extremely modern, that was pointed towards the sky at eighty-seven degrees with an elevation of one-hundred-and-twenty degrees. That would be a clear sign that this was the location of the base station for the Achilles. Only problem was, the city was full of weapons manufacturers, drug dealers, and Pakistan army intelligence. There was also a U.S. consulate in Peshawar, but they were not an option with this unsanctioned endeavor. And there was Laima. I needed to put a note in her pocket with the following message in case I died.

I began to write slowly and clearly: *"Please take this little girl to the U.S. Consulate for safety. Her name in Laima and she will be a U.S. citizen based on the promises of BG Stanton and the U.S. Government. My name is Major River Rochman and I have died locating the Achilles. Please notify my parents in Hippie Hollow, Texas. If her mother is dead in the hospital in Matani, then take her to my parents. God Bless America and the Great State of Texas."*

Phase III: Get into the compound and locate the transmission station. The building structure should give it away. The transmission lines were above the street in this country, so those lines should be running into that location. Communications facilities took a lot of power and needed backup generators to be successful. If they only ran on generator power, then late at night we should hear them running. That would be the dead giveaway. This should be the probable location for the entire hub of the Achilles. At that point, the enemy had the vote on if I was successful or not.

Phase IV: Run like hell to the border. Within a few miles of the border, we would decide how we would get across. If it was by vehicle, that would mean things were going well; if by foot, that meant things had not gone well and we needed to blend in with the mule and camel trains running illegal goods from Pakistan into Afghanistan. This would add days to our travel out of the country. Once across the border, the U.S. military would transport us to Bagram, Afghanistan, to be transported out of the country and into Germany. There we would get medical checkups, and I would be run through the wringer with, "What the hell were you doing and thinking?" This would take place until BG Stanton got me out of it. Then it would be Texas or Bust!

That was a weak plan!

I looked over to Laima. "Hey Laima, what's your thoughts on how good my plan is?"

She just looked at me with disbelief and extreme concern.

Looking back at the steering wheel and the glass in front of me, I pointed the nose of that truck towards Peshawar. Off we went; the next stop was a gas station and a power outlet. It was now almost 0900 hours and it was a cool day for a theft, imprisonment, or death. At least it was not raining. You know that whole "tears from heaven" deal? My mother would be devastated at my death on a rainy day in the slums of Pakistan. She would believe that it must have been a sign of a sad death with no one to care for me as I took my last breath. My dad would hold up some homemade brew and smoke a "J" in my honor, while my mother would cry alone.

I hadn't seen them in more than a few years. Maybe the time I had spent away would ease the pain; time does that sometimes. Daisy, I did not even know what that deal was. Seher and Laima had consumed my mind when it came to caring for another. They had put distance between Daisy and me. Daisy had become a blur.

We drove for about twenty minutes until we hit the Inqilaab Road in the southern part of Peshawar. It was a main road that I assumed would run into a gas station. We drove northeast through a few villages. They didn't have a gas station, only illegal gas stops with gas in jugs. The people running them looked suspicious and scary. If we bought gas here, I would have to talk or play the mute. What I really need was a busy gas station, with a lot of people buying gas. The more people, the less I would have to confront anyone directly. Just mix into the crowd.

So, I continued to drive, staring down at the gauge, just knowing we were on empty and at any minute it would sputter and die. Laima looked over at the gauge, just like her mother, then looked up and pointed at the gauge.

"Yes, yes, I got it. Gas station is coming up. We will be OK, Laima."

We soon came to a crossroads called the Phandu Road, with a sign that showed a gas pump pointed north into the city. "See, Laima? A gas station right ahead." I made the left-hand turn towards the gas station. It took about five minutes before we arrived. The place was packed with cars, tractors, and people with gas cans. Perfect place to blend in; busy was better.

Pulling into line, I was about the fifth car in line to the pump. Confusion set in as to whether to shut the engine off or not. I was afraid that it would not restart. Could you imagine if I had to ask, using the methods of a deaf-mute, for a push to the pump? The truck remained on, for safety reasons, but if we had to speed out of there, I was sure if I pushed the pedal hard down once, all the gas remaining would shoot into the carburetor and that would be it for about one minute.

According to my watch, it took seven minutes to get up to the pump. I got out and told Laima to stay and not move. Walking around to the pump, my worst fears presented themselves; the gas cap was on the opposite of the truck. Could Allah be testing me? My heart had stopped as the gas attendant looked at me like I was an idiot. I shrugged my shoulders and waved my hand over my throat to the attendant. The attendant looked at me strangely. So, I waved my hand over my throat and mouth and grabbed my forehead in a painful way. It worked. The attendant pulled the gas hose over the truck bed and started filling it up.

As he filled the truck up, I stared at the money numbers and not the liters gauge on the gas pump. It was money now and not how far I could get. My assumption and pre-praying preparation believed that the truck would run the distance on about ten dollars in gas to the border. No idea, really!

When the gas gauge hit about thirty-two liters, I banged on the truck bed to warn him that was all I wanted. He stopped and I handed him thirty thousand, five hundred Rupees. If this was U.S. dollars, I would have complained.

Nothing was said. I jumped into the truck and we left, back onto the Peshawar Ring Road headed west towards the intersection of Peshawar Ring Road and Kass Maija Road. The road was a fast country highway that had multiple mosques and boys' schools. The entire time I had not seen one girls' school. The only ones I had seen were along the border with Afghanistan. Those schools were funded by non-governmental organizations and churches from the U.S. Most schools were attacked and destroyed by the Taliban, as girls were not to be educated. Many girls and women teachers had been killed for attempting to be educated.

"Laima, you hungry?"

I rubbed my tummy and then put my hand to my mouth like I was feeding myself. She nodded her head north and south. We continued only a few miles before we hit another gas station with a small store. It was also packed with people so my confidence was high that we could make this our last place to stop before freedom tomorrow in Torkham Gate.

Suddenly, the satellite phone rang. It was BG Stanton.

"Sir, its River."

"River, the CIA arrived at the hospital you gave us and she is already gone. Someone came by and killed everyone. She was not part of the dead. She just wasn't there! Are you sure that was the place?"

"Yes, I am sure. You better not be lying to me, Stanton!"

"River, calm down. She is not there."

"Then you find her!"

Suddenly, my satellite phone beeped three times. Looking at the screen, I saw it was call-waiting. The number was unknown.

"Stanton, someone is calling me. You are the only one I know that has this number."

"River, answer it!"

"Hello?"

Across the phone came my greatest fear.

"River, this is Waba and I have Seher!"

Chapter 30

"Put Seher on the phone!"

"I can't do that, River! She is barely breathing and running out of oxygen from her best friend right now, Mr. Oxygen Tank. It's very difficult to drive and clean the blood out of the mask while I am driving up to see you. Let's meet, River, so I can give Seher back to her daughter Laima. Laima gets her mother and I get you. That's a pretty good deal, don't you think?"

"On one condition: I pick the meeting place."

"OK, where is that?"

"Stand by. I will call you back in five minutes."

In a low, gravelly tone, Waba said, "Do not forget Seher. She is not looking like she will survive through the night. I will wait for your call."

Switching back over to BG Stanton, I said, "Sir, Waba has Seher and he's headed to Peshawar to swap me for her. I have to call back in five minutes with a location."

"You should have left her in Lahore like I told you to. You now have put this woman's life at risk of being murdered in front of you."

"That does nothing for me now. What do I do?"

"You need to meet him at a Christian location inside the city. That way, you have some terrain like buildings, traffic, and people to run and hide. You will need a hospital in case you get her back.

River, you need to get the Achilles back also. Do not forget your mission. I will help you where I can, but you need to complete the mission."

Barely understanding what was coming out of Stanton's mouth, I focused on the map.

"Bingo, there it is—a Christian cemetery not far from my current position. Crossroads are Wazir Bagh Road and Agha Mir Jani Road. There is also a medical clinic there that could help Seher. That's where I will meet him."

"Got it, River, but I cannot get help to you for another few hours. What's your move, River?"

"Waba is in control now. Take care."

Hanging up the phone, I looked down at Laima. She looked hungry and thirsty. Hell, this could be my last day on this earth.

"Hey Laima, let's go get something to eat!" She just smiled and laughed when I rubbed my stomach and made a growling noise. We had only been eating flat bread and fruit for the last two days.

My location in the phases of the operation was at Phase IA. I had gas but no electricity to charge my phone, and I still needed to call back Waba. Time was tight and capabilities were dwindling. I wanted this all to end by tomorrow morning. So, I decided to end all the phases of the operation by tomorrow morning and have Seher in the hospital, surviving with her daughter. Getting her out of the country was now not an option with her injuries.

Would I have to leave them at the mercy of the Pakistani justice system? I had seen in the past that those who had helped the U.S. had been placed in prison with no assistance. She would regrettably get the death penalty.

Looking back at the phone, I saw only thirty percent battery life was left. This gave me about two more calls, at best. Pulling up Waba's cell phone number, I hit dial. *Here we go!*

He answered on the first ring.

"River, you called back. I was getting worried that someone else had killed you instead of me. That would have made me sad."

"Is Seher still breathing?"

"Oh, yes! She looks great with an oxygen mask and her chest going up and down very fast. I hope she makes it, for your sake. Laima will be so sad that you did nothing to save her mother."

"Meet me at Wazir Bagh Road and Agha Mir Jani Road. There is a Christian cemetery by a library and a government school. Meet me in the center of that cemetery in one hour. Can you make it?"

"I am not far away; I will see you in one hour, River. Bring Laima. It will be good for her to see her mother in case she dies. Maybe right in front of her! Goodbye."

It was now close to 1000 hours; the sun was out, yet there was a brisk wind coming from the west. The streets were full of farmers, taxis, and bicycles. Barbers were out along the street cutting hair with a razor blade. Many young boys were selling in the street like carnival workers. Everything from soccer balls, hash, to used tires were being pitched in the streets by children not much older than Laima. Weaving in and out of traffic, children pushed their wares to make money for their families. School was not an option when it came to poverty. Most could not read or write. Poverty here meant barely living with only your bones showing.

In the distance, I could hear the sounds of weapons being fired; bullets fell from the sky around us. Peshawar was the gunmaker's capital of the world. They could make anything that could kill any living thing. All the tools I needed were at my disposal. It was just a matter of getting them when I needed them.

We arrived near the cemetery at 1035 hours. Grabbing Laima, I walked up Wazir Bagh holding hands with her, acting like we were in a hurry and unhappy. Near the public library on Wazir Bagh was a food cart selling beef and flat bread. I looked down at Laima and rubbed my stomach. She smiled and nodded her head with joy.

Dancing around like a cat in a handbag, kicking her legs, she was so excited. My arm was flopping around holding on to her. That was one of the greatest moments of my life; it felt like a father-daughter moment.

I remembered that type of excitement with my dad when the ice pop guy would come around. My dad would take me to get a cherry pop. Man, I loved those things, but what made it even better was that it was something my dad did for me. We would walk away with our ten-cent cherry pops and end up with red lips and tongues for the rest of the day.

Laima would be happy for once today. Her belly would be full. I could not remember when I had seen her eat anything other than flatbread and fruit since this nightmare started. Maybe she forgot her sadness for just a few minutes. Her mother, she would be seeing soon, I hoped.

No one was at the food stand so we walked up and I held up two fingers and then pointed to a picture of what looked to be a meat, mayonnaise, lettuce and flatbread. It came with an orange drink that set us back about one thousand rupees. It was almost the last of our money. There was only about a thousand rupees left, which included some change.

Sitting on the sidewalk to eat, we had now separated ourselves from our truck. Key military and law enforcement were still after us, and I am sure the truck and its description were part of the search. We had about twenty minutes before linkup time. I needed to figure out where I would put Laima so she would not witness this event.

Spending only five minutes to eat, I had completely eaten everything that was in my hand. Finishing the orange drink faster than I could eat the beef, Laima was only a quarter of the way through with hers.

Softly I said, "Laima, let's go."

Walking around the cemetery on the opposite side of the street,

I conducted reconnaissance quickly for an exit route to the hospital and then back to the truck. Soon, we came upon a government school that had a playground, and there were many children playing. Laima looked excited and wanted to pull me to the playground. So, I came along and let her play.

Within seconds, this came as the best idea. I would leave her here to play while I went across the street to meet Waba, kill him, as long as he didn't kill me, and then get Laima back.

My phone rang at 1057 hours, and it was Waba. As the phone rang, it went to reserve power and had less than five percent battery life left. This would be the last phone call I ever made or received. We had to move into Phase II of the operation.

"Waba, how is Seher?"

"River, River!" I heard a low and painful voice. It was Seher and she sounded near death. I walked away from Laima and the playground.

"Seher, I am coming to get you."

"Is Laima OK?"

"Yes, she is fine. We had food and she is playing with other children on a playground. She misses you."

"I miss her too. Please take care of her and run far away—no!"

Waba grabbed the phone away from her; I could hear the phone being smacked against Seher and her moaning in pain.

"You do not want to do that, River, as I will kill her right in front of you and her daughter. Meet me in the center, right now, or she dies. Just leave Laima on the playground; she looks like she is having fun!" The phone went dead.

The game was over. Waba knew everything. I looked back to Laima, and she looked at me and smiled and ran off with some other children. She was so happy, and that gave me time to get her mother back alive.

Looking back towards the cemetery, at first I noticed nothing out of the ordinary. So, I walked across the street and into the cemetery. I had no weapon other than a stick I had picked up under a tree along the street. It was time to be smart and think about how I could surprise him and not let him surprise me. Death was now at my door, a possible black death!

Chapter 31

Phase II was now hours off. A Phase IB needed to be developed in the next ten minutes. I sat down next to a car and a tree along the wooded street of the cemetery. Listening to my surroundings, I began to develop a plan that would allow the element of surprise to get Seher back alive. Hearing cars, children, church bells ringing across the cemetery, and food stand workers trying to get business, I let focus become a religion.

First, I needed to change clothes and blend in with my surroundings. Waba had seen me and these clothes, and they needed to change. Getting up, I began to look into cars along the street for open doors that had what I could use to change my look. By the third car, I found a long white coat and a gray vest. They looked brand new so they didn't match up with my dirty shoes and feet. No matter, it would do.

Looking back into the cemetery, there was no sign of Waba or Seher. My fear was to walk into the cemetery and immediately get shot. In this neighborhood, no one would come to rescue you. They would just linger around your dead body. This was Peshawar, not Beverly Hills. They treated death in Peshawar as just someone with bad luck or karma issues with their gods. So, I continued to walk the outside wall of the cemetery, focusing in on anything suspicious. From people—Seher's blue nightgown that I had last seen her wearing—to dogs and birds being scared away, anything would help at this point. I used these tactics when I hunted in Texas as a child with my father. We hunted for survival. Every shot missed counted as a great loss. Listening to your surroundings allowed you to blend with nature and become part of that community. You had to hide within that sound to fool the animals. A week ago, a man told me to blend in, because that's how I would stay alive.

Ahead of me was a family minus a husband walking into the church. Catching up, I moved into the church and took up a seat in the pews. Several people were praying in Latin and Arabic. I could still speak a little Latin from college so I prayed but with one eye open. Several doors led to the outside cemetery. Grabbing a Bible, I held it against my chest and moved towards the left side front of the church. I reached the first door, but it was locked. The second door was another ten feet away. I continued to act like I was praying and moving to the front to knock out some Hail Mary's when a priest called to me. He waved his hand for me to approach the altar. Moving towards him, I went to both knees and kept my face buried in my chest. Church was not my strong suit, but I had seen movies. Looking up, the priest held out one of those wafers. I stuck out my tongue to accept whatever he was going to save me from. Then all of a sudden, he spoke in a low English tone.

"My son, death is upon you. A man is here with a woman that needs medical help. He will meet you outside the second door. He will not kill you under the altar of God. Do you understand?"

"Padre, you got any ideas on what will happen next?"

"Do you believe in God, my son?"

Tears formed in my eyes. "I am not sure right now. How would God have chosen Seher and Laima to live this life?"

"Some gods do that so you can find them. He put them in your way, River. That's how gods save some people. You are the savior she needed to survive."

"If God did that, I believe in God, Padre. I believe."

"When you go out that door, carry this gun, and this cross. The Christian cross holds a homing device. They will both protect you." The padre winked and nodded.

Then the padre smiled and said, "Kill this man and get to the Achilles, which still remains the mission."

Getting up off my knees, I put the CIA-issued 9MM in my pocket and placed the cross around my neck. Moving towards door number two, I ran into another man hidden behind a pillar. He pulled me aside and told me to be quiet. He placed a Kevlar vest on me and covered me back up.

"Good luck, River. You have no assistance from inside the church. Outside, the Freemasons can help, OK? You look great, so go make it happen."

"Who the hell are you?"

"Your only friend right now, River! The next time you will see me will be at Torkham. Seher needs a doctor now, so get to it!"

"Where is Waba?"

"In a black Range Rover a few hundred feet from this church. It's a real nice SUV."

"Waba is riding in style. Rich daddy, I guess?"

"Yes, his dad is the Kyber rifles commander. You will run into his father if you make it to Torkham. It's a family business, I guess. Get going and best of luck."

The door opened, and I started walking very slowly, scanning for a black Range Rover. The roads were covered by trees and cemetery walls, so he was camouflaged well. Hunching down, I moved towards the center of the cemetery. Soon, I spotted a bloodstained blue head cover that was similar to what Seher was wearing. Ducking down, I pulled out my pistol and took it off safe. I leaned down and started crawling towards the head cover, staying below headstone level. Looking for a hand or a leg, I could see nothing.

"Laima, Laima." What the hell was that?

Looking around, I realized the voice was coming from my left. The voice was close, maybe five or seven feet. It sounded like Seher's.

"Seher, can you hear me? I am on your right. Move your leg or arm." Suddenly, I could see a leg move.

"River, do not come near me. I have a bomb on me. How is Laima?" Her voice shuddered with fright as she laid there, almost bloodless.

"She is fine and playing with some children. We had some food and a cola. Her stomach isn't growling anymore. When we get out of this mess, I am going to go over to the beef and flat bread guy and get you something to eat. They are really good!"

"River, do not come near me. You will die."

"I have some help with me; we are going to make it."

"Death is upon me, River."

"No, I am going to get you to a hospital right after this. It will all work out. Where is Waba?"

"He is hiding in cars on the street. He said if you get too close, he detonates the bomb. It will kill everyone around me, including you. Take Laima and get out of here."

"River, how are you, my friend?" Waba's voice came from the sidewalk. Bushes covered most of the area, so he was unseen but heard.

"Get any closer and I will detonate the bomb. Understand, River?"

"Yes, please leave her alone and take me. I am worth more politically than she is."

"That's not what I want to do. I just want to kill Americans and those that help the enemy. You are the enemy, River, and she is your American assistance. You both will die in a Christian cemetery. That's sounds almost perfect!"

Looking back at the church door, I could see it cracked open and the padre looking out. I used my right hand and made a shape of a pistol and pointed in the direction of the voice. He gave me the thumbs-up sign.

The padre's gesture gave me some courage to move towards Waba. Moving towards Seher was a sure way to get her killed. Moving to my right, getting behind gravestones, I knew Waba knew what I was doing, and he seemed to enjoy it.

"Oh yes, River, move to the right. No, no, no, to the left towards Seher. She needs you, River."

Waba picked up his rifle and gazed through the scope towards me and then back to Seher. He was looking to kill anyone at this point. Waba was exhausted from chasing me across western Pakistan. He wanted it all to end now!

Looking back towards Seher, I could see the padre low-crawling towards Seher. He was still in his padre uniform. His movements were to distract Waba from me. He was an extremely brave man.

"Christian man, I see you getting near Seher. I will kill you if you get any closer!"

I looked back to the padre, and he gave me the signal to run in about thirty seconds. His hand gestures made me believe that he was going to grab Seher. When he did that, I could run and get to the street to flank Waba hidden in the bushes along the street.

"River, you better tell the priest to not think of grabbing Seher, or he will die."

Suddenly, the padre said, "Go!"

He low-crawled quickly to the back side of the gravestone and reached over and pulled over Seher. She screamed in pain as she cleared the gravestone. Shots rang from the bushes; this was my signal to start shooting at the sound of the rifle going off. Waba only got off two shots at the padre and Seher. Running towards the bushes, I could see local people hitting the ground or standing there wondering what the hell was going on. The 9MM was down to about six rounds when I reached the bushes along the street. When I looked back towards the padre and Seher, I could see that the padre was on the ground, shot, and Seher was on top of his chest looking into his face. Blood was on his face and on her hands. No bomb had gone off.

Locals noticed that the shooting had stopped and that the padre had been shot by a man in the bushes along the street.

"Priest, priest, priest!"

Waba suddenly began running as locals came out with AK-47 weapons and sticks. I began chasing him down the street, shooting. The whole neighborhood was shooting at Waba running through buildings and restaurants.

Pakistani Christians and Muslims rushed to the scene to assist the padre. He had taken a bullet to the chest that had pierced his lung. He died instantly. Seher laid on top of him, with a bullet hole that was just above her heart. Blood was dripping from her chest area, her eyes were shut and breathing became faint. Seher was dying.

Running back to the cemetery, I picked her up. I slowly walked towards the hospital that was at the south end of the cemetery. Moving her caused great pain, and she screamed in agony. Laying her on the ground, I told her, "Seher, you are going to be fine. We just need to get you to the hospital."

Coughing up blood, she opened her eyes and said, "River, you cannot tell the truth very well. Please tell Laima that I love her. Take her to America for me, River. Take her to Hippie Hollow and raise her as your own. She loves you; she told me she wanted you to be her father." Her head moved to the side as life began to sink away from her chest. I leaned down and told her, "I will love her as my own. She will know how brave her mother was, and how much she was loved."

Leaning down to her mouth, the last breath from her body brushed my cheek. Seher had now been taken from this world. Tears fell from my eyes like never before. I had never loved anyone this much or felt more responsible for what had happened.

Death was final as far as I could tell, looking into Seher's eyes. My face was cold, confused, and tense. Blood flowed from her mouth and her body temperature was lukewarm, at best. I picked up her limp body, her arms dangling and her head falling backwards to the ground. She died in my arms that day in that cemetery.

Within seconds, CIA agents were standing around me.

"River, do you want me to grab her daughter? She may want to say goodbye."

"No, Laima would not understand. She is my daughter now. I am all she has." I picked up Seher and held her in my arms and said goodbye. "Seher, we will love you always."

The anger of the Christian community in Peshawar towards Waba increased as word had gotten around the city that a priest had been killed by a Pakistani. They had no idea that it was a CIA padre; we left that part out. Waba was to now be hunted by the Christian community and Pakistani authorities. The world community would be notified within the hour that a Christian padre had been killed. Twenty-four-hour news coverage would ensure that!

This now limited my time to get the Achilles and Laima out of Pakistan. Hopefully these people with camera phones had not recorded me. If so, and if social media got involved, we would become identifiable to everyone.

Chapter 32

Crying and becoming inconsolable, I said, "Seher, I am so sorry! I will make everything right, I promise."

"River, we have to go. Leave her here; Waba could reposition himself for a final kill. And all these people hear you speaking English. Now run to the church and get the guns behind the altar. Then go to the right side of the church; there is a truck waiting for you. Get out of here!"

"I have to get Laima!"

"Leave her and get to the Achilles. Stay with the mission." Tugging and dragging me through the cemetery, ducking below headstones, he pulled me through the door of the church to the altar room. He was bleeding; it looked like a kidney shot that looked like it could be plugged by my finger.

Breathing heavy and in pain, he reached into the altar box, and he pulled out two AK-47s and a bag full of cash. Mixed in with the cash were bullets and empty clips.

"Christmas present, River. Use it wisely; I was saving it for Vegas, half on red and the other half on black the next time I was there." Sweating and holding a bloody cloth against his side, he added, "Looks like this is it for me, the end of the line. River, I never had children or a wife. I envy your time with Seher and Laima. We all kind of did. So, go and get Laima in the playground and use the money to get her to safety. Go through north Torkham Gate. That's where the Pakistani Army Brigade is located and not the Frontier Corps. You need to cross there. River, you must do this tomorrow morning by 0700 hours. We paid off the guards and the police in that area. Anytime after that, you are screwed!"

His eyes began to close as the blood drained from his body. It was like he was going to sleep at the altar.

"River, do you believe in God?"

"I hope I believe in something greater than I. I believe you will be at the gate to help me through when it's my day."

He smiled. "Oh great, a gate guard for God. That will work." Those were his last words he would speak.

The air left his body that morning; it wasn't even lunchtime yet. I didn't even know his name, only that he had saved my life. Looking back through the church door into the cemetery, people were gathering around Seher's and the padre's bodies. Women cried and men looked like they wanted no involvement. Even Muslims came into the Christian cemetery to mourn the loss of the religious man. I think Seher laying there was nothing but a distraction. People walked around her. Little did the people know that the padre was a CIA agent working the city's terrorist and weapons trafficking issues for the U.S. government. All this was done for the church.

Before lunch, three people had died, and Waba and I were still alive. One of us should have been dead from all that shooting. Waba had every chance to kill me but didn't. Maybe he was a crappy shot. I doubted it. He wanted to look me in the eyes in the end.

Suddenly, the suspected dead CIA agent awoke and grabbed my leg and yelled, "Get out of here now!"

My heart stopped; obviously I could not tell if a person was dead or not. Staring down at my leg with his hand tight around my ankle, I pulled his hand away.

"Go, go, now!"

Grabbing the weapons and the money bag, I ran for the front door and out to the left. Running into people walking up to the church, I kept my head down and covered my eyes from the brightness of the sun.

Seeing the truck, I quickly walked towards it. There were two Pakistani men standing nearby, smoking cigarettes, guarding it. Jumping in the truck, I started it and popped the clutch. I needed to get over to the playground and get Laima. Many people were watching me, knowing that I was the guy in the cemetery that was speaking English. The Pakistani people are famous for communicating face to face quickly or by cell phone. Keeping my face down, I drove with a purpose.

Arriving at the school playground, I left the truck running and ran into the park. Looking for Laima was difficult; there were a lot of kids playing who were all covered up.

"Laima, Laima, Laima!"

Off in the distance, Laima heard me and began to move towards me. Suddenly she looked at me.

"Momma?" Tears flowed and I ran to her.

Grabbing and holding her tightly, I said, "We have to go, Laima."

We moved back to the truck, I placed her in the truck, and she scooted over. She began to cry just a little out of confusion and seeing the intense rage on my face. She was scared and wanted her mother. How would I tell her?

As we drove, she kept asking about her mother. "Momma, Momma!" That was one of the few words I had taught her. The pain emanating from both of us was extreme. She was suffering from the loss of a parent, a pain I had never understood or felt. How would I tell a child that didn't understand what I was saying? My mother or a padre was not near to gain advice; I had to do this on my own.

Once we had cleared the cemetery and moved into a less populated area, I pulled over. Rolling down the window, I needed air to breathe deeply and needed time to be brave. Killing a man seemed to be easier than telling a child that her mother was dead and she had no one else left in her life.

I looked over to Laima, and she knew it was bad. She crawled over, got on my lap, and began to wipe the tears from my eyes and hugged me tightly. There were no more tears for her. Her eyes were dry and looked determined to take care of me. Grabbing her, I cried and cried, saying I was so sorry.

"Momma, Allah?"

"Momma, Allah."

Laima leaned back and acknowledged that she understood. She had no more tears left; she was just a small child that would never need to cry again. The worst in life had happened before she ever went to school. Emotions from this point forward would only be focused on me.

It was time to leave; we had to get to the Achilles so we could get home. Laima went back to her seat and then put on her seatbelt, something she had never done. Looking determined, she was ready to get this all over with. We were partners for life; the bond between us was strong, like a father and daughter. From this point forward, we were Team Rochman and would guarantee the safety of each other for the rest of our lives. She was now my family.

Chapter 33

I found myself taking chances with everyone involved. This included the CIA padre and Seher, who both died in front of me. Responsibility for their deaths was clearly square on my shoulders and at the forefront of my mind as I drove erratically south through Peshawar. The Achilles was now just four miles from my grasp at Camp Badaber, with death chasing us.

"Laima, do not be scared. Just hold on."

She held on to the door handle and a fabric bag that her mother prized and the only thing she owned. Her mother's death—she knew, from what I could tell; her face was empty. Pakistani female survival meant to adjust to tragedy and accept the next fate. What a horrible human capability at such a young age. She had only death ahead of her until we got into Afghanistan.

My pain and anger mixed, and I sped through the city, headed south, I suppose. This was my therapy: anger, speed, and knowing I was not directly headed into danger that could end Laima's life. This brought some peace to my mind. My blood pressure was off the charts, my chest moved rapidly up and down, and I was dizzy, confused, sweating and missing Seher. Tears started falling. I wiped them from my eyes. Laima reached over and wiped my eye with the sleeve of her dress. Putting her hand on my cheek, she said, "OK, OK." Her small eyes just let me know we would be fine, and she would take care of me. Shaking like a leaf, I pulled over along the road and I grabbed Laima. I held her and I cried! Laima was much stronger than me!

It took twenty minutes to get myself back together. Multiple conversations with Laima took place. She didn't understand, but I knew she understood my sadness for the loss of her mother. Frantic and delusional, I knew it was now the right time to begin my journey to the Achilles, dripping with revenge and the hope that I would be freed from BG Stanton's grasp. My past military–style, phased-attack approach went out the window; Waba ensured that, because the enemy always has a vote. Now it was to make up the plan as I went along.

Now, weapons maintenance and map recon were required. Both items laid on the floor board of the truck next to Laima. Reaching for the map, Laima moved next to me to look also. The map was still marked up with my pencil–written, phased approach.

"There it is, Badader! That's where we need to go, Laima. Once we are done there, we can go back to Texas and live in peace. Would you like that, Laima?" She just smiled with skepticism; Laima was in mourning, in her own way. I now prayed to any god that would listen: Let us live and get asylum for Laima.

Pulling out into the road, headed south to Badader, we moved slowly as if we were locals without a driver's license. My windows were closed as if suspicion was a daily occurrence, with both hands on the wheel showing complete concentration on my task at hand. Laima could barely see over the dashboard but looked calm yet distant. We were now three miles from our objective. It was in the southern side of the city, where a small forested hill to the west overshadowed the camp. We would drive to that hilltop and recon from above the camp. It looked safe, as it only had one road up to the top. This would allow us to see if someone was coming by vehicle and keep out those coming up dismounted. A perfect place to plan and execute from, but did not support an easy exfiltration route out to Torkham Gate.

We needed a high-speed avenue of approach into Afghanistan, but my assumption was we would have to dismount the vehicle and walk over the mountains. This was the hard way but the safest, to go over the Afghan and Pakistan border area mountains known as Tora Bora. Speeding through the border checkpoint at Torkham would be hard to explain since I couldn't speak the language.

The drive through the city to the south took about an hour. That's when we got to the west side of the hilltop overlooking our objective. There were goats with herders and a few milking cows around, but most had not moved towards the top of the hill. Roads in the area were filled with rocks, and the vegetation was sparse at best in the lower areas. Locals had cut down trees for firewood, and the grass had been trampled by the domesticated animals. There was no wildlife in the area; everything seemed to be hunted out. No squirrels, snakes, or ants seemed to exist in this area. In Texas, I would be beating off fire ants and mosquitos and seeing squirrels in the trees. Subsistence living is the way of life in Pakistan.

Climbing the hill in first gear was not an easy task. Laima was bouncing around but her seatbelt held her in place. I just held on to the steering wheel for dear life. Dust was flying as the wheels spun in the loose dirt and rocks until we reached the top. We stopped just short of perching over the ledge, looking into the valley of the Badaber Camp. This is where the Achilles was reported to be for its last day.

Camp Badaber was in the middle of a disputed tribal area run like a mafia-style neighborhood. I surely needed to avoid all human contact once I entered the area. These locals would be the first responders when all hell broke loose. I was also worried about the goat herders; they had seen us climb the hill and not return.

"Come on, Laima." I grabbed her and got out of the truck. We moved into the tree-lined area and sat down to take a break. The truck had been outfitted with water, flat bread, and fruit. Starving, we sat, ate, and listened to the wind blow and the goat herders below talk to their goats. It was a peaceful, comfortable, and safe place for us. I had never felt so comfortable in this society until now. Almost like I belonged here; it had become second nature to dress and act like a local with a child. My nationality had become blurry as my situation and the society I had built with Laima and Seher had changed all that. I liked it!

I soon began my reconnaissance with paper, pencil, and map in hand. Laima remained back with the vehicle, as she could handle it better than anyone. Looking into the camp, I could see the large communications tower that dominated the area off about one mile to my east. Studying the antennas and satellite antennas and horns, I looked for the Achilles receiver. Within minutes I located the dish; it was located off to the side of the tower on the ground, pointed straight to the sky. That meant they didn't have enough cable to reach the top of the tower, or they wanted to be able to pick the Achilles up and move it quickly if required.

There were a total of eight buildings surrounding the antenna. The roads and walkways around the headquarters were limited to dismounted movement. No vehicles could drive through the area. That meant I had to walk in and steal in the middle of the night. Several lampposts dotted the walkways. If they really worked, that would be an issue for movement to the communications building and tower area.

Watching for several hours, I saw workers from the local area flow in and out doing labor-type work. They were getting checked coming in and out for only weapons or stolen items taken from inside the camp. That would be my way in, but I needed to do it soon. This created an issue with Laima staying by herself for that long. There was no playground in this area, so that was out!

I headed back to our vehicle, and I found Laima was sitting there in the trees feeding birds and an old cat. It was one of the ugliest cats I had ever seen. Multicolored, sores, cuts, and limping, it was eating Laima's flat bread like it was its last meal.

"Laima, stay away from that cat. It could bite you!" She just looked at me with her hand out to the cat. Her face said, No, I am going to do it anyway.

"Laima, that thing is going to bite you. Do not come over here crying and holding your bleeding hand." The cat hissed when the food ended, and Laima jumped up and ran to me. I grabbed her as she ran from that cat.

"I got you, sweetheart. I will save you!" My mother called me sweetheart. Was I now becoming parent-like? Moments like these brought me happiness—just for a moment, though. In the distance I could hear every now and then goats and their herders moving closer. This lasted throughout the day. Nervousness and anxiety had become second nature.

Continuing to look at my plan drawn on my map, I looked for holes and mistakes based on vehicle and personnel movement in and out of the camp. I kept coming back to just one plan: Act like a local, get into the workers' line, and act like a deaf-mute. Nighttime was falling and the workers continued to come and go. This was a twenty-four-hour-a-day operation that was perfect to come under the light of darkness.

Hiding as a local in clear view was not an issue at this point. The sun, the dirt, the look of hunger, and the daily stress had already aged me rapidly. I could hardly identify me at this point.

Studying and evaluating leaving Laima in the vehicle was difficult. She had enough food and water to last through tomorrow morning, but no more than that if she kept feeding that damn cat. The gun would not help; she was too small to understand its use. All she could do was scream for help, but no one was around for miles to help. I trusted no one at this point with her life. Everyone but her mother and I had let her down or tried to kill those she loved. Her father, I am sure, she hated with every fiber of her body,

It was almost 1900 hours, and darkness was settling across the hills as the prairie below began to turn on lights. Generators began to be started to provide electricity. The sound was loud enough that I felt it was the best way to get into the day worker line to gain access. Below me was a goat trail that led to the camp fence line that surrounded the camp. Guard towers were placed on all four corners of the camp, while dismounted troops patrolled the fence. Their patrolling movements were not on any set time. That could be good or bad. To me, that meant there was no intelligence leading them to believe they were under any danger. This only left Waba on my tail.

It was now almost 2000 hours, so I told Laima to stay there and not move. Handing her food and water, I laid her down on the floor board of the truck.

"Go to sleep, sweetheart. I will be back in a few hours." She jumped up and kissed me on the cheek and gave me a hug.

"I love you too, sweetheart. I will be right back."

Laima got back down on the floor of the truck. Covering her with a blanket, I reached for the door locks. I wanted her as safe as she could be.

Moving back to the ridgeline overlooking the camp, I got down behind the trees and waited for the right moment to move down into the camp. I had my weapon and knife strapped to my back. With limited ammo, the weapon, once I reached the camp fence, needed to be dropped in order to get in as a day worker. I would leave it in the bushes and come back out once I had the Achilles in hand. The satellite phone was dead, so it was of no use to anyone.

The temperature was about twenty-eight degrees with a slight breeze. Dirty but warmly clothed, with a few pieces of fruit that was all I had. The stars were bright and great for movement. It was now

2045 hours, and I was ready to move. Thinking of home and how BG Stanton got me into this began to fade.

"Hello, River!" The warmth of hands and rope around my throat. Oxygen began to release from my body. My life flashed long enough to see my demise!

"Only Allah will save you from your fate."

Chapter 34

With the oxygen loss and the thought that Laima was so close to me, panic to survive enveloped my body. I must win; I had responsibilities to that little girl. If only Seher was here, she would kill this guy in a heartbeat. She would stab and beat with a tire iron on this guy. Killing to survive seemed easy now that I thought of it. Laima didn't have that blood in her. She was kind and warm hearted.

Blood loss to the brain began to set in. My mind wandered in the past. Suddenly, I had a great release of blood back to the brain. Waba released as I heard him moan from pain as he reached for his back. Turning and spinning like a high school wrestler; I was able to spin away from him.

Waba began to speak into the dark, looking away from me. In the shadows I could see a small figure no more than five feet away. Waba moved towards the figure, speaking in English and Urdu, "You little bitch, you stabbed me!"

In the dark stood Laima with my knife, which had fallen off me in the fight somehow. She had stabbed Waba in the neck. He was bleeding pretty bad and staggering towards her. Jumping to my feet, I ran towards him and jumped on his back and began to bring him to the ground. Blood from his neck got all over my face. Laima ran towards Waba again, leaning forward with the knife in "I will kill you" mode. She stabbed Waba in the stomach. She didn't have enough power to stick it in him for the kill but enough to distract him. Waba grabbed the knife from his stomach area and then raised his arm with the knife to swing at her. I grabbed it, and down to ground we went. Fighting and fighting, I kept one hand over his mouth and the other trying to control the knife. After one minute, Waba started slowing down from loss of blood; he was breathing heavily, and his blood flowing from his neck went to a trickle.

With the loss of blood and bodily functions, Waba stopped moving. He was dying and I needed to ensure that he completely died on this hilltop. So, I jammed the knife into his stomach two more times with him lying on top of me, face up. Both hands filled with blood the consistency of motor oil. I threw Waba to my side and got up.

"Laima, are you all right?"

Her fingers laid in her mouth as tears flowed from her eyes. Drops of blood were on her dress and hands. Laima was terrified at what she had done.

"Laima, you saved me! Thank you, sweetheart. You did the right thing; this is not your fault." She had no clue what I was saying. So I hugged her.

"Laima, we have to get out of here, now!"

Moving to the truck, I placed her in the front seat and off we went, back down the hill. We needed to get out of the area. The commotion that took place should have warned every goat herder around her. The police could get called and could soon find the body. Waba remained dead on the ground amongst the goats and cats on that hilltop as we drove away. Hopefully no one would come up the hill, which meant Waba might not be found until tomorrow morning when the sun came up. Hopefully the animals would eat this guy through the night, just to ensure his death was complete. Twenty-four hours from then, he would be fertilizer.

The road down the hill was dark and rough, yet the stars did provide some light to navigate. Pointing the truck at house lights below, we moved with a purpose. Within ten minutes, we had reached the bottom of the hill and an area filled with some houses. Outside those houses, a few old men and young boys watched us drive by. We just waved as if we were just old neighbors. As we passed, a few men began to head towards the top of the hill.

Looking back, I said, "Oh shit, Laima, we could be in trouble soon. This means we have about one hour to get the Achilles and get out of town. We need a new truck, car, or motorcycle to get us to the border. They will be looking for this vehicle. It's too dark for them to identify us by face, thank God and Allah." Laima only understood the word Allah, from what I could tell!

Circling the hill to the right, we stopped about a quarter of a mile from the gate. I moved into an alley and continued to drive and look for a hiding place for the truck. Again, I would have to leave Laima behind, but this time with something she could handle, a knife! Still a small child, yet she had already helped to kill a man.

Handing her the knife, I wiped off the blood as best I could.

"Use this knife, Laima, if you have to!" She took the knife and slid it under her dress.

"Good girl, sweetheart. I will be back in two hours. Love ya, OK!"

She smiled, as if she understood that I cared and she trusted me.

The truck was hidden between two old jingle trucks that had no engines or tires. They were not going anywhere. It was now after 2200 hours and most people were in bed. The city was quiet, so I heard only whispers and dogs barking. This seemed to be the perfect night to get in and out. Except this time, I had to do this alone. Seher and Laima would not be there to distract and assist. I had no solid plan other than the day worker disguise. I needed to just get to a recon position at the front gate. I would make it up as I moved through.

I reached the front gate in about twenty or so minutes, and day workers were few and far between. Needing to go in with the crowd now required me to wait for the next gaggle to move through. Looking down at my watch, I saw it had now been thirty minutes and still no major movement of workers through the front gate. Plan B needed to be initiated in a few minutes if nothing materialized. I had to keep the momentum, as we had a dead body on the hill and soon he would be found.

Suddenly, an ambulance, speeding down the road, stopped at the front gate. Gate guards came out to inspect the vehicle. Soon, an argument began between the driver and the gate guard as they moved back to the guard shack. This suddenly was my way in. Running over to the back of the ambulance, I jumped in and hid under a few piles of sheets and mobile beds. Lying down, I covered up and prayed.

A few minutes went by before the driver and guard came back. The guard made a few more checks under the vehicle for explosives or people, and he found nothing. I continued to hear arguments as the ambulance moved through the gate. Slowly sliding out from under the sheets and beds, I looked out the back window. The ambulance moved slowly, at times coming to a halt. I thought to myself, *at the next halt, I am going to slip out and become a roaming day worker.*

Within a few seconds, the driver stopped and got out of the vehicle and went inside the small health clinic. Slowly opening the door and checking for anyone coming, I slipped out and walked off towards an unlit area on the camp. It was an old vehicle parts storage area. Multiple fifty-five-gallon barrels were around, some filled with fuel and oil.

I whispered under my breath, "This could be useful." The fuel and oil would make a great diversion when I went to take the Achilles. Start a big fire, snatch, grab, and get out the gate back into the alley.

Wandering through the camp carrying auto parts, I came upon the command center with the antenna outside on the ground.

Staying back, I observed the comings and goings of officers and soldiers moving in and out. It was midnight, with limited visibility to see what weapons they had on them. This place looked professional enough to be of concern with sharp-looking personnel, and the area was clean and orderly. These signs meant it was not going to be easy.

Repositioning myself to look through the front door, I could see the radio room in the back of the building. That's where the antenna was located. That meant that the cable was running into a window or vent into the radio room because it was too short to run up the tower.

Moving to the back of the building, the antenna sitting on the ground was active. The power light was on and the hard drive that ran the Achilles antenna was blinking as it appeared to be receiving data. That was a bad thing; this meant they could possibly be tracking U.S. forces right now. Crouching and looking through the window, I could only see one radio operator staring at a computer screen. I could not see the Achilles handheld controller anywhere in the room.

I thought, "What the hell! Where did they put it? Looking through the window again, scanning the room in a paranoid fashion, I noticed the radio man had radio earphones in his ears. His head was moving from left to right. Soon, he reached down and pulled out the Achilles. He was using it as a music player! I knew the Achilles had the software for audio, but this was one hell of a use of this system. One small cable ran to his ears and the other ran to the computer terminal. There it was, the Achilles, playing Punjabi hip-hop and tracking U.S. Special Forces at the same time.

Backing up from the window, I moved into a safe location to begin the modified planning process that needed to last less than five minutes. Waba had still not been found, but soon he would be. I had only one hour left, based on my personal planning factor.

First, I needed to get that radio man out here to check the

antenna, and that had to be done when he was alone in the room. Second, I had to kill or skull-crush this radio man, take the Achilles, and get out the gate. This had to happen before his superiors came back, found the radio room unattended, and came looking for him. I figured I had just a few minutes.

Moving back to the window, he was still alone, and that was good. Moving back to the antenna, I unhooked the data cable to stop the flow of information going to the Achilles and then stepped on the connector so it couldn't be used again. Moving back to the window, the soldier didn't move a muscle. He just kept moving his head to the music. I waited a few minutes, and he still made no movement. Finally, the soldier reached down to grab the Achilles off his belt; he looked and said something that seemed vulgar. He turned and looked towards the window and got up to look out at the antenna. I crouched down as he looked at the light; it was not blinking. Soon, he walked out of the room to investigate.

As I sat back behind a few fifty-five-gallon drums, the radio man showed up and began to troubleshoot. Using a penlight to aluminate the problem, he was soon accompanied by another soldier. Both looking at the problem, they realized they needed some tools to fix the connector. With none in hand, the second soldier left to find something while the radio man lit a cigarette. This was my only moment now; it was all or nothing. I had the Achilles, a set of matches for the diversion, and a small truck carburetor to beat this guy with.

Slowly, I got up and moved towards him. As I came closer, he was startled but I continued to gesture with my hands for a cigarette. Every now and then, I covered my neck to relay that I was a mute. The soldier continued to say no, pushing me back. On the third push, I hit him with the carburetor, dead in the face. He hit the ground at the speed with which I swung the carburetor. Once he hit the ground, he made no movement. I hit him one more time in the head. His skull was crushed, and blood and brain matter came out of his ears.

Dragging him over to the drums, I hid him behind gas and oil cans. He was really the first man I had ever killed by myself. I didn't know what to think. The second swing was when I wanted him dead. Pulling off the Achilles from his belt, I stood up to move back to the diversion area. Placing it in my back pocket, I looked back just as the second soldier arrived. He called out his buddy's name and heard nothing. Looking through the window into the radio room, he saw nothing. Showing concern, he began wander around the fuel area where I had hidden the body. I was now in trouble if he found the body.

Still carrying the carburetor, I walked back over to the second soldier and scared him. He looked at me and started to talk. He was looking concerned that I was not answering him back. I, playing the mute again, came closer, and I swung with everything I had. He died on the first blow, as his left eye came out of his head and his nose was driven into his face over an inch. Within seconds, blood from his head spread over the dirt like a water hose laid down in a garden. I quickly placed him on top of his buddy and spread dirt over the blood.

"They can go to Allah together as a buddy team!"

Grabbing the matches and cigarettes from the soldier, I took off at a fast pace towards the automotive area where the fuel and oil drums were consolidated. Tearing a piece of my shirt, I dipped it in a fuel barrel, soaking it for a few seconds. This would be the key to deception before they found the dead soldiers. I needed Pakistani focus over here and not at the front gate as I walked out.

A few seconds later, I arrived and placed open fuel cans around the oil barrel. The heat and flames from the oil barrel would soon explode the fuel cans once the flames hit the fuel vapors. I threw the fuel rag into the oil, lit the match, and then the rag. The can began to burn rapidly, with black smoke filling up the area. Soldiers began to look out the windows as I moved throughout the base camp, hiding and moving. Soldiers ran towards the fire to put it out, and within thirty seconds, the whole area exploded, killing at least three guys, from what I could see. Fireballs shot out and landed on top of buildings. It turned out to be a bigger diversion than I had expected.

Running as fast as I could, I cleared over half the camp before the fire department showed up. The gate guards were letting everyone through to assist, and that included locals. The base camp security was nonexistent at this point; the explosion had turned this place upside down. It was time to exit with the Achilles. The time was now 0145 hours, which left me five hours and fifteen minutes to get to Torkham Gate, Afghanistan, over forty miles away. I needed to move out of the camp, get to Laima, and get out of town fast, especially while the Pakistani Frontier Corps was dealing with this fire.

Speeding up my walk to a point that didn't look too suspicious, I picked up hand tools along the way and handed them to soldiers as they ran by me looking to put out the fire. Looking helpful and acting like I was doing something seemed to pay off.

The gate was just fifty feet away and I could smell freedom from this camp. I had killed two people and repatriated the Achilles in just the last few hours. My focus was to get out that gate, even if I had to kill the gate guard. Moving up to the gate, the guards pointed me back towards the fire. They wanted all hands on that fire. I gave the mute hand signal and that I needed more shovels. They let me go through. Once I got out of the light of the fire, I ran like hell through the alleys of Peshawar. I was free, with the Achilles in my pocket, but I soon became lost the further I ran.

Stopping and telling myself to stay calm, I turned back around and ran back to the camp area to regain my bearings. It took me another thirty minutes to navigate back through the alley to the truck and Laima. I was wasting time in a panic, as focus and discipline needed to be the answer to save Laima and myself.

Finding the truck at 0225 hours, I found Laima sound asleep with an apple core on her lap. I rubbed her face and she looked up, smiled, and went back to sleep. Taking the Achilles out of my pocket, I placed it in Seher's old bag that Laima carried. I felt it was safer on that little girl than on me. As I placed it in the bag, I thought about all the people that had died and sacrificed for this thing that a soldier was listening to music on. To him, it was the only music player he would ever have. And to the S.F. guys, this ensured they made it home to their families every day. Americans on the border could sleep easier now. The National Security Agency should be able to see this system not transmitting anymore. Hopefully this would let them know I was headed to the border to be extracted.

Forty miles, one tank of gas, one little girl, and potential freedom. That's all I had left!

Chapter 35

For some apparent reason, as I left Camp Badader in flames, I felt very comfortable about my situation. Good things were happening, the truck started during a panic, and we moved down the alley with everyone else headed in the other direction. Laima was safe and sound, I had enough gas to get to Torkham or just short of it, we had food and water, and best of all, I had the Achilles. It was a great 0300 hours in the morning—actually, the best ever since I started this disaster two weeks ago!

The direction of travel to Torkham Gate was simple: I had to head west to catch N55 north, take a left on the Peshawar Ring Road, to N55 West to Torkham Road, which would take me to the gate. Excitement filled my body, which caused me to begin speeding out of town like a mad man. Driving at speeds in excess of fifty miles an hour, I had my arm hanging out the window like I was headed to the lake with my daughter. Laughing to myself and pushing on Laima like a dad would do with his daughter, just playing around at midnight in the truck. It just felt good and right. Laima was smiling and eating an apple and drinking the rest of the water we had, and we were almost free.

Stopping at the main intersection of the Peshawar Ring Road and N55, I looked over at Laima and smiled and thought how great it was going to be when my mother and father met Laima. I was sure they would love her as they had loved and cared for me.

"RIVER!" Laima screamed and grabbed the dashboard as I looked up to see what the reason was.

"Waba, Waba!" she said, pointing forward of the truck.

There he stood, with bloodstains around his stomach area, carrying a pistol and knife. He stood hunched and in pain in the middle of the intersection of Ring Road and N55. My headlights were firmly affixed to his image of death and his desire to live. He raised his pistol, he pointed it at me, and yelled, "River, come here now or I kill the girl." Shifting the weapon in mid-conversation to Laima, he moved towards her. With hands trembling, he looked over to me and said, "You thought you had killed me on that hill, River. The little girl was a surprise. I never thought she could do it. Killing her when she was sleeping, I should have done that first. Turn the engine off, River; you are not going to go anywhere but to your God. Laima will see Allah but will burn for her young sins. Now, stop the engine and throw the keys out the window."

There was only one option at this point: run him over while taking the chance that Laima could be killed.

"Waba, do not kill Laima. She has done nothing; she is just a small child!"

"Yes, a small child that has the capability of revenge. Years from today she will look for me and gain revenge for her mother. I will not look behind my back, ever. She must die and the seed of revenge will be buried in the earth for the worms to devour. Now, get out of the truck."

"Come on, Laima."

"No, River, she stays and burns to hell in that truck. This is her deathbed. Now, get out of the truck, now!"

Nothing in my life was clearer than this moment. I was prepared to die right along with Laima. If we die, then we both go together to God and Allah, and he will handle Waba. Seher will be there waiting for us, and we will all be together again. I was cool with that plan!

Waba could barely stand at this point; the blood had reached his knees, while his hands that held the gun had stains. He was at his weakest, and this was our time. Waba was within five feet from the driver's side headlight with the gun pointed at Laima. Figuring I had one second to run him over before he launched the first round at Laima, I put my foot slowly down on the clutch. I put both hands on the steering wheel, and made sure I was in first gear.

"OK, Waba, I will get out of the truck, but let me say goodbye to Laima, please!"

"You Americans are far too caring of little girls. She is worth nothing, and no one will ever miss her."

Speaking softly, I said, "Laima, hold on and keep your head down."

Laima just looked at my eyes and could tell that she needed to hold on and duck as the gun was pointed at her. She was so smart; she knew what to do without me even telling her.

"Come out, River, that's enough."

The minute I looked back up into his eyes, I hit the gas and let the clutch out at the same time. The vehicle lunged forward; I could hear the wheels losing traction and then catching on the street. Waba's eyes became alert as the gun came up to kill Laima. Shots began to ring out and enter the window into the cab. Laima began to scream as Waba was hit by the grill and hood. Grabbing hold of the hood below the front window, Waba looked at me through the window as I drove into the intersection with him attached. I slammed on the brakes to throw him off, but he continued to hang on.

Yelling and smiling, he said, "River, you cannot kill me. I will live forever!" He pointed the gun at me, and the gun rang out as the bullet hit me in the shoulder. As the bullet entered my body, I jerked the steering wheel to the left into oncoming traffic. Within seconds, I collided with a Pakistani cab parked on the side of the road. Waba ejected into the cab window at about thirty miles an hour.

The vehicle and body impact shoved Waba through the cab window into a sleeping driver. Laima was thrown onto the floor board as I hit the steering wheel. Blood flowed from my nose—it was broken, I assumed. Glass exploded all over Laima on the floor. She was crying and trying to get up back in the seat.

"Laima, you OK, sweetheart? Please be OK. Are you hurt?"

Laima looked at me and was crying with no sound coming out of her mouth. The intense look on her face told me she was scared and hurt. I grabbed and held her, and she screamed with pain from my squeeze. Shaken up and bruised, but still alive. That was a good thing.

My blood continued to flow all over my shirt and Laima as we hugged. Looking up, I saw Waba, his skull pumping blood and brain matter just like Seher's husband. Setting Laima back in the seat, I got out with my gun to look over the destruction and ensure Waba was dead this time. Looking into the driver's side window, I reached in and checked the pulse of the cab driver; he had none. Moving over to Waba, I touched his throat and then his hand for a pulse; there was none. I continued to check his pulse for over minute. I wanted him dead. Suddenly, his eye opened up, looking directly at me.

Bang! Bang! Bang!

I fired three shots into his head and neck. The bullets ripped through his skull and throat. This exposed every bit of evil his father had placed in his DNA. It all now lay in the seat of that cab.

Laima cried out after the shots went off. Looking up at me, she got out of the truck and limped slowly to me. Hugging my leg, she cried as I stared at Waba—dead! Waba died at the crossroads of N55 and Peshawar Road. How fitting that he died in his hometown where it all started.

There was no one on the road that night. It would have been pitch black if it hadn't been for the one surviving headlight of the truck. The truck was still running but smoking. Radiator fluid, oil, and gas were spread all over the road. We were walking and hitchhiking at this point, because the truck was beyond driving. Reaching into the truck, I pulled out Seher's bag loaded down with the Achilles and our last remaining supplies. Food, water, maps, and my dead satellite phone, was all that remained. We were close enough to call for help, but my satellite phone needed a charge.

It was a cold night. I believe the day was December 11, and it was after midnight. Standing on the road, I looked both ways, east to Peshawar and west to Torkham, Afghanistan; it was a long walk home. With the mountains of Tora Bora, the Pakistani Frontier Corps and the Pakistani army ahead of us, I had now only six hours to clear the Afghanistan border with a paid passage for only two people. Only two tickets left!

"Let's go, Laima, we have a flight to catch to Texas." As we began to walk, I heard a cell phone ring. Looking back at the cab, the ringing was coming from the front seat.

"Let's grab that cell phone; we will need it at some point." Reaching into the cab, I noticed the phone was ringing from Waba's coat pocket. Grabbing the phone slowly, I then backed away from his lifeless body. The phone continued to ring. Looking down at the screen, I noticed that the number looked to be a U.S. cell phone number that had a 571 area code. I knew only a few people with that area code. I know who!

Chapter 36

In the middle of the night, in any country, traffic in rural areas is few and far between. Waiting to hitchhike is exactly that, waiting. After one hour of walking, it was evident that we needed to steal a vehicle to make the journey in time. Just as I was ready to violate a ten-commandment sin, I could see a convoy of trucks coming our way. There must have been at least twenty of these trucks carrying large loads of goods. Jingle trucks running through the night, how fitting.

"Laima, we need to jump on one of these trucks. They look to be going our way."

We stood on the side of the road, close enough to be in the glare of the headlights. We waved at the first, second, and third trucks to get a ride, but none stopped. Looking on the side of the vehicle, there was a cardboard sign with the letters UNOPS. That stood for the United Nations Operations. This was a great sign that help could be given by this organization. Yet, we waved for assistance and the drivers continued to drive by us and not even glance. By the time the end of the convoy was ready to go by, a small UNOPS truck stopped and someone spoke to us in Urdu. I could not understand, so I played the mute option again. He could see the blood on our faces and clothes.

"Oh my heavens, you are hurt!" The driver got out with his

first-aid medic bag and told us to sit on the tailgate of the truck. Taking out his flashlight and pointing it into my face, he looked stunned.

"OK, why don't we start speaking English here? You are not Pakistani, Afghani, Indian, or anything else other than American or British. So which is it, chief?"

"American and she is Urdu. Her mother was killed by the Pakistani government and I am all she has."

"Are you a spy, adventurer, or a lost soldier?"

"Hard to tell at this point! I need your help; we need to get out of Pakistan into Torkham Gate by 0700 hours."

"Why by 0700 hours?"

"The U.S. has paid off the guards. They change guards at 0700 hours, so that's why I have to get there soon."

"OK, I can get you as far as five miles before the border checkpoint. We are supposed to cross at 0645 hours and pick up U.S. and Afghani military convoy support from there to Bagram. Will that work?"

"Yes, but I will be late."

"I know but that's the best I can do without getting everyone here injured or killed. Do you understand?"

"OK, that's better than nothing."

"Please check Laima. She hit the floor board pretty hard."

"Hell, she is tougher than both you and I put together."

After fifteen minutes, the convoy continued with Laima and I riding with UNOPS. Laima fell asleep in my lap. Feeling her heartbeat was the best feeling ever at that moment. The only other heartbeat I could feel was in my face. My nose was broken and my nasal cavities were damaged. I sounded like I had a gas mask on as I breathed. Mostly, I could only breathe from my mouth. It hurt the more I paid attention to it.

"What are you going to do with the girl?"

"I plan to adopt her and take her back to Texas. I promised her mother I would do that."

"Like a daughter?"

"Yes, I feel she is my own now. I love her with all my heart. Her mother died to protect us; she was very brave. When she is old enough, I will tell her of her mother's bravery and how she gave her life to save ours."

"What's your name?"

"River. That's all I can tell you for your safety."

"You know, River, there is a story floating around Islamabad about a young woman, her small child, and an American that is wanted for murder and government theft. Is that you?"

"I have no idea what you are talking about. We are just weary travelers that ran into some bad luck."

"Really, there are two dead Pakistani men back aways. One is all shot up and the other looks like he was hit with a freight train. Not you, right?"

"No, not me!"

"OK, River, here is the deal. I will help you get through the border, but we have to hide the girl in the supplies and you need to be an American UNOPS officer. Can you do that?"

"Yes, but I need clothes, and one of those drivers needs to be in on the deal."

"No, I will just separate the drivers at the five-mile marker and that's when you stash her in this back truck."

"But the drivers will know I am not with you. They could rat us out."

"I will figure something out, trust me. When we arrive at the Jamrud Fort along highway N55 we can make the transition there. We only need little Laima to stay quiet for a few more hours. Can she do that?"

"Yes, I have no options at this point. Our lives are in your hands."

"And you need to listen to me. Read this operations order from UNOPS. This tells you our mission and every other thing you need to know if asked. Got it?"

"Yes, I got it!"

We continued to drive for another forty-five minutes. Coming onto the Jamrud Fort, it was almost 0400 hours in the morning. The sky was cloudy with very little light from the fort. This was a perfect place to make the transition from River the soldier conducting an immigration infraction of a known murderer and thief to the United Nations Operations Officer conducting convoy operations. Laima just needed to hide for another two hours and we would be free.

Jamrud Fort was a fairly large Pakistan Frontier Corps maintenance checkpoint for vehicles headed into Afghanistan. Moving into the Tora Bora Mountains, all trucks would be inspected for vehicle maintenance and weight. A lot of bribes were paid to inspectors here.

Still, up to this point, I had no idea what the UNOPS guy's name was. Probably best not to know if we got caught. Knowing nothing is better than knowing something at this point. But, then again, I was a deaf-mute, right?

Getting me a set of clothes, the UNOPS guy handed me some old dirty clothes that he had been wearing for the last month, which was all he had. They were dirty, smelly, and fit loosely. Looking into the vehicle mirror, I had lost a lot of weight. My beard and hair were unkempt. Hopefully this would work. I had to remember to speak English from this point forward.

Driving back up to the convoy, we pulled up close to the last jingle truck. I picked up Laima and said, "Laima, you have to hide in the truck, OK?"

She was still very tired; she lay limp in my arms. Her stomach sounded of hunger. Laima was weak from lack of food and water at this point. Maybe this was a blessing from God or Allah. With her so tired, I got onto the back of the truck and made a bed hidden in the supplies of food and towels.

"Laima, lay down here! This is a great bed."

Laima opened her eyes and looked at me, confused. To solve the confusion, I jumped up into the truck and acted like I wanted to take a nap on the makeshift bed. Laima reached out her arms to me; she wanted to lie down. Laying her down, I said, "Stay, Laima." Showing my hand to lay down, she did. Fast asleep she went, looking like she had done this before. After she went to sleep, we covered the bed area back up to hide her position in the truck. We prayed she did not awaken.

"Do you think she will be found?"

"Only if she wakes up and they hear her."

Pakistani policemen and Frontiersmen roamed the vehicle line, getting in the cabs and climbing on top of the cargo with long, pointed sticks, plunging sticks down into the cargo of the trucks and then pulling them out, looking for the blood of any hidden human. Laima was in the last vehicle. When the policeman came to check, he was too exhausted and fat to climb anymore on the vehicle, so he only visually checked. Laima stayed quiet, as I was sure she was asleep. He wiped his head with a rag and said, "OK, you can go!"

Suddenly, Laima must have moved and moaned. We were all startled by the policeman's reaction: "Open now, drop all cargo now!" We were caught and there was no place to run and hide. I was not leaving Laima.

The UNOPS guy jumped forward, speaking broken Urdu and English together. Working to calm him down, I looked for anything that could be substituted as the noise he had heard. There it was, a baby goat that had been placed in the back of the truck with tape wrapped around its mouth. It had broken free of the tape and wanted out. I grabbed the goat in excitement, showed the goat to the UNOPS and policeman. They initially laughed and then the policeman whipped the driver for bringing the goat in without permission.

For the policeman's trouble, I handed him the goat and we all waved goodbye. UNOPS yelled down to all drivers to load and begin movement. Within ten minutes we began to move through to the border. The Pakistanis did not check UNOPS members for anything here. Thank God, as I had not even made up a name to call myself. The name River was spreading all over Pakistan due to our movements and activities in the last few weeks. Saying the name River was a death sentence at this point in this country. I looked forward and waved goodbye and gave the head nod as we pulled out of the fort.

The road to Torkham Gate was only about thirty-five kilometers to our west. At our rate of travel, it would be two hours or so to get there at twenty-five miles an hour. Rocking back and forth as we crossed many dry stream beds, Laima must be shaking to death back there. This was the first time we had been separated for this long. I was like a worried parent wondering if she was OK or not.

"Are we going to stop anywhere soon?"

"No, we cannot if you plan to make the border before 0700 hours. At this rate, we will cross with only fifteen minutes to spare. That leaves us with very little time for a breakdown or refuel of the convoy if required. We need to continue!"

"OK, I just need her to not be scared."

"I am worried also about Laima, River. But, I assure you, that little girl is tougher than both of us put together. She could survive anything."

"OK!"

"If you make it across into Torkham, Afghanistan, what will you do then?"

"I need to make a phone call to a BG Stanton and have him get us picked up."

"And the girl, what happens to her?"

"Asylum."

"Asylum, really? You think it will just happen like that? This BG Stanton, do you trust him to get that done this quick or at all? Asylum seekers take years to get into the U.S. legally. You know that, right?"

"He owes me. I saved his ass and now he owes it to Laima and her mother. It was her mother's dying wish and I intend to make that happen, no matter what it takes!"

"OK, we'll see how that works for you."

All I could think about was, "Do I trust BG Stanton, and whose 571 area code number was it on Waba's phone?" I had seen this number somewhere; I just couldn't put my finger on it. Could someone in Virginia be leading Waba to me? He sure kept finding me fairly easily!

"Get some sleep, River; I will wake you when we get within five miles of Torkham."

That was a good idea; even a thirty-minute power nap would be a good deal. Within minutes, I fell asleep like a rock hitting the ground, but it was a stressful and tense sleep.

"River, wake up. We are here at Torkham Gate."

Coming out of a deep sleep, I looked straight forward to the truck with Laima in it. "Is she OK, you think?"

"She is fine; I just hope she stays asleep through the border. You need to wipe your eyes and get ready to lie your way through this border with the Pakistanis and then the Afghani police and army. Focus on that!"

"OK, I got this! I have too much to lose to come this far and blow it. I was a deaf- mute, a husband, and father to a little girl for the last two weeks. I can do this."

"So what's your name? It's not River, right?"

"What do you think I look like, a Steve or Joe?"

"Let's go with Frank Ingram. Your job is an assistant driver. You have worked with UNOPS for the last six months. Frank is actually a real person that we left in Islamabad because he got the flu. So, if they call UNOPS, they will confirm that you are supposed to be in country. Got it, River?"

"Got it, Frank Ingram it is."

"Get ready, here comes the first checkpoint."

Chapter 37

We arrived at about 0630 hours just short of Bacha Mena. Bacha was a village just about a quarter-mile from Torkham Gate. This was where they would check the vehicles for explosives prior to going into Torkham. Torkham was a much larger town with buildings and businesses positioned right up against the N5 route into Afghanistan. If a bomb went off here, it would kill thousands of people.

"Guards with metal detectors will be here soon. We need to get out and move to the front of the convoy to act like we are interested in what is going on. Are you good with that, Frank?"

"Yes, I am good. Let's just get this done."

"Frank Ingram, do not rush this or we will look suspicious. This better be an Academy Award performance! And, do not look or say anything to Laima when we walk by that truck. I know this will be difficult, but you have to act like she is not there. Now let's go."

Getting out of the truck, my legs were weak and my eyes were straining to see anything. I stumbled as my legs seemed to not want to move forward. I thought to myself that I needed to stay calm because Laima was depending on me. The Achilles, to hell with it! If they looked at it, it would be a music player and nothing more. My name was Frank Ingram and I was a driver! I continued to tell myself this over and over again until I believed the lie. The lie became truth the minute I looked back at the truck Laima was hidden in.

Ahead of us, soldiers with handheld metal detectors and undercarriage mirrors began their search for anything unusual. They were professional, from what I could tell. A lot of experience and patience was being used creating extra time at the border; I needed to be across by 0700 hours.

Scanning the crowd of policemen, I wondered who was the individual that had been paid off by the CIA. It had to be one of the officers in charge at the gate that signed off on each UNOPS convoy. The border office was ahead of us by over a mile. Pakistani officers were not going to march down the road this far, no way. Hopefully he had already approved the movement earlier before we arrived. I had many questions running through my mind.

"Frank, let's move up to the front to sign some paperwork!"

"OK, let's go."

Moving to the front of the line, I passed by many officials checking for explosives. Bomb and agriculture work dogs were also being used. They moved up and down the line fairly quickly until suddenly, the dog locked onto the truck Laima was in. It barked loudly and continued to bark and lay down. It was excited about the contents of the truck. Did the dog smell Laima, or was there something wrong with the vehicle?

I turned to run back to the truck when UNOPS said, "Frank, stay here and I will handle this." My heart raced and I hoped this would all blow over. Looking frantic and sweating to death, I continued to show concern.

"Frank, go sign the paperwork for the convoy. Do it!" I turned back towards the front to do what I was told. Laima was in his hands.

Reaching the front of the convoy, there stood a Pakistani officer with a pen and clipboard sticking out to me. "What is your name?"

"Frank Ingram!"

"Frank Ingram, are you sure? I thought you may be Mr. Stanton. Is that your real name, or is Frank Ingram your name?"

"It's Frank Ingram!"

"You are sure of that, Mr. Ingram?"

"Yes!"

"You sign here, please. Now, leave this country with what you came for, and do not return. Do you understand?"

"Frank Ingram will never come back, I assure you of that. Sir, will Frank Ingram make it through the next checkpoint?"

"I do not know."

The officer then notified everyone over the radio that the convoy was cleared for movement across to the Afghani checkpoint. UNOPS was still talking with the dog handler. He soon departed knowing something was illegal about that truck.

UNOPS yelled out, "Get in your vehicles now!"

Within minutes, we pulled out to move into the town of Torkham. We had cleared Pakistan but still had to clear Afghanistan.

"River, when we get across to the Afghani truck checkpoint, there is a U.S. Special Forces camp across the street. When we get there, you need to judge when you run for the camp. It's about four hundred meters or eight o'clock. It's a closed–in, walled compound. That's where you will find final safety. If your BG Stanton is an honest guy, that's where your assistance will come from."

"Honest, I am not sure what that word even means anymore. Right now, you are the only person that has really helped me other than Seher and Laima."

"Where is Seher, River?"

"Dead. She was killed by a Pakistani assassin in a Christian cemetery in the middle of Peshawar two days ago."

"Where is the child's father?"

"Dead. Seher and I killed him over a week ago. He was trying to kill her and the child so I stopped him."

"Are you going to kill me?"

"No, you're safe!"

We crossed into Afghanistan at 0658 hours. Torkham, Afghanistan, looked like a town that did nothing but strip stolen cars. There was every car part and engine ever purchased in Pakistan sitting right here. Stacks of metal storage containers could be seen for hundreds of yards. Diesel trucks used to transport car parts into Afghanistan were parked on the side of the road. This was the largest multimillion-dollar chop shop I had ever seen in my life. In Texas, junk yards are huge, but not like this.

"Welcome to Barter Town, River."

"You aren't kidding; I have never seen anything like this before."

"Maybe even freedom for Laima and you."

"Freedom, huh!"

By 0715, we had come to a halt inside Afghanistan. Afghan National Army soldiers were out in force. Yet, mixed in with them were S.F. soldiers assisting. Could this be true? Was I actually going to catch a break?

Getting out of the vehicle, I located the S.F. camp. From my vantage point, the time was now to grab Laima and run for it. Seeing freedom within the walls of the S.F compound was like an extreme shot of excitement and courage. The time was now; no soldiers or policemen were around between me and the compound.

"OK, it's time. I am going to do this now!"

"You sure, River?"

"Yes, thanks for all you have done and I wish you the best. You will be on our Christmas card list."

"I can't wait to see that family picture next year."

"Me too!"

I moved up to the truck where Laima was sleeping. Pulling the supplies back, I could see her foot as it moved. Pulling her out by her feet, she was still asleep and severely dehydrated. Drenched in sweat, she moaned and fell limp into my arms. I turned to look for my path to freedom. As I moved around the back of the truck, there stood a Special Forces soldier. Looking at me, startled, he said. "Follow me, sir!"

Three other soldiers surrounded Laima and me as we ran back towards the compound.

"Run, sir, run as fast as you can and do not look back!"

I did exactly that. Hearing nothing but combat boots hitting the ground and Laima's heart beating, my eyes were focused like a laser on the gate. It took only one minute to get into the compound. Once through the gate, I dropped to my knees with Laima in my arms and began to cry. That was the best and worst day of my life. It was the best day because Laima was now safe, but the worst day because Seher did not gain her freedom and I had let her down.

"Sir, is your name River Rochman?"

"Yes, yes, that's my name."

"Welcome home, sir. I need the Achilles to verify."

Handing him the Achilles from my cargo pocket, I couldn't believe how that thing changed my life. Yet, I was glad that part was over.

The S.F. officer went back to his command post and made a call. All I heard was, "The Achilles is in our possession."

Laima was taken straight to the medics where a female doctor nursed her back to health over the next three days. She came through with flying colors. While I waited each day for Laima to come out and play in the compound, I decided to charge the satellite phone just in case it all went to hell. Also, I still had the area code 571 stuck in my head. Why did that number ring a bell somewhere?

Turning on the sat-phone, I looked through the pre-programmed phone numbers and found nothing. When I went through the past calls, there it was: 571-555-1175. In the heading it said "COL Stanton's Office"! Going back to Waba's cell phone for that missed call, I realized it was the same number!

Chapter 38

Why would Stanton be talking to Waba? Was it an intelligence move to gain information, tracking cell phone signal, or was it something a little more dangerous for me? My gut told me Stanton was on the wrong team and I was the scapegoat. Waba seemed to always be ahead of me, waiting. Even in the middle of an intersection in Peshawar, how did he get information that accurate? Google Earth sure the hell isn't in real time!

"Hey, sir, BG Stanton says you did a great job and says he will meet you back in D.C. Great job, really!"

"Stud, I need you to do me a favor. I need you to call this number and tell me who answers the phone."

"What's the number?"

"571-555-1175."

"Sir, is this a joke? BG Stanton will kill me if I call him at this number. I did that once before and he took me to task!"

"OK, thanks."

Getting up from the steps to the tactical operations center, I walked over to Laima playing with a little dog that was the mascot for the team. The dog just continued to lick her face and Laima just laughed and continued to try to push the dog away. I wished Seher was here to see this moment. I bet Seher had never seen her daughter play with a dog and be this happy. Leaning down to Laima, I picked her up and held her tight.

She looked flustered and emotionally distant, and I said, "Laima, you having fun with that dog?"

Laima smiled and said, "Dog?"

"Yes, dog!"

No tears flowed from my eyes. I was through with that.

Yelling from the operations center, the S.F. officer said, "Sir, BG Stanton needs to talk to you ASAP!"

"OK, I will be right there." Moving slowly back to answer the phone, I was formulating my conversation and how it would flow. Should I start yelling or play nice to ensure Laima and I made it out of country by tomorrow morning? *Let's play nice until I am back in D.C., then I go game on.*

"This is Major Rochman. How can I help you?"

"River, thanks for all you have done for your country. They really appreciate it. You saved many lives by your bravery."

"Yes, sir, many brave people died unnecessarily for other people's past mistakes, wouldn't you say?"

"What does that mean, Major?"

"It means you lost the Achilles and needed an unknown to take the blame for the loss and the death of all those soldiers and civilians. You hung me out to dry! If I failed and was caught by the Pakistanis, you would have claimed I was rogue and was a traitor to my nation. I was the fall guy. But, since I was succeeding, you contacted Waba and gave him my location once I got into Pakistan. By the way, Waba is dead and I have his cell phone. When you called him last night, he was dead in a taxi west of Peshawar. I took his cell phone and, funny enough, your phone number was in the screen. Interesting outcome, isn't it, sir?"

Silence, silence, silence, that's what I heard from Stanton's end. "So, what's next, sir?"

"River, we can work this out."

"Yes, I want asylum for Laima now and then safe travel out of Afghanistan to Europe."

"What will you do in Europe?"

"Hide and live our lives in peace."

"You will never live in peace. As long as you have that cell phone, I will continue to hunt you down until I have it."

"Bring it on, brother!"

"And I will, River."

"Sir, this is the deal: asylum and safe travel for Laima and I. I am officially retired with full pay and benefits for the rest of my life. Simple stuff, that's all I ask for. You are a general; you can make that happen."

"When do I get the phone?"

"Once I have all that I have asked for."

"Don't screw me, River; it will not end well if you screw me. If you do, I swear I will come after Laima just like I did Seher in that hospital."

"Give me what I need, now, or else I turn the phone over to CNN, Fox News, and every hick town paper in the United States and Pakistan. You won't be able to take a dump without being recognized anywhere."

"River, you are nothing but a major. I am a general. Who do you think they will believe?"

"We'll see how that information operations campaign goes, sir! Now get me what I have asked for by tomorrow morning. Out! Did you get that, soldier?"

"Yes, sir, I have it all on tape."

The officer handed me a memory chip with BG Stanton confessing his sins. This was my ticket through the next five years, at least. "Stud, keep a copy for yourself. You may need this someday."

"Major Rochman, what's next?"

"Revenge, and only revenge!"

The asylum message came through at 1700 hours that afternoon for Laima. We were to fly out of Kabul by commercial airline the following morning. My mission was unsanctioned so there was no military support. Laima had to be given a temporary passport. We took a picture of her with a digital camera; it was her first ever. She was beautiful as the soldiers went into Torkham to buy her some clothes for the picture. Prancing around, she was excited and kept looking in mirrors at herself. It was a proud moment in both our lives.

The next morning a Blackhawk came in and picked us up and flew us to the same NATO Airfield at Kabul that I started at. We were treated like royalty by the S.F. community. They bought me a two-piece suit made by a Turkish tailor and some Italian black leather shoes.

I shaved and took a shower that night. Looking unrecognizable, Laima could still see me, as she laughed and rubbed my cheeks. Laima was now my daughter. Her passport said her name was Laima Seher Rochman, and she was an adopted child from Pakistan. Her birth date was December 11, 2001, the day and month I first had seen her. The rest of the details, like hair and eye color, just meant beautiful.

Thirty-two hours later, we stopped overnight in Washington, D.C., to clear customs and the adoption organization. Laima was given a physical, and as expected, she was as healthy as a horse. She stayed in Walter Reed Hospital through the night for observation. I stayed in the room with her and only left for a few hours to take care of some old business. Just know, you should never leave your child on Christmas Eve for any reason, except to protect them.

The next mornings, December 25, 2004, the *Washington Post* stated that BG Stanton, a respected army general, had been murdered in his bed in Arlington, Virginia, that night. No suspects were noted.

I never went to the funeral—just Texas!